Penguin Books
Come to Dust

Emma Lathen

Come to Dust

Penguin Books

Penguin Books Ltd, Harmondsworth,
Middlesex, England
Penguin Books Inc., 7110 Ambassador Road,
Baltimore, Maryland 21207, U.S.A.
Penguin Books Australia Ltd, Ringwood,
Victoria, Australia

First published in the U.S.A. 1968
Published in Great Britain by Victor Gollancz 1969
Published in Penguin Books 1974

Copyright © Emma Lathen, 1968

Made and printed in Great Britain by
Cox & Wyman Ltd, London, Reading and Fakenham
Set in Intertype Times

This book is sold subject to the condition that
it shall not, by way of trade or otherwise, be lent,
re-sold, hired out, or otherwise circulated without
the publisher's prior consent in any form of
binding or cover other than that in which it is
published and without a similar condition
including this condition being imposed on the
subsequent purchaser

Contents

1. Auditors Will Be Admitted 7
2. The Class Will Be Divided into Discussion Groups 14
3. No Credit 22
4. At the Pleasure of the Instructor 30
5. Papers Will Be Required 40
6. Supplementary Reading on Reserve 51
7. Field Trips Are Scheduled 57
8. Students on the Accelerated Programme 63
9. Counselling Is Available 74
10. The Department Must Approve 81
11. Numerical Grades Are Not Given 89
12. Commencement Address 100
13. Indoor and Outdoor Sports 107
14. Chapel Is Required 119
15. Student Body 126
16. Midterm Examination 134
17. Bachelor of Arts 143
18. Classes Will Not Meet 152
19. Candidates for Degrees 160
20. Seminar for Majors Only 170
21. Independent Work 179
22. Visiting Lecturers 186
23. Please Read Instructions Carefully 194
24. Final Results Will Be Posted 204
25. The Sheltering Pines 215

1. Auditors Will Be Admitted

The Sloan Guaranty Trust is a jewel in the crown of Wall Street. No expense has been spared to provide a physical setting worthy of the third largest bank in the world: Italian marble, hand-woven draperies and Barcelona chairs are the outer show of inner capital grace. Moreover, the grandeur so manifest in the lobby fronting on Exchange Place waxes with each ascending floor: up on Six, the trust department is swaddled in careful splendour, from the offices of John Putnam Thatcher, senior vice-president of the bank and head of the department, to the cubbyhole of Sheldon, the messenger boy. Higher still, the tower is a virtuoso fusion of elegance and costliness beyond the ken of ordinary mortals.

John Thatcher, who had schooled himself to temper his response to modern interiors, was in conference in the tower suite with the chairman of the board, George C. Lancer. The subject at issue, a projected cut in the Sloan's prime rate, not only concerned many millions of Sloan dollars, it vitally affected larger questions of public policy. Thatcher and Lancer were weighing pros and cons that would subsequently exercise the Investment Committee, the Loan Policy Board, and, in time, the Wall Street money markets, the U.S. Government and the financial press of the entire Western world.

So, when the telephone on Lancer's desk buzzed, he halted his comments with a look of mild surprise on his conventional, handsome face. Just as the Sloan's physical plant was engineered to promote maximum efficiency, particularly among eminents like George C. Lancer and John Putnam Thatcher, so the personnel was trained to protect that efficiency. In practice, this meant keeping telephone calls from impinging on important policy discussions.

'Yes, Miss Evans?' Lancer responded without undue curiosity. It was not necessary; the telephone apologized at length, and Thatcher saw Lancer's eyebrows rise slightly. 'Well ... er, yes. That's all right, Miss Evans. You might as well put him on, since he's on the line,' he said.

Thatcher sketched a willingness to depart but Lancer motioned him to remain. 'It's Gabe Uhlein,' he said before returning to the phone. 'Yes, Gabe. No trouble at all.'

Thatcher settled back. Lancer's side of the conversation consisted of those uninformative noises that indicate comprehension. Uhlein was doing the talking, as he usually did. It was scarcely surprising that Miss Evans could not withstand him. Persuasiveness was Gabe Uhlein's stock in trade: by profession he was a fund raiser, the president and guiding spirit of Target Associates, a large organization devoted to helping good causes get adequate moneys.

'Now Gabe, I don't know about that,' Lancer was saying doubtfully, shooting an amused look at Thatcher. Clearly he had been braced for a plea for funds; but whatever Gabe Uhlein currently wanted, it was not money. 'There are a good many difficulties.'

Again the conversation shifted. Thatcher was not surprised when, some minutes later, Lancer wearily nodded, picked up a pencil and said, 'All right, Gabe, what was that name again?' It was not that he lacked decision; on the contrary, Lancer was a notably strong executive, in contrast to Bradford Withers, the president of the Sloan, who was currently representing the bank at a conference in Paris. But Lancer, like many another before him, had found that the only way to get rid of Gabe Uhlein was to yield to his blandishments. In addition, Uhlein was an important customer.

'Fine, Gabe,' Lancer was saying firmly. 'I'll have one of my people call you. Fine.'

He put down the receiver and shook his head. 'An Elliot Patterson seems to be missing,' he told Thatcher.

Thatcher was ahead of him. 'And Elliot Patterson works for Gabe, and Gabe wants us to take a quick look at Elliot Patterson's bank account?' he suggested. This was simple enough and common, if slightly irregular. Banks, like the rest of us, do little favours for friends.

'That's it,' said Lancer, resuming the phone to give directions to Miss Evans. 'Elliot Patterson,' he told her distinctly. 'Works at Target Associates. Home address is 203 Walnut Street, Rye. Have Benson check his personal account, will you, Miss Evans? Call me before the afternoon is out.'

The phone was down again but Lancer hesitated before returning to the prime rate of interest. 'Elliot Patterson?' he said, savouring the name. 'Sounds familiar, somehow. Have you ever heard of an Elliot Patterson, John?'

But John Putnam Thatcher did not know Elliot Patterson. He did not fully realize how fortunate he was. It was a warm pleasant Tuesday in October, and would be the last time he could say this. Soon the name Elliot Patterson would be ringing endlessly in his ears. The pealing began several hours later the same day.

Thatcher was booked to dine with the Lancers that evening, then accompany them to an exhibition of European gouaches at the Gary Museum of Modern Art. Like so many social events, this was both good and bad; on the credit side of the ledger was an excellent dinner produced by the Belgian cook whom Lucy Lancer cherished with unceasing vigilance, and Lucy herself, a poised and practised hostess whose enviable competence on all fronts was leavened with redeeming glints of humour.

'But, much as I value both your company and your dinner, Lucy,' Thatcher said with the freedom of an old friend, 'I think perhaps European gouaches are too high a price to pay.'

Lucy Lancer did not try to defend a weak position. Instead she directed her husband and Thatcher to bring their drinks to the table since Matthilde was particular about the fish. Obediently they followed her into the chandelier-lit dining-room, where the trout proved well worth Matthilde's solicitude.

'By the way, George,' Thatcher inquired idly as they waited for the roast, 'how did that man of Gabe's turn out? Did he strip his account?'

Lancer carefully tasted the Beaune and decided it was

potable. 'No,' he said. 'Elliot Patterson's personal account has held steady at $1,400 for months now. No unusual deposits or withdrawals. Gabe said it was just what he expected ...'

He was interrupted by an exclamation from Lucy.

'Elliot Patterson?' she asked with lively interest. Admirable woman that she was, Lucy tolerated business talk at her table and rarely descended to feminine changes of subject. 'Why are you checking on Elliot Patterson, George?' she demanded.

He nodded in self-congratulation. 'I thought I recognized that name! We do know an Elliot Patterson, don't we, Lucy? I knew it, but I can't place him.'

'Brunswick, dear, Brunswick! But what is all this?'

Exchange of information occupied the rest of dinner. Brunswick, of course, was Brunswick College, in Coburg, New Hampshire, that select Ivy League institution of which male Lancers had been alumni for five generations and benefactors for three. When Brunswick College emulated its compeers and installed a youthful dynamo as president, he had, in the richness of time, descended upon New York for the inevitable introduction to the most important and affluent collection of Old Brunsies extant. Equally inevitably, Mr and Mrs George C. Lancer had contributed to the round of festivities with a large party in his honour.

'Elliot Patterson was at our cocktail party,' Lucy informed her husband. 'Then we met him at the Armitages' dinner ...'

'Lucy, you're a marvel,' said Lancer. 'Of course. I remember now. Thin, serious fellow with a good-looking blonde wife. I remember thinking that he was a far cry from Gabe Uhlein.'

Lucy murmured something about hoping that no harm had befallen him, but her husband was pursuing his own train of thought to another conclusion. 'Well, he's only been missing since yesterday afternoon,' he said tolerantly. 'Myself, I can think of a good many explanations.'

'Shame on you!' said Lucy severely. 'Elliot is devoted to his lovely family. He told me so himself.'

Thatcher received this with deep suspicion, but George Lancer said, 'Well, the one I wish would disappear is this little twerp you're dragging us out to see tonight!'

Lucy explained that Neil Marsden, curator of the Special Collections of the Gary Museum of Modern Art, of which she was a trustee, was yet another Old Brunsie. 'George doesn't approve of curators of art museums.'

Thatcher was not the man for sweeping condemnations, but two hours later he was forced to conclude that much could be said for Lancer's position. The Gary, an eccentric exercise in spiralling ramps, was boldly flaunting hundreds of European gouaches, sizzling with hot reds and purples, against raw cinder-box walls. Occasional relief for the overstrained eye was provided by ominous foliage and, in the great rotunda, by a lowering granite sculpture. The Friends of the Gary, enjoying a private view of the collection touted by *Time* Magazine, sported full evening regalia; Lucy's notable diamonds did not sweep the field without rival. Thatcher decided that the overall effect suggested a debutante cotillion in a reformatory.

Nor did the curators, a mixed lot, commend themselves to him. Thin to a man, they boasted eclectic accents from BBC to Tidewater Virginia and embodied, as it were, a living rebuke to all America west of the Alleghenies.

'And this is Neil Marsden, dear. You remember,' said Lucy Lancer with a charming smile that held a tiny glint of malice for Thatcher and George.

'Ah, Mrs Lancer,' said Marsden enthusiastically. He greeted Lancer and Thatcher with warm approval, causing Thatcher to recall something forgotten during ten years as a widower. Marriage, even with the best of women, has its drawbacks.

Marsden had a well-bred face; in clipped accents he delivered an encomium to somebody called Bruno Brunei, using beautiful hands for punctuation. Thatcher thought that his mannered enthusiasm probably rested on a low-keyed but pervasive fretfulness. Although he was balding, he could not be much older than thirty.

'... tremendous trouble with the customs people, for some incomprehensible reason,' he was saying, to round out an anecdote designed to place art curators in the ranks of the world's indefatigable toilers. 'All in all, it has been quite a day! Why, we didn't get completely hung until five o'clock!'

Since her companions maintained unencouraging silence, Lucy responded. 'No!'

'Yes, indeed,' Marsden assured her. 'And if that wasn't enough' – here he became confidential – 'there has been this flap about Elliot Patterson. I can't imagine why everybody suddenly wants him today.'

He captured the attention of an audience two-thirds of which up to now had been reluctant if not hostile.

'I simply do not have time – certainly not when I am hanging the most important show we have ever had at the Gary – to waste hours on the phone. I'm sure you have this sort of trouble frequently, Mr Lancer?'

But Lancer only retorted, 'What connection do you have with Elliot Patterson?'

Neil Marsden evinced no resentment. Thatcher had a strong feeling that the chairman of the board of the Sloan Guaranty Trust and his lady could ask Neil Marsden anything without impairing his burning desire to please.

Still, Marsden was somewhat disappointed. 'Why, the Committee, Mr Lancer,' he said. 'The Brunswick Admission Committee.'

Lancer confined his alumni activities to munificent contributions and broadly spaced hospitality for visiting academics.

'What's that?' he asked.

With her husband bent on extracting information, Lucy smiled brilliantly and slid away to join friends, leaving Neil Marsden to fend for himself.

'Oh, I thought you knew,' he said with deference. 'Elliot is on the Admission Committee with me.'

And others as well, Thatcher presumed. The Brunswick Admission Committee, he soon learned against his will, was a branch of the Brunswick Alumni Club of New York. For most of the year it concentrated on a never-ending quest for funds. But in the fall, the Committee conducted preliminary interviews with the young gentlemen of the Greater New York area who aspired to become freshmen at Brunswick College.

'Of course, the college makes the final decision, but they

tend to follow our recommendation,' Marsden said, revealing the exalted view he held of his own role in the scheme of things.

'Gabe didn't mention this Brunswick connection,' Lancer commented to Thatcher.

'Which doesn't mean that he doesn't know about it,' Thatcher replied, amused.

Marsden projected enough tempered curiosity to require response.

'Elliot Patterson seems to have disappeared,' Lancer told him shortly. 'Went to a meeting of some sort yesterday afternoon and nobody's seen him since.'

Marsden was startled out of his languor. 'Disappeared? What do you mean, disappeared? We met at the Ivy League Club just yesterday! So that explains why Sally Patterson has been calling to ask if I've seen Elliot today! But what could have happened to him? Elliot is the last man on earth to do anything out of the ordinary!'

'Apparently he didn't go home last night,' Lancer said, beginning to look around for Lucy with more frankness than courtesy.

One might have thought, Thatcher mused, idly watching the passing parade of elegance, that someone young Marsden's age could take a more lighthearted view than Elliot Patterson's employer of escapades, domestic spats or whatever.

But not at all. Neil Marsden was just as mystified as Gabe Uhlein.

'Good Lord! I hope . . .' He broke off.

Thatcher inquired if Elliot Patterson had been himself at the meeting of the Brunswick Admission Committee. Odd this discussion might be, but he and George were being spared gouaches and Bruno Brunei.

'Mmm . . . what? Oh, oh yes. Elliot was perfectly normal. We cleaned up some of the details about a donation from Mrs Curtis, you'll be happy to hear, Mr Lancer. Then we interviewed four boys applying to Brunswick . . .'

Again Neil Marsden broke off.

'A blonde?' Thatcher suggested. 'A binge?' Suiting action to words, he accepted a drink from a waiter. Neil Marsden dismissed these suggestions as frivolous.

'Not Elliot Patterson!' he said with a hint of contempt. 'He's a model family man. As a matter of fact, he's a pretty wet fish.'

'You know him,' Thatcher conceded.

Lancer was still searching the throng when Marsden frowned again, then rather hastily excused himself with the plea of responsibilities elsewhere.

Seasoned self-control kept Lancer and Thatcher from comment upon either Neil Marsden or Elliot Patterson. Instead, with the air of men doing their duty, they removed from the line of vision of a substantial matron who was intent upon the production hanging behind them.

Finally, with a really savage look at them, she said, 'I don't care what you say, I think this is disgusting!'

With deep appreciation, Thatcher watched her sail away.

'George, she thinks we're curators!'

2. The Class Will Be Divided into Discussion Groups

George Lancer and Thatcher spent the rest of the evening inspecting such gouaches as they could not avoid, conversing with acquaintances similarly victimized by culture-minded womenfolk, and waiting for Lucy to detach herself from the vivacious conversations she enjoyed despite the daunting background of inchoate paintings, angular sculpture and hovering curators.

Meanwhile, the great Elliot Patterson snowball began gathering momentum.

Neil Marsden, his smile firmly fixed in place, proceeded through the gallery with practised half-bows in the direction of various Friends of the Gary. He was heading, as fast as he could, to his own office and the telephone. Marsden's limitations were obvious. His talents were less obtrusive but considerable. These included a developed social sense allied to a powerful feel for self-preservation. News that Elliot Patterson was missing activated both.

The phone rang twelve times, giving Marsden ample opportunity to listen to the convivial sound filtering through from the gallery. Finally somebody answered, and he said, 'Hello! Oh yes, Mrs Armitage. This is Neil Marsden. Is Ralph there?'

Automatically, Marsden had assumed a light, engaging tone although he knew perfectly well that Ralph Armitage did not like him. As a matter of fact he did not like Armitage, a prosperous middle-aged insurance broker. But Armitage was a fellow Old Brunsie, and another member of the Brunswick Admission Committee. At the moment he represented a pair of shoulders to help with the problems that Marsden saw shaping.

'Ralph? Good! Listen, have you heard that Elliot Patterson is missing? Nobody has seen him since our meeting yesterday.'

In a comfortable ranch house in East Orange, New Jersey, Armitage settled at the desk in his study and gazed at the framed diplomas, certificates and trophies decorating the wall above. The voice on the phone was excited enough to be unpleasantly febrile. Marsden was quite correct. Armitage did not like him at all.

'So?' he said gruffly. 'So he's gone out of town.'

'That's not it at all.' Marsden was impatient. 'Everybody's being discreet. Sally called me today and didn't really breathe a word about it. But Elliot has dropped out of sight. He didn't go home and he didn't turn up at work. They have no idea where he is.'

'Didn't get to work?' It was a commentary on the American businessman that Armitage was more impressed by Patterson's failure to arrive at his office than by his truancy from home.

'Exactly.'

There was a long silence before Armitage whistled appreciatively. 'Skipped, eh? Have they called the police yet?'

'My God, I hope not. Think of the scandal,' Marsden said passionately. 'Sally wouldn't like to start that, would she?' Unspoken was the fact that Neil Marsden wouldn't like it either: it is one thing to use clubs and committees as part of a calculated assault on cultural and social fortresses; it is another to be associated with missing men and police inquiries.

Armitage was weighing it. 'They're going to have to do it, sooner or later. And Sally isn't the only one involved.'

'They must be hoping it's an accident,' Marsden said doubtfully. 'Although that doesn't seem possible with all the identification he carried. I suppose you're right. George Lancer was telling me that Uhlein's putting out feelers.'

Even in the midst of his preoccupation, pride at the source of his information was discernible. The next time he referred to Lancer, it would be as George.

'I'll bet Gabe Uhlein is putting out feelers,' Armitage said heartily. 'You remember all those independent accounts Elliot got last spring? He could have made off with millions!'

'No!' This was not what occurred to Neil Marsden when he thought in terms of scandal.

'And you can kiss good-bye to the idea of an accident,' the other continued. 'He was going straight home, wasn't he? Nothing happened to him between Fifth Avenue and Rye that wouldn't come to the surface in twenty-four hours.' He retreated into his thoughts, emerging to say, 'Elliot! Of all people!'

Neil Marsden was appalled.

'I'm surprised to hear you say that, Ralph,' he said pettishly. 'To accuse Elliot of stealing! Why, it's absurd! For heaven's sake, he's oppressively virtuous.'

Armitage acknowledged the moral disadvantage. 'No, no,' he said hastily. 'I'm not accusing Elliot of anything. I'm just saying that people may suspect it...'

Marsden projected superiority until Armitage, goaded, was driven to ask, 'Well, what the hell are you up in the air about, if you think it's vulgar to worry about a couple of million dollars?'

The question was rhetorical but he got an answer. He was still thinking about it when the conversation ended.

'Business?' his wife inquired placidly when he rejoined her in the living-room. It was an all-purpose word to her, embracing the arcane activities that accounted for the many good things in the Armitage life.

'Mm,' said Armitage, still deep in thought. 'What was that, Joan? No, not business. It's the Brunswick Committee. Elliot Patterson seems to have disappeared. That was Marsden, calling up all in a twitter.'

Mrs Armitage put down the magazine she was using to pass the time until the eleven o'clock news. Her husband, accustomed to thinking aloud, found he had an attentive audience. It was understood between the Armitages that his activities as an alumnus of Brunswick were properly a part of Ralph Armitage's business life rather than part of the Armitage social life. Nevertheless, over the years, Joan Armitage had met some of his colleagues. She remembered Elliot Patterson.

'We met yesterday at the Ivy League Club,' her husband continued. 'Marsden says that Elliot walked out – and simply disappeared. He didn't go home. He didn't turn up at his office this morning.'

Mrs Armitage clucked disapprovingly. Ralph Armitage interpreted this correctly.

'No, Joan. Or at least I don't think so. Elliot's the serious type. I handle his policies, and I can tell you he keeps up top coverage for that family of his. He's got three little girls, I think.' Then he added a clincher. 'They've got a nice place up in Rye.'

Mrs Armitage had not read the ladies' magazines for nothing. 'It's the quiet ones who always break out, Ralph,' she quoted. 'And besides, if Elliot's so quiet – what is he up to?'

He scratched his head. 'God knows.'

She pressed home her advantage. 'And what was Marsden calling up about?'

Armitage made a gesture of distaste. 'Oh, him,' he said.

'Well?' she demanded implacably.

'Oh, he's afraid – of almost everything. Talk...'

'Blondes, women, drink!' Mrs Armitage finished triumphantly. Her own life had been mercifully free of these curses, but she had read a lot.

'Not Elliot,' said Ralph Armitage. 'I'd stake my life on that. Still, he could get his hands on a lot of money...'

With womanly dignity, Mrs Armitage rose to tune the TV.

Suddenly her husband said, 'Marsden's a strange duck. He's afraid that it won't look good for us if Elliot broke out. Publicity, all that sort of thing. He jumps to the conclusion that Elliot's run wild but refuses to believe he could be low class enough to steal.'

'How perfectly terrible all of this is for Elliot Patterson's wife,' Mrs Armitage said.

Her sympathy, as it happened, was misplaced. Things were not so terrible for Sally Patterson as they were for her guests.

'And what did Neil want to say to you?' she asked with iron control the minute her visitor put down the phone. The Patterson living-room in Rye, like the Armitage living-room in East Orange, was eloquent of above-average income, social respectability and decorum. Subtle differences existed. Instead of *Better Homes and Gardens*, good books graced the end tables. The décor was uncompromisingly colonial instead of a bastard modern. A grand piano in the corner displayed a heavily starred 'Merry Farmer' on its music rack. On the mantel were the photographs: Sally Patterson, blonde, sweetly maternal, draping protective arms over three small blond replicas. Staring sightlessly back at his brood was Elliot Patterson: gentle-eyed, bespectacled, with a thin sensitive mouth and a general air of piety.

'I said, Jim, why did Neil Marsden want to talk to you?'

The rising note was not lost on Jim Dunlop, youngest member of the Brunswick Admission Committee. However, he felt unable to relay fears of scandal and worse, so he lied.

'Neil wanted to know if there's anything he can do to help,' he said.

Sally Patterson sniffed. 'That's what he said to me,' she said, putting her finger unerringly on the weak spot. Fortunately her own concerns overwhelmed her. 'Besides, how can he help? Oh dear, what can have happened to Elliot?'

Jim exchanged a speaking look with the third person present in the neo-Revere living-room, his young wife Lou. She looked as bewildered as he felt. The impulse to comfort a troubled wife had seemed simple enough, and, as Lou had pointed out when Sally called, the Pattersons had had the Dunlops to dinner. The obligation to provide comfort was clear.

But Sally Patterson defeated them.

'This isn't like Elliot,' she said, troubled but thoughtful. 'You see, at first I thought he was simply out of town on a business trip, and I had forgotten. Or he had forgotten to mention it. But that's just silly. I don't forget, and Elliot always tells me when he's going to miss dinner.'

Dunlop nodded vigorously. He had come to regard Elliot as a walking compendium of all the domestic virtues.

'Then, when he didn't come home last night, I was really at a loss,' said Mrs Patterson, who had the trick of overemphasizing some words. She did not sound at a loss.

Once again the Dunlops exchanged troubled looks. They had arrived with laudable intentions to say 'there-there', to offer tissues for tears, to make helpful suggestions about going to bed, calling relatives, and hoping for the best. All of this self-possession baffled them.

'So I called my brother-in-law,' the recital continued. 'He said . . .'

The Dunlops already knew what the brother-in-law had said and what Mrs Patterson had done. First she had called Target Associates, ascertained that her husband was not at his desk this morning and left a message asking him to call her when he got in.

'But at noon, Marian Knightley called,' she continued. 'Elliot wasn't in by then, so they wondered. I've always thought Marian was not really sympathetic, but she could tell that I was worried. I simply had to tell her that Elliot hadn't come home. It turned out that Target didn't know where Elliot was either . . .'

In short, at the time Gabriel Uhlein was first approaching the Sloan with delicate inquiries, Mrs Patterson had begun her own; an engagement pad revealed that Elliot's last appointment had been a Monday afternoon meeting of the Brunswick Admission Committee, at four-thirty.

Mrs Patterson turned calm eyes on young Dunlop.

'Well, he was there all right,' he said, flushing slightly from a general sense of discomfort. 'He was perfectly fine, I mean, as far as I could see. In fact, he was feeling pretty pleased about getting Mrs Curtis to contribute $50,000 . . .'

'Oh yes,' Mrs Patterson said intelligently. 'Elliot is so pleased about that! Mrs Curtis was a challenge to him. It took him days to convince her that her husband should be honoured by that new reading room. But, of course, Elliot is so sincere. Even people like Mrs Curtis recognize that.'

Jim Dunlop did not think that this was the time to discuss Elliot's excellences. His experience was severely limited but he thought he saw his duty. With an assumption of male authority that he was far from feeling in Mrs Patterson's presence he said, 'Yes, we sat around discussing Mrs Curtis for a few minutes, then we went out and looked over those kids who are applying to Brunswick. Then Elliot stayed behind to talk to one of them and that's the last we've seen of him. Now, Sally, the thing to do is call the police. Elliot might have been hurt.'

Lou leaned forward. 'He might have amnesia,' she said thrillingly. She had been a psychology major at Bennington.

Sally Patterson looked kindly at her comforters. 'I don't know,' she said without any indecision. She did not need to add that the Patterson life, neatly ticketed, held room for the League of Women Voters, the Citizens Committee to Preserve the Elms, Sunday School, the *Saturday Review*, but not for the police. 'I don't know,' she repeated.

Pure cowardice led Dunlop to waver. 'Well, maybe you should give Elliot another day or so . . .'

She insisted on giving them a cup of coffee before they set off for the city.

'Jim,' said Lou in a small voice as they sped back to their tiny apartment near Sutton Place. 'Didn't it seem that Sally wasn't really – I mean, she seemed awfully calm about things, didn't she?'

'Mmm,' said Dunlop. Calm and excitement are relative; the

Dunlops were still newly married enough so that a burned piece of toast could ignite dramatic emotional scenes, followed by dramatic emotional reconciliations.

'I mean, if you were missing, I'd go crazy!' Lou said. 'I'd scream to the police, to anybody who'd listen.'

Dunlop pointed out that Mrs Patterson had been troubled enough to call her husband's employers, his friends, his colleagues.

Lou was not impressed. 'Of course, they've been married for ages, haven't they?'

'Ten years at least,' said her lord and master. This was agreement.

'And they've got three children, haven't they?' Lou persisted. She was still trying to fill in the gaps left by that psychology major.

Dunlop said that they did.

'I suppose it's possible that after all these years, they still haven't learned to communicate,' she mused. 'You'd think they would have found that out a long time ago.'

'Yes,' Dunlop agreed, obscurely disturbed. Himself a sociology major until graduation from Brunswick one year ago, he was inclined to listen to Lou's technical pronouncements with respect. But twelve months as a worker in Manhattan were beginning to leave their mark. For the first time in his life he was moving in a circle that was not composed exclusively of his age peers. The facile judgements of the Delta Kappa house at Brunswick seemed almost irrelevant when brought to bear on other generations. He had a dim sense that considerations of communication and identity might not be the best tools with which to embark on a thorough analysis of relations between the Pattersons.

'And, of course, if Elliot Patterson hasn't been able to establish a sense of identity, he wouldn't feel any commitment to his family,' Lou continued.

Jim Dunlop came to a startling conclusion. These were murky waters, and there were more things in heaven and earth than were dreamt of in Psychology 201. In a word, Lou was talking nonsense about a situation she couldn't begin to understand.

But being an affectionate young man whose instincts were naturally kindly, he said, 'I guess so, Lou,' and resolutely tuned out his wife's chatter.

The Dunlops had just passed a milestone, though neither of them realized it. The honeymoon was over and the marriage had begun.

3. No Credit

Despite their excesses of the previous night, John Putnam Thatcher and George C. Lancer spent a decorous Wednesday with the Loan Policy Committee, mulling over the proposed changes in the Sloan's prime rate. The calm dialogue that had characterized their deliberations of the day before now gave way to a new script, accommodating a larger cast of characters and more colourful exchanges.

'I'll tell you who won't go along,' announced Walter Bowman, the Sloan's chief of research, its most conscientious intelligence gatherer and one of Nature's warriors. 'The Second National for one. A quarter of a point, if that . . .'

'Now hold it, Walter,' said an adversary from International.

'I happen to know . . .'

'What about U.S. Bakeries? Where can they take their business? Hmm?'

The dispute swirled on. George Lancer, as usual, remained silent, maintaining the fiction that as chairman of the board his was a nonoperating role. Thatcher remained silent because he had long since heard all the details of the opposing arguments and was not, at this stage of the game, going to be caught trying to reconcile the irreconcilable.

An incautious reference to the Federal Reserve Board forced a luncheon adjournment. As Lancer had obligations to a visiting crew from the Banking and Currency Committee, Thatcher adjourned to Massoletti's with Bowman. As usual, Bowman fuelled the inner man with the Falstaffian portions necessary to sustain his considerable bulk and entertained Thatcher with a series of pungent anecdotes about a Wall Street researcher grown so inflated by his press coverage that he had plotted a coup d'état in his own firm.

'And what happens to Jacques now?' Thatcher inquired.

'Bounced,' announced Bowman with satisfaction. 'What did you expect? Just because *Fortune* wrote him up, he went haywire. I expect he'll have to go to Boston.'

It could have been Siberia.

Bowman rattled on. Not until dessert did suspicion darken John Putnam Thatcher's mind.

'Walter!' he said suddenly, looking across the table at his companion, now bathed in unconvincing innocence. 'Your job is to root out information and transmit it to me, not to try to fish news *from* me.'

Bowman remained unrepentant. 'Habit,' he explained airily.

Thatcher eyed him with severity. It would be interesting to learn precisely how Walter Bowman had learned of Gabriel Uhlein's request for a check on Elliot Patterson's bank account. It was certainly not from Donald Benson. But Thatcher, a realist to his core, knew he never would learn.

'Then I ran into Gabe himself last night,' Bowman explained.

'Worried, was he?'

'Hell no! Full of bounce! Cheerful! Everything's coming up roses! Naturally, the whole thing made me suspicious. You know what a sharpie Gabe is. He was too damned hearty, if you know what I mean. What's up? Did this Patterson run off with the petty cash?'

Temperately Thatcher replied that one of Uhlein's employees seemed to be out of touch with his office and turned the subject. This did not satisfy Bowman, but he was too experienced to argue. Thatcher knew other sources would soon be tapped. And, although Walter was the best intelligence agent on Wall Street, he was not the only one. Clearly the tenuous web of communication that spun up and down Wall Street was beginning to quiver.

As Gabe Uhlein could have testified. He had spent a miserable morning on the phone, turning away casual and not so casual inquiries. Now he put the receiver down once again and glared at it. A small, round-faced man with guileless blue eyes, he was Dickensian in build. Nature might have designed him to be a professional fund raiser. At the moment, however, his customary cheerfulness was conspicuously absent.

Then, decisively, he jumped to his feet and hurried out to his secretary's desk.

'I'll be with Mrs Knightley if any calls come, Doris.'

He strode down the corridor. Target Associates was not the kind of institutionalized establishment where the head of the firm summons assistants to stately conferences. Give and take was the order of the day. Uhlein often dropped in on his subordinates. Quite at home, he would prop his legs against the nearest piece of furniture and transact business. Today he was trying to show the staff that he was his usual insouciant self. But the minute he got to Marian Knightley's office, he shut the door behind him and said, 'Marian, I think we've got trouble on our hands.'

Marian Knightley looked up from the folder she was studying. Uhlein was not prone to cry wolf. Indeed, if he had a fault, it was his tendency to assume that the wolf all too visible on the horizon was somebody's well-trained pet. It was not like him to admit trouble. She ran through a mental list of possibilities.

'Has something come up about Elliot?' she asked calmly.

Uhlein shook his head and hooked himself on to the corner of her desk.

'No, still no word. God knows what . . . No, I was just talking about it to Sally Patterson. Marian, she's wondering about going to the police.'

Marian Knightley was torn between amusement and irritation. 'For heaven's sake, Gabe, of course she is! After all, her husband has disappeared – '

But Uhlein interrupted impetuously.

'I don't like it,' he said with a rush. 'It won't do us any good, Marian. People are already asking questions. What if Elliot gets picked up drunk? Maybe he was in a gambling raid. He may be hiding behind a false name. My God, if it comes out – well, you know what scandal would do to us!'

The frown on Mrs Knightley's brow did not follow a well-etched path. She was in her early forties and looked ten years younger. Obviously she did not do much frowning.

'I know,' she said thoughtfully. 'But if Elliot had been picked up, he would have contacted one of us, to raise bail if nothing else.' She did not add that she had been half expecting a cry for help from Elliot; it would not be the first time he had come to her. 'But Gabe, Elliot isn't much of a drinking man. And, as for gambling . . . well, that's absurd.'

Gabe Uhlein brightened and took heart. 'Of course it is,' he said. 'Elliot is the quiet kind. He's not the type for the bright lights, is he? Why, just the other day Senator Verender told me that we were lucky to have him. And after all, the Sloan says that his bank account is absolutely normal,' he wound up in a burst of conviction.

Marian looked at him and remained silent. Under her gaze, Gabriel Uhlein's conviction oozed away. Marian was always the most helpful of colleagues, but you had to play by her rules. And her most stringent rule was that she would not voice suspicions for you. When Uhlein first began to fear that one of his employees was getting lazy to the point of irresponsibility, or taking to drink in a big way, he could always rely on Marian's sound advice. But it never came in a form he could like: something to let him believe that she had first raised the whole unfortunate matter. Their battle of will had been fought out long years ago. Uhlein recognized this by capitulating immediately and falling back into uncongenial anxiety.

'Now, of course it's absurd to think that Elliot could be any kind of crook,' he slowly edged into his subject. 'After all, you and I have worked with him for years. But people who don't know Elliot – why, they might wonder if he hasn't skipped.'

'They might,' Marian Knightley admitted.

'Our answer to that would be: *Look at his bank account. He did not empty it out. That's not the action of a cheap thief.*'

For a long moment Marian looked at him. Then: 'We gave

him those independent accounts last June, Gabe. They're what I'm a little worried about. And you are too.'

Uhlein winced. 'He's been at Target ten years, Marian,' he pleaded.

'Election accounts,' she continued ruthlessly.

Uhlein groaned. 'I knew those damned things were going to spell trouble.'

Target Associates was a pioneer in the field of nonpartisan management of campaign contributions. The move, like most of Gabe Uhlein's moves, had been financially successful from the start, but it introduced donors fighting for anonymity, erratic cash flows, and books in hopeless confusion until November elections were past – in other words, an embezzler's dream world. Gabe Uhlein and Elliot Patterson had been enthusiastic about it; Marian Knightley had not.

Absently she pushed a cigarette pack across the desk. 'All right, Gabe. Let's get right down to it. Neither of us can see Elliot as a thief...'

'Hell no!'

'But we're in no position to take any chances, are we? We'll have to call in the auditors. Elliot's accounts are going to have to be checked – fast.'

Uhlein closed his eyes in very real pain. 'And everybody in the office will know. And the word will get out, too. Oh, God! Marian, don't you think Elliot's bank account means anything?'

Compassionately she said, 'Not really, Gabe. After all, if Elliot has simply walked out on Sally, he might have left the money for her. Or maybe his own bank account was too small to bother with – after he cleaned us out.'

In an agony, Gabe Uhlein pushed himself to his feet and took an agitated turn around the small office. 'And if he walks in on us, what then? If he finds us auditing his books?'

Marian Knightley was, in her way, bracing. 'Gabe, if Elliot walks in tomorrow, he's going to have a little explaining of his own to do.'

Uhlein departed for lunch as depressed as it was possible for him to be.

*

In contrast, Thatcher and Bowman left Massoletti's contentedly and joined the Loan Policy Board milling casually outside the Sloan's conference room. With an inward sigh, Thatcher watched his ebullient companion greet a colleague with zest; his own well-being was plummeting. He was, he reminded himself sternly, being paid for this sort of thing, but offhand he could think of twenty occupations preferable to prolonged and indecisive committee meetings – including an attack on the items currently littering his desk. He was, therefore, not displeased when Miss Evans rounded the corner with a message for him.

'Of course,' he replied. 'Oh, Vaughan, I think perhaps you and the Committee had better carry on. Lancer and I are going to be delayed briefly.'

'Fine,' said Vaughan, revealing ferocious determination to extract results from his confrères.

'And keep a weather eye on Bowman,' Thatcher advised paternally, departing. In expert hands, a brief delay could be made coterminous with this meeting.

Still he wondered, as the elevator bore him towerward, what accounted for Lancer's courteous request. Unlike the absent Bradford Withers, Lancer was not given to fits and starts. On the contrary, he was almost painfully dedicated to discharging each of his duties and obligations to the best of his very considerable ability.

'Oh, John,' he said when Thatcher reached his office. 'I hope you don't mind. Frankly, I don't see that the Committee is making enough progress to require our presence.'

'That's one way of putting it,' Thatcher commented, carefully drawing up the one comfortable chair he had located in Lancer's office.

Lancer nodded, indicating to the knowledgeable a fact received and docketed: at some time in the future, the Sloan would be reevaluating the effectiveness of the Loan Policy Committee.

Hoping he could avoid the committee inevitably charged with this task, Thatcher inquired about the departure from routine.

Lancer got up and walked over to the window. Something was troubling him. Thatcher reserved judgement.

'You know, John, Gabe Uhlein has a lot of good reasons for wanting to keep the police out of this,' he said without turning.

Thatcher groped for a moment before recalling the missing Elliot Patterson. 'Certainly he has,' he agreed. 'Professional fund raisers have to have impeccable reputations. Or, at the least, they have to keep the police off the premises.'

'Yes,' said Lancer.

'Although I would be willing to bet that Uhlein is calling in the auditors right now,' Thatcher continued reflectively.

This was not omniscience but experience. Books can be audited in decent privacy – without alarming potential contributors and clients.

Lancer pressed on. 'He said yesterday he was urging Mrs Patterson to hold off calling the police.'

Thatcher waited.

'Then I ran into the Brunswick Committee having lunch at the Club,' Lancer went on.

'That curator,' said Thatcher appreciatively.

'Yes, Marsden. And Ralph Armitage. You know him, don't you? Runs that big insurance brokerage up on Lexington Avenue.'

Thatcher did, vaguely.

'And a youngster who's just starting out in some public-relations outfit. Dunster, or Davis or something like that...'

Thatcher, who knew George Lancer, accepted this without comment, knowing that somewhere on his person a memorandum book contained the correct name, the precise business affiliation and any other relevant details.

'These people all have good reasons – or what they think is good reason – to let things drift,' Lancer said censoriously. 'Marsden, as you might expect, is terrified of being involved in scandal. He seems to feel that if Patterson emerges from some lost week-end, the press will seize on his connection with Neil Marsden. That young man has a very inflated conception of his own news value.'

Gravely Thatcher agreed.

Lancer resumed his indictment. 'As for Armitage, I'm surprised at him. I would have expected a higher degree of responsibility. He's obviously picked up news about an audit at Target Associates. There's no problem about the kind of scandal he anticipates. And there's no denying that Brunswick isn't going to look good if its fund raisers turn out to be embezzlers.'

Thatcher's guess during lunch with Bowman had been justified. Lancer and Armitage had their ears to the ground; others did too.

'And what is the upshot of all this?' Lancer asked severely. 'Everybody is grinding his own axe. No one is advising the wife with a view to *her* best interests. It's high time Mrs Patterson went to the police. This has passed beyond the realm of a night out and a hangover the next morning.'

'Yes, it has,' Thatcher said reluctantly. It was all too clear where his agreement was going to take him. He had been victimized by Lancer's strong sense of duty before.

'I'm glad you agree,' said Lancer, consulting his watch. 'But if this poor woman is getting all this advice from Uhlein and the others – she may well be confused. I gather she has been convinced not to call the police so far. I thought what I would do was run up and talk to her. In fact, go with her, if that's necessary. I think that's the right thing to do.'

That tore it. If only Lancer were going forth as an Old Brunsie, Thatcher was safe. But the right thing to do?

One older, wiser, man of substance, bent on lending a helping hand and moral support, spoke to another.

'I'd be glad to have your company, John.'

Never had the Loan Policy Committee looked more inviting.

4. At the Pleasure of the Instructor

Newspapermen, perhaps understandably, constantly tout the power of the press; in fact, the power of banks should not be despised. An hour after George Lancer unveiled his intentions to Thatcher they were speeding up the New England Thruway in the Sloan's opulent limousine, en route to Rye. With them, respectful but dazed, was Jim Dunlop, who had been ruthlessly winkled away from his desk at Pruett, Pruett & Mayberry by dint of a telephone call from Lancer's Miss Evans to Mayberry's Miss Howes.

'It was good of you to join us, Dunlop,' said Lancer with his usual meticulous courtesy.

Dunlop, who had been offered no alternative, murmured that he was pleased to be of service. If he was too youthful to pull this off without showing curiosity, he at least refrained from outright question. Thatcher was inclined to give him high marks.

'We felt we should talk to Mrs Patterson, who must be having a difficult time,' Lancer continued. 'It occurred to me that it might be easier if we arrived with someone she knows. I myself have only met her on social occasions, perhaps two or three times.'

Dunlop listened hard, then, with care, said, 'Yes, Mr Lancer. But perhaps I should point out that my wife and I are not – have not been terribly close to the Pattersons. They're . . .'

He broke off. Amused, Thatcher guessed that he had been about to explain that the Pattersons, in their mid-thirties, represented an older generation to the youthful Dunlops. An awkward point to make among one's seniors.

'It's really Elliot I know,' Dunlop continued doggedly. 'We're on the Brunswick Committee together, of course. And he helped me out when I first came to New York job-hunting.'

'I see,' said Lancer tolerantly. 'Still, you do know the Pattersons better than I do. You may be able to help convince Mrs

Patterson that she should report her husband's disappearance.'

Thatcher thought that Dunlop looked daunted. He did not blame him.

Lancer, however, continued, 'Now, from all reports, Patterson is a respectable man – not the sort to have dropped out of sight before. Right?'

'Right,' Dunlop said.

Thatcher broke a promise he had made to himself and joined the discussion. 'You don't sound enthusiastic,' he remarked. 'Do you have doubts about Patterson's respectability?' Even as he spoke, he recognized his essential unfairness; young Dunlop was already outweighed and outmanned. There was no justification for further harassment. Thatcher tried to mend matters. 'Or do you oppose informing the police?'

But George Lancer relieved Dunlop of the need to reply.

'Nobody wants to call the police,' he said. 'It's only natural to hope you can put it off. After all, Patterson's friends must want to avoid the inevitable speculation that any publicity will involve. And there's the fear, too. But, no matter how reluctant people may be, this situation can't be allowed to drag on. It is adding needlessly to Mrs Patterson's anxiety. And for all we know, it may be adding to whatever difficulties Elliot Patterson is in.'

Lancer, Thatcher could tell, was thinking along standard, almost-respectable lines: innocent mishaps like street accidents, medically inexplicable attacks of amnesia, venial sins which had come to grief.

Jim Dunlop, on the other hand, was not. Little could Thatcher be expected to realize that Jim Dunlop, having resolutely faced up to his ignorance of adult life as it is lived in America, no longer had any guidelines. The sky was the limit, as far as he was concerned. Elliot might have defected to Peking with the lastest fund-raising techniques; he might have joined the Peace Corps; he might be making a living by mugging people in Central Park; he might be holed up in a cold beach cabin on Fire Island with a teen-age sex kitten.

'Well, I think we're here,' said Lancer, peering out.

The chauffeur had indeed turned on to Walnut Street and was searching for the right number. This did not prove insuperably difficult; the Patterson home, architecturally indistinguishable from its fellows, was a house apart. For one thing, two cars were pulled up in the driveway although it was only the middle of the afternoon. The lawn was carefully raked and the drapes cheerfully drawn, but already people had pulled up and gone indoors, then hurried out. Coming and going had continued for almost two days. Unremarkable as such departures from normality might seem in an urban setting, in suburban circles they were equivalent to a small-scale riot. Not a soul could be seen on the pavements; no curtains twitched at neighbouring windows. Yet Walnut Street was breathlessly, if invisibly, keeping tabs on every new development at No 203.

Mrs Patterson herself answered the musical chimes. A small trim woman, she was dressed in a handsome woollen shift. Her hair was a sleek golden cap. Yet her cheeks were pale. She had been crying, but she seemed to have herself well in hand now.

'Oh, Jim,' she said in welcome. 'Yes, of course, I remember Mr Lancer. And Mr Thatcher? How do you do? Won't you come in? I'm afraid everything is upset just now.'

Now, when it had become inevitable that this party was to descend, armed with unsolicited good advice, on a woman whose husband was missing, a woman described as confused and distraught, Thatcher had reasonably enough experienced distinct premonitions. His forebodings were correct; where he had gone wrong, it developed, was in the detail. Mrs Patterson had an unalterable commitment to gracious living. It was more chilling, under the circumstances, than hysteria.

'It is kind of you to come,' she said in a clear sweet voice, transforming their visit into a social call. Thatcher was wondering if she was practising for the funeral when he found himself enmeshed in a second round of introductions.

'My brother-in-law, Mr Consett. And this is Susanna. This is Andrea. This is Caroline. Say hello to Mr Dunlop, Andrea...'

Mrs Patterson made it velvety clear that Susanna, Andrea and Caroline were going to exhibit their beautiful manners.

This caused a delay, since the little girls had grown big-eyed with shyness on the arrival of the newcomers. They were lovely children, with much-brushed Alice-in-Wonderland tresses combed back from angelic brows and streaming to the shoulders of their charming little frocks. They were also under three feet tall, and, acting on principle about human beings that height, Thatcher extricated himself and moved over to the brother-in-law, who was less endearing but adult. A red-faced overweight man, he showed signs of strain.

'Helluva thing,' he confided in Thatcher's ear. 'I can't understand what El's up to!'

This indiscretion was probably due to relief at being liberated from a suffocatingly feminine atmosphere. 'Still, we decided the girls better come home with us, in case Elliot turns up the worse for wear. You never know!'

Elliot's wife admitted no such lack of confidence.

'And now we're going to go with Uncle Bill to see Aunt Karen and Jimmy and Donny and Mary Louise!' she exclaimed sweetly, ignoring mounting sullenness among her daughters. 'We'll put our coats on . . .'

It was a full ten minutes before order was restored, a ten minutes during which Mrs Patterson was driven to tell her offspring that she was deeply disappointed in them all. But finally the coats were donned, and Consett, Susanna, Andrea and Caroline sped off towards Long Island. Consett's parting injunction that his sister-in-law remain calm seemed, to the disinterested observer, totally unnecessary.

Mrs Patterson gallantly waved at the departing station wagon, then rejoined her guests in the living-room with a brave smile.

'I thought it was better to send the girls to my sister,' she informed them. 'Of course, they don't know that anything is wrong, I've been very careful about that. I told them Daddy is on a trip. But children are so sensitive to atmosphere at that age. And I don't want them to see Mummy worrying!'

Jim Dunlop, very newly married, was respectful. But Lancer, who like Thatcher had raised a family, was made of sterner stuff. He got down to business.

'Yes, of course. Now, Mrs Patterson, the reason I asked if we might come to talk to you was that I had heard about the difficulty you are having.'

Thatcher waited for the questions. How had Lancer heard? How many people knew? Were people talking?

They did not come. Mrs Patterson settled herself opposite them, sighed, and looked at her visitors with sad patience.

'You do understand,' she said, underlining her words with approval. 'It is terribly difficult. I have been trying to keep a grip on myself for the children's sake, but I am just frantic!'

Now, frantic was precisely the word Thatcher would not have chosen. In his day he had seen women who were frantic; the price of black emotional abandon was higher than reddened eyes.

'I simply tell myself that Elliot will walk in any minute. This whole horrible dream will be over!' She produced a spanking white handkerchief and raised it to her face.

Lancer leaned forward and spoke gently. 'That is what we all hope, but, Mrs Patterson, we can't rely on hope. After all, Elliot has been missing since Monday.'

She withdrew from her handkerchief and looked at him for a moment.

With kind authority, Lancer said, 'You must call the police.'

There was absolute silence.

Then, with equally kind authority, Mrs Patterson replied, 'Oh, I'm afraid that is out of the question.'

Briefly puzzled, Lancer launched into his sensible argument. At intervals Mrs Patterson replied. As the exchange continued, Thatcher derived unholy glee at Lancer's increased difficulty in keeping acerbity at bay. Thatcher had never questioned George's purity of motive on this errand of mercy. Yet there was no doubt that he had been moved, however unconsciously, by visions of a frail woman whose helplessness called for manly protection. Instead, with motives equally pure, Mrs Patterson was explaining things to him with softly perfect self-assurance.

'You see, Mr Lancer, I know that Elliot wouldn't like that at all,' she said with bewildering certainty. 'And, of course, I have complete faith in Elliot. Just as he has complete faith in me.'

Thatcher took pity on Lancer, who was frankly at sea.

'Mrs Patterson,' he interjected cautiously, 'exactly why wouldn't your husband want you to call the police?'

In considerable detail she told him. Sally Patterson, it developed, had cultivated that highly articulate manner which sheds a specious gloss of rationality over the wildest absurdities. In fact, there was no logical underpinning to her moral certainty; it was a matter of revealed truth. On the one hand, recourse to the police, they learned, was tantamount to accusing Elliot. On the other hand she, Sally, did not wish to expose Elliot to vulgarity of this sort.

'You see,' she said, intelligently persuasive, 'what I am determined to do is keep everything as it is, the way Elliot and I love it. When Elliot returns, he will find things just as he left them.'

This proud proclamation left Thatcher, who was nobody's fool, disinclined to add anything further. Fortunately young Dunlop, benefiting from more recent exposure to women in their prime of silliness, took over after this rout of his elders.

'We know how you feel, Sally,' he said inaccurately. 'But look at it this way. What can have happened to Elliot? He may have had some sort of accident. Calling the police about him would just help us check out these possibilities.'

Without rancour, Mrs Patterson corrected error when it crossed her path. 'Oh no, Jim. Bill has called all the hospitals for me. So there's no need to worry about that!'

Perhaps this accounted for the brother-in-law's badgered air. Thatcher could think of less charitable explanations. At any rate, he settled back, leaving the impasse to others. Lancer, unwilling to believe his ears, summoned up heavier guns. But Sally Patterson remained unmoved while her duty was defined, while her intelligence was appealed to. She appreciated Mr Lancer's concern, but she knew exactly where her duty lay. Her duty was to Elliot. And despite terrible anguish of spirit, she had thought about things very carefully. She knew she was doing what Elliot would want. Argument only reinforced her assurance. She remained quite kind.

'I know you mean well, Mr Lancer,' she said in tones reminiscent of those she used with Susanna, Andrea and Caroline. 'But Elliot and I – well, we have always made it a rule to work out our problems together, not with outsiders. Elliot is as important in raising the girls as I am. And I have always helped him with his business decisions. We talk things out and we don't go running to others, the way so many people do. We've always said that if we didn't have perfect confidence in each other, why, we wouldn't have anything. So now, when something like this comes up, I am not going to lose my head and rush off to the police.'

George C. Lancer, Thatcher was happy to see, was getting a little punchy as Mrs Patterson's gentle but inexorable aria unwound.

'And I know and trust my husband. Of course, I have worried that perhaps he had an accident. But, thank God, I've come to my senses. If Elliot had been hurt, I would have been notified. Elliot is always very careful to carry identification – just in case. He always has been. And as for these insinuations that Elliot could have done something wrong...'

She shook her head at the absurdity. Words, unfortunately, did not fail her.

'Oh, I realize what some people are saying! Mr Uhlein phoned and said something about not calling the police. And the Brunswick Committee too, Jim. Oh, nobody said anything. But I'm not a fool. I know what they're thinking. That Elliot might have ... oh, taken money. Or run off with another woman.'

Mrs Patterson's sentiments might be vehement, but her control never faltered. 'That's utterly ridiculous,' she said with quiet conviction. 'Elliot is a sensitive human being. His whole life is devoted to service. He is not out for all the money he can get. He wants the good things for his family – but only the good things that count. Elliot wants to help people – young people. You know that, Jim. His whole life is dedicated to spiritual awareness. Whatever these people are saying – well, it reflects on them, not on Elliot.'

In sum, Elliot Patterson was not common clay. To Thatcher he did not sound quite human either. Sally Patterson was also making it clear, as she genteelly harangued Lancer, that Elliot's wife was cut from the same superior web. Lesser souls might experience shame and mortification. Poor insecure creatures! Where there is real knowledge, there can be no suspicion, no fear, no shame. Thatcher had no trouble making his diagnosis. Mrs Patterson had spent ten years perfecting her role as all-understanding, all-forgiving earth mother. It was now far more essential to sustain that role than to find Elliot. Happily, neither Sally nor Lancer suspected this state of affairs for one moment.

Even the door chimes did not break her pace. While Jim Dunlop obeyed an unspoken request and went to the hall, Mrs Patterson continued to provide further analysis, secure in some inner conviction that it was not her husband on the doorstep.

And she was quite right. It was not Elliot Patterson. Thatcher, whose attention was inclined to wander, could hear the low rumble of several masculine voices. Surely they were spending a long time on hallway preliminaries? Young Dunlop seemed to be protesting.

It was several minutes before he returned. What he trailed in his wake did succeed in putting a period to Sally's remarks.

Two gigantic, bronzed, armed and booted State Police troopers stolidly took up positions in front of a cobbler's bench, looking wildly out of place surrounded by pine panelling and chintz. Suddenly the room became very low-ceilinged.

Mrs Patterson's self-possession was not shaken. She bent on Dunlop a look that nicely blended comprehension and forgiveness. She had charged him with insubordination, convicted him and then suspended the sentence – all in the blink of an eyelash.

'But, Sally! We didn't call them,' he protested.

Sally shook her head indulgently.

'You're Mrs Patterson?' the older and senior of the troopers broke in to ask. 'Mrs Elliot Patterson?'

'That's right. And I do wish you to understand that whoever has reported my husband's disappearance has done so without my permission.'

To those who knew her – and even after one short hour Thatcher had no hesitation in including himself on that select roster – this anxiety to set everyone straight came as no surprise.

Its effect on the police, however, was nothing short of sensational. Until now they had been exuding stately benevolence. At Mrs Patterson's magic words they both stared dumbfounded at their hostess, momentarily off guard, before every vestige of human expression disappeared as completely as if shutters had fallen over a loaded shop window.

'That's not surprising,' the sergeant said heavily as he pulled out a notebook and pencil. 'Now, you say your husband has disappeared?'

Sally Patterson stiffened at his scepticism. She had met many reactions to her news about Elliot – amazement, sympathy, horror, reassurance. This was her first encounter with disbelief.

'Certainly!' she said with a ladylike snap.

'And when did he disappear?'

'On Monday night.' Sally eyed the sergeant with cold dislike.

'And Mr Patterson is the owner of a green Oldsmobile, licence number 317–48?'

Sally contented herself with a nod. She had become a visual rebuke to uncouth intrusiveness. She was sitting, gracefully erect, on the sofa. As no one had suggested that they sit, the troopers, very correctly, continued to loom overhead.

'And I suppose the car disappeared with him?' the sergeant suggested softly.

Mrs Patterson, whose preoccupation with the more civilized aspects of life had severely impaired her instinct for survival, did not hesitate.

'Certainly. Elliot drove the car into the railroad station every morning. It isn't there now.'

Thatcher was conscious of his own surprise seconds before it was mirrored by his slower-witted companions. But within a very short time all three men were gaping.

Sally exploded this piece of dynamite with serene unselfconsciousness. She was absorbed in her silent battle with the sergeant. But for everybody else, Elliot Patterson ceased to be a man who had disappeared on Fifth Avenue in the middle of Manhattan. Now Elliot Patterson had disappeared five minutes before reaching his own home. Or five minutes after?

Thatcher told himself sternly not to leap to conclusions, even if Mrs Patterson suddenly seemed too stereotyped to be true, even if the whole Patterson ménage suddenly seemed too upright to be real. Remember, this was a house with three children in it. Thatcher's efforts at self-discipline received an assist from the object of his suspicions.

'Sergeant,' she said clearly, 'we must have one thing understood. I have no intention of permitting a police search for my husband.' She grabbed for an attitude which had stood her in good stead that afternoon. 'No doubt you mean well—'

'Mrs Patterson,' the sergeant interrupted unceremoniously, 'there's no question of your permitting or not permitting a search for your husband.'

Sally was looking more animated. Anger had brought two bright patches of colour into her cheeks and sharpened her jawline. She also permitted herself a looseness of phrasing that would have been unheard of an hour earlier.

'And who else wants him? Whose business is it?' she demanded.

The sergeant was very grim. 'Well, we want him. We want to question him in connection with the hit-and-run killing of two high-school students on Monday evening.'

5. Papers Will Be Required

Sally Patterson came to the rapid conclusion that the police, after all, did not mean well.

'Don't be silly!' she spat with a kittenish ferocity that stripped away assurance and years and left a gauche girl in her place.

'It would be easy enough to prove it's silly. Just produce that car so our lab boys can go over it,' the sergeant said evenly.

'How can I produce the car?' Sally demanded wildly. 'I don't know where it is! I don't even know where my husband is! You're just taking advantage of the fact that he's not here.'

Now that Mrs Patterson was visibly distressed, the sergeant moderated his bulldozer tactics. As a sign of his new approach he seated himself and beckoned his junior to do likewise. At chair level they were simply big men, not threatening presences.

But Sally Patterson, biting the corner of her handkerchief, stared at them as if they were two savage panthers let loose in her living-room.

'I know this isn't easy, ma'am, but, believe me, it's best to get the whole thing cleared up. Now, don't you think your husband should come back and cooperate?'

Whether the real tragedy of the situation had at last come home to Sally or whether she was simply undone by being on the receiving end of gentle authoritarianism, Thatcher never knew. But quite suddenly she went to pieces.

'No!' she began in a low guttural voice as her back arched alarmingly. 'No, I won't listen to you!' she stormed. 'No, no, no!' Spreading rigidity brought her heels and palms slapping down in a ragged drumbeat.

Fortunately a neighbour, maddened with curiosity by successive arrivals of a limousine and a squad car on Walnut Street, materialized on the doorstep just in time to be impressed into service until a doctor could be located. But Thatcher could see that prospects for departure were not good.

Common decency required that Mrs Patterson be supported

during this awful time. And even after sedatives turned her hysterical denials into the moans of a wounded animal, release did not come. The police now seized on Jim Dunlop as a source of information about the missing man. Common decency required the august presence of George C. Lancer and John Putnam Thatcher during the questioning of Dunlop.

'After all, we dragged him into this thing,' Lancer said. 'Wouldn't do to walk out on him.'

Thatcher was stung by the plural pronoun. 'It might be more useful to send out for some food,' he retorted.

The police were reviewing Elliot Patterson's last known movements.

'And all of you left this Ivy League Club together?' the sergeant was saying.

Dunlop was very unhappy. 'Marsden, Armitage and I left with three of the boys we had been interviewing. Elliot stayed behind to talk to another one of them. That was the last I saw of him.'

But the police were far more interested in where Patterson might have gone after the accident than where he had been before. Did he have a summer place? Where did he have relatives? Did business take him somewhere frequently? Did he have a mistress? If Dunlop didn't know the answers to these questions, then who did?

Well, the search for Patterson had now passed into professional hands, Thatcher reflected. Certainly the mystery of his disappearance could cease to trouble his family and friends. A hit-and-run killer's reasons for going to ground spoke for themselves.

And presumably this evening would produce food sooner or later.

'I am sure,' George Lancer said with as much slow sincerity as if his dinner time were not long past, 'we all hope this is a terrible mistake.'

The sergeant was not unsympathetic. He looked around the carefully middle-class living-room and tried to find the right words.

'Sometimes this kind of thing happens so fast people don't

really know what they've done. Say, Patterson had a drink or two. Somehow, he hits these kids. Before he knows what he's doing, he steps on the gas. Then, when he comes to his senses – he's stuck. He's afraid to go back. He knows he lost his head ...' He shrugged fatalistically.

This was cold comfort, and Thatcher was happy to see that nobody was maintaining that Elliot Patterson was incapable of having a drink or two. Still, he reminded himself, he had come along to lend George a helping hand. He might as well try.

'What took you so long, officer?'

Hitherto largely ignored, he became the focus of attention. Young Dunlop frowned in his direction. Lancer looked his question. The troopers were silent.

'I gather that the survivors gave you an accurate description of Patterson's car and the licence plate. Yet here it is Wednesday. And I think you said that two youngsters were killed on Monday. I know that our police are a good deal faster-moving than that ...'

'Of course,' Lancer mouthed silently as a look passed between the policemen.

Then it came: A group of eight teenagers, eddying out of a beer hall just over the line in Putnam County, had spilled onto the gravel driveway. They were somewhat the worse for drink. At any rate, headlights suddenly roared out of the darkness and brought horror to the scene. After the screaming and the cries were past, after glass and blood were removed, six shaken high-school boys were still alive. Two of them were too injured to be of any use and two, in shock, were released to their parents who whisked them under a doctor's care. This left two boys to be interviewed; they agreed it was a late model Oldsmobile. Bloodstains and enamel fragments from the torn trousers of one of the corpses told the authorities that the car was jade green. Not until yesterday had a further item appeared. The licence plates were New York State; the first three numbers were 317. The boy was certain because his own were the same.

'So we pulled a list, Mr Thatcher,' said the younger trooper with a slow, humourless smile. 'We're checking out 275 cars. Over a hundred are clean already.'

Everybody present was too realistic to fall upon this. Even Lancer was very temperate. 'It could still be a mistake,' he said.

'It could,' the officer agreed. 'But you see why we want to see Patterson – and his car.'

They did. The party that finally set off for New York was not in good spirits. On the other hand, they were in better shape than Uncle Bill Consett, who wearily pulled up just as they were leaving. His wife hurried purposefully indoors. Consett lingered.

'That, I don't believe,' he said, upon hearing an encapsulated male interpretation of the police charges. He waved away polite professions of faith. 'No, I mean the business about roaring out of the darkness. El is not only the worst driver I've ever known, he's the slowest. I doubt if he's gone over fifty in his life. Not' – here he paused, struck with a new and unwelcome thought – 'not unless he's gone stark raving mad.'

This time there were no polite professions at all.

Emboldened by two miles and the darkness of the car's interior, Dunlop broke the silence. 'I suppose that's possible, isn't it? That Elliot has temporarily lost his mind.'

Since there was nothing else to do, Thatcher set out to learn what was in the young man's mind with a question of his own.

'Have you ever observed signs of abnormality?'

The negative was hasty and emphatic. Overemphatic?

'It's tragic,' Lancer said. 'If only Patterson had gone right home after your meeting, Dunlop, this would never have ... er ... arisen. Why on earth was he driving around Putnam County?'

'Outside a beer hall,' Thatcher murmured, with intent.

He was right. Dunlop restrained himself only with difficulty.

At 68th Street Lancer roused himself from his sombre thoughts and courteously invited his companions to join him in a late supper. Thatcher truly regretted having to beg off, and he was sorry to deny young Dunlop the opportunity to taste Matthilde's notable cooking. Still, consoling himself that he was doing an unknown wife a considerable favour, he refused

George's invitation, neatly cut Dunlop out, and bore him away. It had been a long trying day. But he did not propose to let it end without knowing what was weighing so heavily with the young man.

George Lancer rounded off his evening with a better dinner than John Thatcher was enjoying. Then, over brandy, he told Lucy about the trials of the day. As usual, she listened with interest and produced one excellent suggestion: that he alert the Sloan's public-relations man first thing in the morning. Newspaper coverage of the search for Elliot Patterson could be moderated, if not eliminated.

'Not that I think the police will release anything to the papers until they have something more definite,' said Lancer, making a note of it. 'But you're quite right, Lucy. Publicity will only add to that poor woman's distress. And to be quite selfish about this, I could wish that Patterson had not been so active in the Brunswick Club – that is, if things turn out to be what they seem. I'd be sorry to see Brunswick's name dragged through this kind of mud.'

'I know, dear,' said Lucy. 'And speaking of dragging, what a shame you had to let John in for all this.'

Blissfully unaware that Thatcher was laying up information that would enable him to repay in kind, Lancer agreed that he regretted it very much, then inquired about Lucy's day. Like Gaul, it had been divided into three parts; unwed mothers and the preservation of landmarks in the morning, the Friends of the Opera in the afternoon.

Despite these creature comforts, however, Lancer did not enjoy an untroubled night's sleep like, for instance, John Putnam Thatcher. This was not because he was less unregenerate but because of fundamental differences between the two men. Thatcher had perfected the art of compartmentalizing his thoughts, so that he could put the most nagging problems out of his mind at will. Lancer, on the contrary, positively enjoyed turning things over ruminatively during odd hours, searching out details that had been overlooked. He was not a worrier but, as Lucy put it, a ponderer.

Then too, Thatcher was a senior vice-president of the Sloan, which, given the current president, gave him considerable responsibility for day-to-day operations while Lancer, the chairman of the board, normally functioned as the bank's outside man. With Bradford Withers on the premises these lines frequently blurred, but in theory it was Lancer who maintained liaison with other banking notables, with government officials, and with those members of the business community worthy of the Sloan's attention. He was a specialist in choosing the best and most dignified way for the Sloan to do and say exactly what it wanted. Accordingly he had developed a certain feel for the big vague forces that shape men, events, and opinion. At the moment he felt nothing but disquiet.

Nevertheless the Sloan received his undivided attention the following morning. This was fortunate, since in his and Thatcher's absence, the Loan Policy Committee had erupted into overt warfare, with Walter Bowman evincing determination to grind Vaughan and the whole of International Division to dust beneath his heels. Peace was restored by lunchtime; harmony was yet to come.

'Dining upstairs?' Thatcher asked.

'No,' Lancer replied. 'I think I'll drop in on the Brunswick Club for lunch.'

'George,' Thatcher said bluntly, 'you're a sucker for punishment.'

This Lancer, taxiing over to the Ivy League Club, could not honestly deny. He did not expect to enjoy lunch: the food was execrable and he did not have high hopes for the conversation. Yet, because of all the Lancers who for so many years had attended Brunswick College, he felt some obligation to keep a watching brief.

There was, at least, no need for delicate introduction of the subject troubling him. The first person Lancer saw after he entered the gloomy lobby was Ralph Armitage. He was coming down the great staircase, looking shaken.

'My God!' he burst forth instantly, so shocked that conventional greetings were superfluous. 'It's true, George. There's a cop up there. He won't let me into the Brunswick office. Says that somebody is going to come down and search it. I didn't believe it. I really didn't.'

Lancer, trading away his topcoat, found that Armitage was waiting to join him on the way to the dining-room. There was, in short no need to ask; the Brunswick Club had learned that the estimable Elliot Patterson was now a fugitive from justice.

'I just heard about this,' said a new voice. 'Oh, you're here too, Mr Lancer? Excellent.'

Neil Marsden, a symphony in conservative tailoring, had hurried up. 'To be quite truthful, I find it very difficult to believe that Elliot is a hit-and-run killer.'

'You'd believe it,' Armitage interrupted, 'if you went upstairs and tried to get into our offices. They've got a cop standing guard, big as life.'

Marsden was horrified.

They had reached the dining-room and were being escorted to a corner table by an aged steward. A table for four, Lancer noted. It was assumed, on all fronts, that he had rushed to the Ivy League Club to join Brunswick Committee deliberations. This, in fact, was why he had come, but nonetheless he was nettled.

'... even on the Expressway, police terrify me,' Marsden was babbling in a high nervous voice. 'But here, at the Club!'

Lancer could not decide whether this was an ill-timed stab at humour. Whatever it was, it succeeded in restoring Ralph Armitage. Glossing over his own shock, he glared at Marsden across the top of his menu.

'Keep your voice down,' he said sourly. 'No use letting the whole dining-room know. And this isn't a ticket for speeding. This is a manslaughter charge.' He turned to Lancer, one man of sense to another. 'Why the hell couldn't the damned fool stop? Bad as it was ... oh, what? Oh, I'll take the vegetable soup. Then, the leg of lamb ...'

After a stately pause for ordering, battle was resumed.

Marsden was openly spiteful. 'That's very easy to say, Ralph. Elliot was probably drunk as a fish.'

'He doesn't drink much,' Armitage retorted. 'Look, no matter what happened, speculating about it isn't going to get us anywhere. The thing is, Elliot seems to be on the run...'

'I suppose you think we should ask him to resign,' said Marsden nastily just as young Dunlop hurried up, full of apologies for his tardiness and a new constraint.

Lancer was not the man to let a lack of official standing keep him from taking a hand. Clearly time for that hand had come.

'This is tragic,' he said calmly. 'I think the best thing we can do is hope that Elliot's connection with the college will not be blown out of proportion – and in the meantime, ignore the entire affair. Of course, we all hope that this is simply another misunderstanding.'

Marsden nodded but Jim Dunlop studiously kept his eyes on his grapefruit.

Armitage said, 'I took that line too, until I got upstairs and saw that cop.'

Lancer continued to counsel prudent inaction, unsurprised by Armitage's disproportionate response to the presence of one lone policeman. On the contrary, he understood it very well. Hit-and-run murder is like famine in India and the atom bomb; dreadful, but remote. The mind registered but the spirit remained aloof. Only when the world's evils touch homely details do most of us respond: the single charred doll at the holocaust; one torn letter on the battlefield; a shovelful of dirt at the graveside.

'I never thought I'd see the day when we had cops at the Club,' said a portly gentleman pausing at their table. 'What's this I hear about your Patterson killing his wife and kids?'

Surprisingly, Neil Marsden took up the cudgels. 'We had the police here during the New Year's Day Open House, you recall,' he said. 'And Elliot has been in an accident. This is simply a formality.'

He was quelling enough to repel the portly gentleman, who had misbehaved disgracefully during the aforesaid open house, but his departure revealed a middle-aged man with a meagre face and shrewd eyes that brooked no nonsense. Pulling up a chair, he joined the party.

'Now what is all this?' he demanded testily. 'I've been hearing more damned nonsense about Patterson. What exactly is going on?'

Whelby Kitchener, treasurer of the Brunswick Club, was a highly expert real-estate appraiser. His usual manner of barely suppressed moral outrage made it a kindness as well as a pleasure to convey bad news to him. Armitage did so.

'We're not broadcasting it' – here Kitchener bridled at the implication – 'but Patterson appears to be wanted by the police for a hit-and-run accident. From the little we know, it seems that he's taken it on the lam. At any rate, no one has seen him since last Monday, when we had our meeting.'

Kitchener looked at him without enthusiasm. 'So that explains why I have not received the bond.'

The silence was complete. Then: 'What bond?' Lancer asked with a sinking heart.

Kitchener eyed him snappily. 'The bearer bond for $50,000 that Mrs Curtis has donated to Brunswick College.'

The committee came to life:

'That's right! I remember!'

'Of course!'

This litany soothed Kitchener. 'I understand that Patterson picked up the bond from Mrs Curtis some time over the weekend – although why these old women insist on keeping valuables in their homes ...'

Marsden nodded. 'That's right. He said you'd have the bond on Wednesday. Remember, we congratulated Elliot on pulling it off? We sat around discussing it.'

'I missed most of that,' Dunlop mumbled, but Marsden went on.

'Elliot was tickled pink to finally have his hands on the bond, and we kidded him about how great he was with old ladies until the boys arrived ...'

Marsden's garrulity struck Lancer as forced and out of character, but Kitchener merely demanded, 'Well, where is the bond now?'

Dunlop looked up. 'Maybe it's upstairs in the file cabinet, Mr Kitchener. I remember scooping up those folders and putting them away before we went out to the waiting-room to see the kids.'

'And,' said Ralph Armitage, not giving Kitchener any opportunity to deprecate such arrangements, 'that office is now locked and guarded by a policeman. You will have to wait.'

Kitchener rose. 'I should very much like to see the policeman who can keep me out of an office containing a $50,000 bond for which I am in any way responsible.'

He strode off.

'Hurrah for the old team!' said Neil Marsden.

'As I was saying...' Lancer recommenced.

For fifteen minutes they discussed the repercussions, probable, possible and avoidable, of Elliot Patterson's difficulties. It was agreed to bend every sinew to keep newspaper coverage to a minimum, and failing that, to keep references to Brunswick altogether out. It was decided that the Brunswick Admission Committee would continue to interview applicants, acting for the time being as a three-man body. It was decided that flowers for Mrs Patterson were premature. Indeed, the grating personality conflicts that characterized the committee were temporarily put aside over the question of how to indicate appropriate support and sympathy. Somebody had mentioned a book when Kitchener reappeared.

'Hah!' he said in triumph.

'Did you?'

There was no real need to ask. Only difficulties overcome could produce that self-satisfaction. Telephone calls, contacts in the Mayor's office, sheer force of personality finally put Kitchener into the Brunswick Club's files. Striding through the waiting-room, he had stalked into the inner office, ignoring the resentful policeman at his heel.

Then, he had fronted the filing cabinet: 'And did I find a $50,000 bearer bond? I did not! I found no Curtis file at all! Do you know what that means?'

Again Neil Marsden surprised George Lancer with his readiness for combat. 'Of course we know what that means. It means that Elliot Patterson was too careful to leave that bond here overnight. He took it home with him, just as right and proper as anybody could want. Unless, of course, it means that you simply didn't look in the right drawer.'

Before Kitchener could riposte, Armitage raked his flank. 'Elliot is extremely careful about financial details, Whelby. We should have thought of that. He certainly wouldn't leave anything of value in a file cabinet.'

Whelby Kitchener gave ground. 'You're right,' he admitted. 'At least that fits in with my previous dealings with Patterson. He's always been very careful. He was the one who insisted on receipts for every transfer. First-rate methods.'

Lancer contributed his own soothing syrup. 'And remember he may have left that bond in the safe at Target Associates,' he said. 'Or did any of you actually see the bond itself?'

After thoughtful reconstruction of the recent past, the Brunswick Committee agreed that the discussion of Mrs Curtis's donation had centred on suitable ways to express gratitude rather than on the bearer bond itself.

'In fact,' said Marsden, reaching for a cigarette, 'when I heard you were thinking of a letter from the president, I remember suggesting that the old lady might like being invited up for a week-end.'

Nods concurred, but Kichener was impatient. 'Well, I shall certainly be in touch with Uhlein immediately. But' – he brightened slightly – 'have you considered what may have happened if Elliot had that bond with him? For the most upright reasons, of course?'

Ralph Armitage sounded hollow. 'If that's so, Elliot is trying to escape from the police and just happens to have a $50,000 bearer bond to help him.'

Given the current situation, it was not surprising that there were no testimonials to Elliot Patterson.

'I think the best thing to do,' said Lancer falling back on a time-tested technique, 'is to wait and see.'

After all, as he later reported to Thatcher, sufficient unto the day . . .

6. Supplementary Reading on Reserve

The fact that Elliot Patterson, until days ago a model husband, devoted father, public-spirited citizen and exemplary employee, had become a hit-and-run killer did not prove newsworthy enough to distress the loyal sons of Brunswick. There were no headlines. But the brief, uninformative article about two dead teenagers (one of them an honour student) describing police inquiries as vigorous was not inaccurate. A uniformed policeman on the second floor was enough to tell the whole Ivy League Club that Elliot Patterson– and the Brunswick Club – was in trouble. Sally Patterson, after her initial shock, knew she must break the bad news to Target Associates. She was taken aback to discover that her call came hard on the heels of two detectives. Target already knew.

'Yes, Sally,' Marian said in her cool voice. 'No, they just asked routine questions ... Of course, there was nothing to say ... Yes, I agree this is some sort of mistake. No one knowing Elliot could believe it for a moment. I told them so ... No ... Yes ... Now, is there anything we can do for you? Oh, yes, Gabe wants to know if you're all right for money? Fine. Well, I'll keep in touch. Bye.'

She put down the phone and looked at her employer. 'Gabe, you're a coward.'

He admitted it frankly. 'I usually like the wives,' he said truthfully. 'But Sally ...' he shrugged.

Marian was amused. Gabe's approach to women, from thirteen to ninety, was playfully, tenderly flirtatious. Marian had seen a member of the Senate Armed Services Committee blossom under it. But even the most decorous lovemaking requires some response. Marian treasured the memory of an evening, a Target Associates dinner for a departing colleague, when Sally smiled kindly at Gabe's performance, then turned the discussion to the antipoverty programme in Westchester County.

Marian herself had passed from woman to colleague within six weeks of her arrival at Target Associates.

'Sally still has faith in Elliot?' Gabe asked.

'She knows he could never leave the scene of an accident,' Marian quoted. 'I agree with her.'

This last said something to Uhlein. He wriggled slightly. 'Of course! Of course! Still, if he was drunk . . .'

He peeped at her, then subsided. In many ways Uhlein and Mrs Knightley knew Elliot Patterson better than his wife did; his notorious temperance did not require comment from them.

'But where can he be?' Marian was talking almost to herself. 'Poor Elliot. Poor, poor Elliot!'

As his employees and competitors had good reason to know, Gabe Uhlein was not really Mr Pickwick, despite his appearance.

'Now listen, Marian. I know you can't explain it. But believe me, the police don't send two detectives up here on a wild-goose chase. Crazy as it seems, it looks as if for some reason or other Elliot was driving down Putnam County last Monday night – God knows why! And he did have an accident. And he did drive on. I agree, he wasn't drunk. You heard me tell the cops that. But other things can happen. Maybe he got sick. Maybe he had a blackout.'

She listened. Gabe's persuasiveness was directed to a goal. Nevertheless, she would not finish his argument for him. 'I suppose you must be right, Gabe, but I'm not really convinced. So . . .'

Glumly he finished it himself. 'Maybe he had a million dollars of Target money on the front seat.'

'It's possible.'

'So you think we ought to go on with the audit?' he fired at her.

She nodded.

'The poor fish. Innocently he gets into a helluva mess – God, we could all do it – and you will still think we should audit every penny. Marian, it's a shame you don't follow the horses – although I'd fire you if you did. You'd make a great long-shot player. I'll say that much.'

Marian relaxed and watched Gabe go through a familiar

performance. He was whipping himself into a frenzy, pouring scorn and contempt on a proposition which, in his heart of hearts, he knew to be reasonable.

'... so, we'll audit Clayton's books too, while we're at it,' he declaimed. Clayton was five years dead. 'We'll call in the FBI. We'll ...'

The phone rang.

'Yes, he's here, Doris. It's for you, Gabe.'

The voice announcing Uhlein here was free of tension, creamy with smooth promise. 'Yes, Mr Kitchener? Yes ... oh yes. Fine ..'

The conversation lasted ten minutes. Uhlein confined himself to monosyllables. They were enough to tell Marian he was growing unhappy.

'... all right, Kitchener. I'll check and call you as soon as we find out. How do I know how long it will take? That's the best I can do!'

He slammed down the phone, glared at Marian and said, 'Well, there you are.'

'Where?' she asked.

She listened to the story of the missing $50,000 bond, which Uhlein told with great care. She and Uhlein knew Elliot Patterson far better than the members of the Brunswick Committee knew him. To them, it was unthinkable that he might have left $50,000 in an unsecured office, but it was equally unthinkable that a professional fund raiser should casually shovel the equivalent of $50,000 in currency into a dispatch case and drive off for a merry evening tooting around Putnam County.

'You're going to check the safe?' she asked as Uhlein started for the door. There was no need to ask: the care of other people's money was the vital core of Target Associates' being, despite Gabe's little eccentricities.

'Of course, he might have taken it to a bank during the day,' he said over his shoulder as he left.

So he too did not expect to find the bond in the office safe.

Marian shook her head. She should have learned her lesson. She thought she knew what Gabe was expecting, but did she?

Until the last few days, she would have said she knew what Elliot Patterson was thinking. Certainly ten years of their working side by side had given her ample opportunity to learn. Elliot was serious, high-minded and just a little dull. In bits and pieces, over lunch, during ten-minute chats, in unguarded asides, Marian Knightley had followed his dull life in a detail that would have infuriated Sally Patterson. She had weighed the decision to leave the Peter Cooper apartment for a house in Rye. She had listened to confidences about how many children the Pattersons wanted to have. She had given her opinion on the advisability of purchasing a second car. She had heard about nursery schools, slipped discs, vacation plans. Without saying much, Elliot had told her all.

Or so Marian Knightley had thought.

But suddenly she pulled herself up. Not only was she a successful and highly paid executive, she was the wife of a busy, well-known architect and the mother of a son beginning to follow in his father's footsteps at Harvard. Her life was full enough to occupy her; her colleagues at Target were restful interludes, not the answer to private emotional needs.

She listened to tales of mortgages and getting children into bad colleges with friendly detachment. But had she really listened to all that Elliot Patterson had to say?

And had she even noticed when he stopped saying it?

She shook herself. One thing was certain. Elliot might be a hit-and-run driver; he might be hallucinating; but he might also be on the way to Brazil with Target Associates' money.

There was no room for any doubt about the last.

The police inquiries, meanwhile, were vigorous but fruitless. Elliot Patterson's features and description were telephotoed to law-enforcement agencies up and down the East Coast, but this did not produce a rash of erroneous identifications. It produced nothing. Business executives in their late thirties with thinning hair, horn-rimmed glasses and anonymous clothing are so common as to be invisible. Patterson's relatives, including a sister in Elmhurst, Illinois, and an aunt in St Petersburg, Florida, denied having seen Elliot recently and insisted that

Elliot had always been an exceptionally good boy. The representatives of several Target Associates clients, including the Secretary of the Westport Home for Unwanted Cats as well as Mrs Florence McBee, candidate for the State Assembly, all averred that Patterson had been his usual, slightly reserved, but very helpful self when last seen – and had not been seen since. Neighbours in Rye all swore that sounds of strife had never emanated from the Patterson home and managed to insinuate that Rye is zoned against sounds of strife. Regulars on the 8:15 due at Grand Central at 9:07 recalled Elliot, who regularly read *The New York Times* and *The Wall Street Journal* like all the other regulars, but they were divided, fifty-fifty, over whether he had been aboard (and reading) on the Monday in question.

Finally an exasperated detective came up with a brainstorm. A moment's thought told him that a 1968 jade-green Oldsmobile (licence 317487) was on the whole more noticeable than Elliot Patterson. Accordingly he altered some orders to subordinates. Within hours, the inquiries to friends, relatives and business associates slackened while fuellers, parkers and passing admirers of the car were sought.

All this took time.

During this time, John Putnam Thatcher put the deteriorating situation in the Loan Policy Committee from his mind at judicious intervals by debating the question of right and wrong. Since he was long past adolescence, this was not a customary self-indulgence, but he was motivated by his regard for George Lancer, and more important by his approval of Lancer's behaviour.

Lancer had already apologized for exposing Thatcher to their trying afternoon in Rye. Thereafter he avoided entangling Thatcher further. Thatcher knew, from Lancer's altered luncheon habits and a stream of disruptive incoming calls, that the Elliot Patterson storm had not swept out to sea. But Lancer remained punctilious and proffered information only in response to direct questions.

So, it was Thatcher's own curiosity that hooked him. Dissimilar as he was in every other respect from Gabe Uhlein, Thatcher shared with him a professional interest in money and negotiable instruments. He heard without much interest the surprising fact that Elliot Patterson was still at large, days after he had become the object of a widespread police hunt.

'Makes you wonder,' Lancer commented. 'Nobody describes Elliot as a cloak-and-dagger type. How on earth can he be keeping out of sight?'

'Contacts with the Mafia?' Thatcher suggested. 'Remember, the underworld is going respectable, George. Patterson probably raises millions from sinister figures in Chicago and Providence.'

His secretary, Miss Corsa, overhearing this, directed a censorious look at Mr Thatcher. When a wonderful family man like Mr Patterson got into this sort of trouble, Miss Corsa could not countenance frivolity on Mr Thatcher's part. Fortunately her duties called her elsewhere, and Lancer, by referring to the missing $50,000 bond, pricked up Thatcher's ears.

'Missing, George? Oh, come now! Fifty thousand dollars doesn't get mislaid like a pair of glasses!' Thatcher said.

'We are not saying that,' Lancer said. 'There is still a possibility that it will turn up in Patterson's accounts. Uhlein's got the auditors in . . .'

'Oho!' said Thatcher.

George continued to explain why it was felt that the bond might turn up at Target Associates. Then honesty compelled him to add that the Brunswick Committee also entertained hopes that Elliot Patterson was safeguarding the bond, wherever he was.

'George,' said Thatcher, quite seriously now, 'when I hear talk of missing bonds, warning bells ring for me.'

Although they were quite alone, Lancer glanced around Thatcher's office.

'Me too,' he said.

'And Uhlein makes three,' said Thatcher.

Lancer could not dispute this. There is no valid reason to audit the books of a perfectly respectable employee who has simply strayed, without premeditation or preparation, into a life of crime and flight.

'I tell you, I don't understand it,' Lancer finally said in a burst of confidence. 'First Patterson is a perfectly ordinary breadwinner. Then Patterson is a crazy hit-and-run killer. Then Patterson is a big-time crook who has run off with money belonging to Target – and to Brunswick.'

Not the sort of career that Brunswick hopes for in its sons, nobody had to add. Lancer relapsed into a sombre study, and Thatcher was back with right and wrong. Was this the moment to inform George C. Lancer that at least one member of the Brunswick Committee scented something even more malodorous?

John Putnam Thatcher was not the man to shirk duty, no matter how unpalatable. He did, however, find himself grasping at straws. If Elliot Patterson were simply a terrified victim of accident, then the point need not arise.

He would postpone his revelations and hope strenuously that the worst Elliot Patterson had done was run amok in Putnam County with somebody else's $50,000.

7. Field Trips Are Scheduled

Day followed day.

At the Sloan Guaranty Trust, the Loan Policy Committee adjourned *sine die* (and *sine* results, for that matter), leaving Thatcher and Lancer free to return to their desks. At Target Associates, Weaver Colby & Colby, certified public accountants, tortured Gabe Uhlein by demanding and getting confidential details concerning fund drives by the Macedonian Freedom League. In Rye, Sally Patterson collected her daughters from her cowed sister and brother-in-law who found their charming feminine ways overpowering, and not only shopped at the Westchester Shopping Centre but attended a meeting of the Rye Kindergarten League Parents Association. The Brunswick Committee, without much enthusiasm, resumed the process of interviewing lanky unformed youths whose only goal in life, they claimed, was to prove worthy of Brunswick College. In Brewster, New York, two teenagers were interred after a sermon centring on the slaughter of the innocents which confused the bereaved friends and relatives among the mourners.

And still there was no sign of Elliot Patterson.

'The police have stepped up the search,' said Lancer over lunch at Whyte's. 'Carruthers has a friend who knows the Commissioner, and he says they're giving it all they've got. He says they expected to pick Elliot up within ten hours.'

Everybody had expected it, Thatcher thought but did not say aloud. Certainly, after the state troopers had fractured the glacial calm of the Patterson home, he had expected a swift resolution, whether in the form of arrest or suicide. But quick or dead, Elliot Patterson was still at large.

'The police have even been asking questions up at Brunswick,' Lancer continued. 'Elliot went up for a visit this spring, and sure enough, the police checked it out. Todd, he's the new president, you know, called me about it.'

'Mmm,' said Thatcher.

More and more he felt he should have a little talk with Lancer. Less and less did he want to. He seized on what he knew of the modern college president. 'Tell me, has that $50,000 bond turned up?'

Lancer caught the mild mockery. 'Not yet. But they haven't finished the audit over at Target Associates. We're hoping it will turn up there. And also' – he grinned suddenly – 'and also hoping that Mrs Curtis won't get wind of this. Then there *will* be hell to pay!'

Thatcher decided that he was not the man to dash hopes. Events, however, were conspiring to force his hand.

The first was unfolding at 333 Madison Avenue.

'It's a helluva position,' Gabe Uhlein complained, savaging his fourth cigarette although he had recently given up smoking. 'Oh, come in, Pete. What's this? Oh yes. Yes, that should do it. Tell Blakesly to run off oh, say, twenty thousand of these brochures. And tell him we can't use "Give Until It Hurts!" Somebody else already has . . .'

Marian watched him take Pete's outline, shake error from it, whip it back into shape with pencilled emendations, then speed Pete off with his usual decisiveness.

'Good boy, Pete.' Uhlein commented. 'Coming along fine. Need watching, of course. Where was I?'

'You were in a helluva position,' Marian told him.

The two senior members of Target Associates were waiting for the final report from Weaver Colby & Colby. Other members of the staff maintained routine; outside Uhlein's inadequate little cubicle, phones rang, typewriters chattered, as contributors to college building funds were circularized, $1000-a-plate banquets were arranged, and exhaustive lists of tax advantages were compiled. But for two days Gabe and Marian had been cut off from such activity as they held themselves ready to aid the accountants in a whirlwind of record gathering, telephone verifying and conferring.

'That's right,' Uhlein agreed. 'Either Elliot planned to skip and cleaned us out, God forbid, or he's a hit-and-run murderer. Either way, it's not going to do Target Associates any good.'

Before Mrs Knightley could comment, Doris opened the door and announced Mr Colby.

Uhlein instantly shed concern and became his usual expansive self. 'Ed, come on in! Sit down. Sit down. Let's get this off our chests and get back to work.'

If Ed Colby detected the undercurrent of suppressed hysteria, he was kindhearted enough to resist the temptation to prolong it.

'As far as we can see, Gabe, everything's fine,' he said, digging into a bulging briefcase. 'Not a penny missing. In fact, Dad was saying that he'd be surprised if your own accounts were in such good order. This Patterson was a fanatic on keeping everything in beautiful shape.'

Colby continued. 'Here's your summary,' he said slapping down a thick bundle of documents. 'The fund holdings of the Upstate Democratic Committee, those escrow funds of Wentwood University. Amalgamated Blood Banks keeps three checking accounts, and the Armenian Apostolic Diocese has this large debt ... and so on, and so on ... and here are the current income statements, notarized treasurer's reports and the receipts we turned up ...'

Colby dealt briskly with Elliot Patterson's Target accounts;

he finally produced a signed statement saying, in effect, that Weaver Colby & Colby were satisfied that everything was hunkydory.

'I have always had complete faith in Elliot's probity,' Uhlein said with dignity.

'Sure,' said Colby with a grin. Everybody invariably had faith in the financial probity of employees and partners. Still, Weaver Colby & Colby were kept jumping with emergency audits. 'Say, what's this I hear about Elliot getting into some sort of trouble about running somebody down?'

It took seven minutes and all the skill of two experts to lever Mr Colby out of Target Associates without hurting his feelings.

'Well, thank God for that!' said Gabe after he returned from escorting Colby to the elevator. 'But you see, people are already talking.'

'Of course they are,' said Mrs Knightley. 'Just wait until the police catch up with Elliot.'

Uhlein was a pragmatist to the bone. 'I guess we'll have to take things as they come. At least Elliot didn't touch a penny. That's something.'

But Marian Knightley was still frowning. 'It makes things more mysterious than ever, Gabe.'

'Well, it proves that he innocently got into his car and had this accident, doesn't it?' Uhlein argued.

She pushed aside the Colby report with dissatisfaction and leaned forward. 'But what was he doing driving around Putnam County?' she demanded. 'Was he up to something Sally didn't know about? Or is Sally keeping something from us?'

Uhlein said nothing.

She continued, 'You know, Gabe, something about this doesn't ring true for me.'

Before he could say anything, she rose and elegantly strolled out of the office. To keep from thinking about her past comment, Uhlein set about fulfilling a promise. 'Doris, get me Kitchener, will you?'

When the call came through, he was terse. 'Kitchener? Uhlein here. The accountants have just left. Elliot's accounts are in perfect shape.'

The telephone offered tempered congratulations, then Uhlein continued:

'No, no sign of that bond. Here's the list' – he riffled through papers – 'United Missionaries, Free Cuba ... No sign of any $50,000 bond. None at all.'

The telephone erupted.

'Kitchener,' Uhlein said urgently, 'Elliot probably had that bond with him, when he had his accident. You'll get it when ... when he turns up.'

This did not hearten Kitchener, and Gabe, even as he offered assurance, acknowledged the accuracy of Marian Knightley's comment. The whole thing was as phony as a three-dollar bill. After he had hung up, he sat lost in thought. He was so silent that Doris thought he had left his desk. She barely restrained an alarmed cry when she bustled into the office and found him sitting there.

Whelby Kitchener was also troubled but not also immobilized. On the contrary, he girded himself for action. He was not at all happy to think of a $50,000 bond belonging to Brunswick College in the hands of a fugitive from justice. Not happy at all. In fact, he was so unhappy about it that he decided to exhaust the last remaining possibility. The bond was not in the filing cabinet at the Brunswick Club; it was not deposited in any known Elliot Patterson bank account; there remained Rye.

Kitchener was gripped by a strong sense of ill-usage as he grumpily entrained for Rye at the most inconvenient hour of the day. No consideration for Mrs Patterson's feelings led him to make the trip himself – it was perfectionism.

He wanted to preside over the examination of Elliot Patterson's study himself. He regarded all women as incompetent ninnies, and he did not trust any young mother to make a thorough search. The browbeaten women in his own life, ranging from secretary to wife to widowed sister-in-law, had grown accustomed to meek acceptance of his masterful judgements and unending strictures. Whelby Kitchener, in a word, was ill-prepared for Rye.

Mrs Patterson greeted him graciously, made small talk without referring to her absent husband, and showed unmistakable signs of wanting to have an intelligent chat about college financial problems.

Kitchener was firm.

'I am pressed for time, my dear lady,' he said accusingly. 'The afternoon trains all seem to be locals. I really must get down to this.'

'I insist on helping you, Mr Kitchener,' said Mrs Patterson with the same firmness. 'Elliot doesn't keep many papers at home, but I know what he does have here. We always discuss his more interesting cases.'

Kitchener restrained a shudder. This vision of wifely helpfulness and support so grated him that he let slip what he had not meant to reveal.

'It is not a question of papers, Mrs Patterson,' he said frigidly. 'It is a question of a $50,000 bond.'

Mrs Patterson compressed her lips slightly before replying. 'Oh, you must mean Mrs Curtis's donation. We were so happy for Brunswick. But, Mr Kitchener, Elliot would never have brought the bond home. He is exceptionally careful to keep money and stocks and bonds in safety . . .'

Kitchener had not come this long way to listen to another encomium to Elliot Patterson's impeccable business methods.

'Yes indeed, Mrs Patterson,' he interrupted, 'but the fact remains that the bond seems to be missing.'

She took a deep breath. 'Why don't you ask Marian Knightley? That bond is probably at Target Associates. That's where it must be.'

Kitchener did not waste words by denying this but repeated that he was pressed for time. Fortunately for him, as Mrs Patterson was just as determined as he, a sudden childish treble in the back yard claimed her attention.

'Of course, you may look through Elliot's papers,' she said with conscious courtesy. 'I can assure you that there is nothing to interest you, but you have my permission. Here, in here. This is our little library-study . . .'

Kitchener fought down resentment. He intended to look at Elliot Patterson's papers no matter what Mrs Patterson said. As for her permission . . .

With a final malediction on the modern woman, he settled down to work.

It did not detain him long. Elliot Patterson's papers were all neatly docketed in file folders. In spite of one or two forays which were a tribute to Kitchener's general nosiness (he looked into the tax folder to see how much Patterson was making – really, young men were grossly overpaid these days!), he was able to do the job in fifteen minutes. Then, frowning unhappily, he did it all over again. This time there were no side excursions. He had eyes only for one thing, and at the end of twenty-five minutes he knew that Mrs Patterson was absolutely correct.

There was nothing resembling a $50,000 bearer bond in the room.

8. Students on the Accelerated Programme

In the end, a bad-tempered old lady propelled John Putnam Thatcher into the discussion he had hoped to avoid. Mrs Warren V. Curtis, aged eighty-nine and the terror of family and neighbours in Greenwich and Palm Beach, was not a rose to bloom in the desert.

'Good heavens, that woman must have gotten wind of things!' George Lancer exclaimed, putting down the phone. 'She's been calling Brunswick, trying to find out why she hasn't heard anything from them about her donation. Really, considering how much money Curtis must have left, it's disgraceful that the old harridan is only giving the college $50,000 . . .'

It was one point of view, of course. Thatcher leaned back and considered Mrs Curtis. The police search for Elliot Patterson might stretch out indefinitely; no octogenarian has time to throw away.

'Lyman Todd calmed her down with some story or other,' Lancer continued. 'But sooner or later, she's going to find out what's happened. And when she does . . .'

To avoid thinking of those perils, Thatcher asked if the dowager had made efforts to contact Elliot Patterson. He was the one, after all, who had managed to extract a bequest from her in the first place.

She had. Both home and office parroted unconvincing tales about out-of-town trips. But if Elliot remained unavailable, the evil news would reach even such sequestered ears as Mrs Curtis's.

'And let me tell you, she's a woman who likes nothing better than kicking up a fuss,' said Lancer. 'There's no use appealing to her loyalty to Brunswick, as I told Todd. Besides, they still have hopes from her will. Personally I expect she'll leave her fortune to a home for distressed gentlewomen.'

The whole rationale of storm watching is to anticipate catastrophe with a view to intelligent preparation. Thatcher, after considering and rejecting the notion of enlisting Lucy's assistance, took a deep breath.

'George, may I say a few words about this whole Patterson situation?'

Lancer looked at him disarmingly and said, 'I wish you would, John. I'd be interested to hear your opinion. You've been very forbearing with me. I've appreciated it. I can't help feeling somewhat troubled.'

'Yes, I know.'

Lancer twirled a pencil. 'I don't claim to be a professional alumnus, you know. But I do feel obliged to help Brunswick when it's involved in unsavoury publicity – which is inevitable with hit-and-run murders. And unless that bond turns up pretty soon, Mrs Curtis will be creating a storm of her own. I hope we can avoid it.'

Thatcher hardened his heart.

'George, I don't know Patterson, of course, but certain aspects of this whole episode have struck me as rather unusual.'

Lancer could not deny it.

Thatcher continued: 'Here, I take it, is a perfectly commonplace businessman who first disappears, which is odd enough. Then last Monday, he gets involved in a hit-and-run accident, kills two teenagers and is now trying to escape a police dragnet, which is odd too. Then, as you yourself have pointed out, he seems to be pulling it off, which may be the oddest part of all.'

Lancer said cautiously that the whole thing was very strange indeed.

'Now, George,' Thatcher went on, 'in addition to everything else, it appears that Patterson just happened to have a $50,000 bearer bond with him when all of this occurred.' He broke off to direct a shrewd glance at Lancer. 'To be quite frank, George, I feel that when Elliot Patterson is located, the answers to several questions may come out in a way to stimulate the very public interest you are trying to avoid. It may well prove far more damaging to Brunswick than anything you have contemplated.'

The pencil twirled faster.

Thatcher steeled himself. 'In the interests of completeness, I think I should add another item to this unfortunate hopper – something else you may want to prepare for. You recall that on our return from Rye I took Jim Dunlop off with me. Well, I pumped him.'

Lancer was intrigued. 'And you found out why he's been looking so damned sheepish? My God, you don't mean *he's* got anything to do with all this?'

'No, no!' Thatcher assured him. 'No, Dunlop is simply embarrassed, I think.'

'Embarrassed?'

'George, you know that one of the duties of the Brunswick Committee at this time of the year is interviewing young men who are applying for admission to college.'

George did.

'From what Dunlop said – and I confess that the martinis may have led him to speak more frankly than he intended – most members of the committee regard this as a boring chore. But not so Elliot Patterson. I gather he has been conspicuous by his deep interest in these boys. He spends hours with them, hours of his own time, apart from committee meetings. He has long talks with them. He phones them to follow up interviews. Dunlop says that it is quite striking.'

Rather blankly Lancer spoke of Elliot Patterson's widely

known interest in young people, education and character moulding. Thatcher saw that he would have to be more explicit with this distinguished son of Brunswick. He took a deep breath.

'Dunlop, it appears, is a native of Putnam County. His parents live in Carmel and he knows the entire area very well. Until a year ago it was his home.'

Thatcher was investing even these innocent words with sinister significance. Keeping the bass pedal down, he continued, 'In particular, Dunlop knows the reputation of this tavern where the hit-and-run took place. It is extremely unsavoury.'

Lancer searched his experience for something relevant and rightly concluded that he must fall back on imagination.

'I thought it was some kind of teenage hangout. Good God, if the books they publish these days are anything to go by, all those girls in miniskirts and those boys in long hair are carrying on like Greta Garbo and John Gilbert.'

Lancer, Thatcher decided, read the wrong kind of book. And he honoured him for it.

'No, that is not what I mean. This tavern is not frequented by girls, George. It is quite shabby and run-down and has no music. No one spends an evening there. But the boys do drop in for a beer and pizza on the way home. This in turn has attracted another element. Known perverts stop by in the hope of making contacts with some of the boys. The tavern is regarded as a blot on the county by the residents, but it hasn't been closed down, not yet. They maintain that the undesirables it attracts come from far and wide.'

Comprehension, speedily followed by other reactions, produced an expression that nearly upset Thatcher's carefully preserved sense of gravity.

Lancer was croaking. 'You mean . . .?'

'That's it, George,' Thatcher told him. He cast about for consolation. 'Now, Dunlop was very quick to say that there's never been a hint that Patterson lives the . . . er . . . gay life. Nor has Dunlop ever witnessed any trace of impropriety with one of the Brunswick boys.'

He was grateful that Lancer was capable only of strangled protest. It spared them both discussion of the dutiful wife, the three lovely daughters and the beautiful home in Rye. With the worst behind him, Thatcher pushed on.

'Dunlop's discretion has been praiseworthy, I think. You can follow his growing disturbance. Patterson was last seen – before the accident, that is – deep in conversation with one of the boys the committee was interviewing. Everybody else left, you recall, and Patterson remained behind to talk with a Carter Sprague.' Thatcher broke off, recalling Jim Dunlop's heated description of young Sprague. There was nothing in it to make Lancer feel better. He went on: 'There was that. Then it developed that Patterson turned up, in the most unfortunate way, I grant you, outside this place in Putnam County, hours after he should have been home to dinner. You recall the accident actually occurred in the driveway. To top it all off, Patterson decamps after a collision that must have left the place looking like Omaha Beach. Naturally, one thinks he may have been in such a compromising position – because of his companion, say – that he could not afford to remain. In any event, Dunlop has seen all sorts of interpretations in this – all of them, I regret to say, bad.'

Lancer struggled back to the surface. 'I took Dunlop for a clean-minded young man!'

'Oh, he is, George, he is,' Thatcher assured him with a smile. 'In fact he seems excessively clean-minded. I understood that today's young people were all liberated souls. Dunlop sounded positively Victorian the other night.'

Lancer, as nearly agitated as he ever would be, wasted no time reflecting on modern youth. 'Good God, if it turns out that Patterson is homosexual ... And he's on the admission committee of Brunswick! Oh Lord, do you realize what that means? Do you suppose it's possible ...? I mean ...'

Not unkindly, Thatcher pointed out that Lancer was gabbling. Then, in an equally helpful spirit, he sought to relieve his mental strain by concrete facts.

'It scarcely matters what kind of man Patterson is,' he said, 'although I confess I'm beginning to wonder. The fact is, he's in a mess, and that's that. No matter what he turns out to be, he won't look good when – and if – he turns up.'

Lancer pounced. 'But this is the worst possible thing that could happen to a men's college. Hit-and-run – what's that? It's nothing, I tell you. Even stealing a bond ... but this would be a crippling blow. That boy. I wonder ...'

Thatcher pointed out that the police had no doubt already approached the last person to have seen Patterson, young Carter Sprague. All unknowing, he sounded a call to action.

Praying aloud that the only thing on the police mind was hit-and-run killing, Lancer remembered that the newspapers would not be that high-minded, not if they were given any choice.

'I'd better have a look at this kid,' he said resolutely. 'I can always tell him I'm part of the admission interview process. The Brunswick Club will back me up.' He stabbed for his secretary, carefully avoiding Thatcher's eyes.

Thatcher sighed. 'You feel you have to, George?'

'I do.'

Thatcher feared as much. Grounds for his fear were all too real; this was no time to abandon George C. Lancer.

Two hours later, their host was trying hard to exude an alien wholesomeness.

'It's impressive, it really is. Two busy men like you from the Sloan, giving up your time this way. That's what makes Brunswick the college it is.'

His wife agreed. 'You're right, Andy. And, Mr Lancer, Lucy has told me how hard you work for dear old Brunswick.'

George Lancer, in spite of his intimate knowledge of Brunswick's capital needs and building programmes, was behind the times when it came to college placement. These days the parents of a potential freshman rally behind him. They know the names of college trustees; if possible, they get to know their wives. What's more, they regard themselves as under even severer examination than their offspring. Carter Sprague's parents were giving their all. For half an hour they had been exchanging artificial chitchat which suggested that two hard-bitten, middle-aged New Yorkers had just been snatched from their Brownie troop.

It was now well on towards five o'clock, but neither Thatcher nor Lancer had been offered cocktails. Everybody dutifully ignored the large bar in the corner. Furthermore, Mrs Westerveldt was not smoking. For, of course, Carter Sprague's mother was no longer Mrs Sprague. It was Willard Sprague, the pineapple millionaire in Hawaii and a loyal son of Brunswick, who was making himself felt over ten thousand miles. Andrew P. Westerveldt was a shipping magnate, but both the Westerveldts were going along.

The air of unreality hovering over the assembly was accentuated by their surroundings. They sat in the living-room of a large cooperative apartment high in the sky of the East Seventies. Mrs Westerveldt had not been content to summon an interior decorator; she had called in an architect as well and had indulged in massive construction work. Either she or the architect had been to North Africa; the apartment abounded in Moorish arches, cool tiles, slim colonnades and carved Spanish chests. On a raised platform a fountain supplied the background tinkle of falling water. No doubt, thought Thatcher fair-mindedly, it was a pleasant sound in the desert. Unfortunately the fine September weather had taken a turn for the worse, and now rain was beating against the wide glass doors overlooking the windswept terrace. The combination of tiles, gale winds and dripping water everywhere made the natural man yearn for Scotch.

Since it was obvious that he wasn't going to get any here, Thatcher was happy to see the Westerveldts make winsome adieux and take their innocence elsewhere.

This left Lancer with young Carter Sprague, at last. Thatcher eyed the boy. He was, of course, in a difficult position. While his parents were projecting virginal purity, he was playing the blasé man of the world. Now he roused himself from the Byronic silence he had been maintaining and exerted himself to put his visitors at their ease.

'Unfortunately, I haven't had a chance to meet Mrs Lancer,' he said with a delicate wave of the hand betokening distant places. 'I'm away so much.'

Lancer had done some homework. 'St Mark's, isn't it?'

Carter stiffened slightly. 'Only in the winter,' he said repressively. 'Summers I'm abroad. Usually Paris. And I take in Chamonix for the skiing.'

Lancer was inclined to grasp at straws. 'You like skiing, do you?' he asked, interpreting Sprague's comment as an offering of athletic interests.

'It's the thing to do,' Carter told him gently. 'One meets one's friends.'

Clearly one didn't meet them at St Mark's.

'Our Admission Committee is always busy at this time of year,' Lancer said doggedly. 'That's why we've been called in as extra help.'

Carter inspected him, then John Putnam Thatcher.

'The fall is a bad time of the year,' he agreed. 'I can't imagine why these tiresome interviews are scheduled just when everybody is away. Normally I wouldn't get back to New York for another two weeks.'

Lancer, breathing hard, resisted the temptation to apologize for interrupting a busy social calendar. He was noticeably short.

'It's the most convenient time for the college. Now, if you'll just go over your last meeting with the Committee, we won't duplicate their efforts.'

Carter crossed his legs, leaned back and blew a contemplative smoke ring.

'Let's see. It was the usual sort of thing, you know. They had four of us in for this session. We had to wait a good bit, I'm sorry to say,' he said, kindly drawing Lancer's attention to the shortcomings of his underlings. 'The Committee was meeting on its own across the hall and they kept dashing through our waiting-room to that inner office. Finally they had all four of us in for a general pep talk about Brunswick. Then we went back to the waiting-room and they called us in, one by one, for our interviews. I explained that I've never been too interested in maths or science, which accounts for my marks there. I told them the kind of education and environment I want. I dare say you can tell I'm interested in a humanistic, liberal approach to the arts. The kind of thing I could get at Harvard – but that's neither here nor there, with Father insisting. At any rate, Mr

Marsden was quite helpful about the Brunswick artist-in-residence programme.'

Thatcher feared for Lancer's blood pressure. 'Did you talk with Mr Patterson much?' he asked. 'I understand he's very interested in this sort of problem.'

Carter Sprague was gripped by internal struggle. 'Patterson? Oh, you mean the one the police came asking about?'

A charitable interpretation would be that Carter Sprague was suppressing a boy's perfectly normal excitement at police inquiries. There was something about him, however, that did not encourage charitable interpretations.

'The police wanted to know if he seemed abnormal,' said Carter, resuming superiority. 'He didn't. He seemed like all the others.'

Thatcher was moved to sternness. 'You spoke with Patterson after the others left, didn't you? Why was that? What did he want?'

Carter scored a point.

'He didn't want anything. I asked to speak to him.'

'Why?' Lancer demanded.

Carter was now perfectly at ease. He tapped ashes delicately. 'I'll confess to you that I was doing a little conniving,' he said, inviting appreciation of his adroitness. 'Things will be a lot more comfortable for me if I am admitted to Brunswick. Father – my real father, that is – is insane on the subject. In fact, my allowance from him hinges on it. So, it's worth my while to go along, although I'd prefer ... well, I took a long look at the committee while I was there. I could predict their reactions quite well. Neil Marsden is a civilized human being. We understand each other. He'll recommend that Brunswick accept me. Then there's Mr Armitage. He might care for my type, then he might not. But he's the kind who is impressed with Sprague pineapples and Westerveldt Steamship Lines. That's the kind of background he likes to see at Brunswick. Dunlop? Well, Dunlop is still immature. He's hostile to me. He'll get more tolerant when he's older.'

This cool analysis floored George Lancer, who saw it as almost obscene – which in many ways was fortunate as it deflected his attention from other problems. For the first time, however, Thatcher was amused. Carter Sprague, he suspected, was quite accurate.

'And Patterson?' he asked.

'Now there's where I really played the right cards,' said Carter Sprague with a sudden, brilliant smile. 'Patterson's the type who wants to be a father figure. I knew it wouldn't make any difference to him what I was like. He'd eat out of my hand if I asked his advice. So I decided it would be a good move to ask him to stay and talk with me for a few minutes. Then, all I had to do was have a big problem deciding on the right kind of college. And the right sort of programme. Should I deepen the interests I already have, or should I broaden out to other interests? It's simple and foolproof. In no time, Patterson was arguing that I really should go to Brunswick. Even though he was in a hurry to get somewhere, he couldn't resist playing up to my questions.'

'A hurry?' Thatcher asked, to draw Carter's attention from George C. Lancer, who was rigid with outrage.

'So he said,' Carter replied, 'when I asked to talk to him. He said he could only give me a few minutes. I caught him in the hallway, when they were all on the way out. But he came back into the waiting room and sat down for about ten minutes. Then he said it again and started to shove everything into his briefcase. Half the stuff fell on the floor, and I did my helpful boy act and helped him pick things up. He left at a trot. Oh yes, he was in a hurry all right. But I managed to make an impression.'

'I'll bet you did,' said Lancer grimly. 'Where did you leave Patterson?'

'The corner,' said Carter, indicating he had lost interest. 'We walked half a block east to Fifth. Then he turned south and I turned north. I gather from what that cop said, that's where Patterson dropped out of sight. Does anybody know...?'

'Where were you going?'

Carter was surprised but smoothly produced the Librairie Française as his next appointment.

'And then?'

For the second time during the interview, Carter was rattled. Only after a moment's thought did he say, 'Some friends and I were driving out to the country for dinner.' His vagueness was almost defiant.

Thatcher wondered if the police had elicited further information. At any rate this inquiry was at an end. Lancer could not control himself enough to continue. Indeed, he could barely restrain himself until they were out of the apartment.

'Have you ever heard anything like it?' he exploded at last. 'So that's what St Mark's is producing these days!'

'It was pretty bad,' Thatcher agreed, 'but for your purposes it could be a lot worse.'

'I suppose you mean because he's not an outright pervert?' Lancer shot back.

'More precisely, he doesn't give the impression of being one. On the contrary, he sounds like a precocious satyr!'

'Bah!' said George C. Lancer. 'And let me tell you, those friends of his and that dinner in the country . . .' Speech failed him.

It was true. There was no hard evidence that Carter Sprague could not be involved with teenagers and vice in Putnam County. On the other hand, it seemed hardly likely. Even more unlikely was any connection, healthy or otherwise, between Elliot Patterson and Carter Sprague.

'I am prepared to believe that Elliot is a killer. I am prepared to believe he is a thief!' George said heatedly. 'But no matter what you say about him, I cannot believe he would have spoken to Carter Sprague for ten minutes except for the strong call of duty and loyalty to Brunswick.'

Thatcher reached for the door of the taxi that pulled up.

'Unless, George,' he said as gently as he could, 'unless Elliot Patterson was too stupid to notice.'

9. Counselling Is Available

Things never seem so bad as just before they are about to get a good deal worse.

With a whisper here and a confidential mutter there, those to whom Brunswick College was dear had braced themselves for the revelation of Elliot Patterson as the monster he was. Sooner or later the press would fall on the situation. Then the balloon would go up with a vengeance.

There was no widespread relief when the result of the Target Associates audit percolated down to its own level.

'If only Elliot were a thief,' groaned Jim Dunlop. 'That at least would be normal.'

His wife reminded him of Dr Kinsey's findings.

As for the missing $50,000 bond, Whelby Kitchener alone could delude himself that it was of paramount importance.

'It's irrelevant,' Neil Marsden snapped. 'He happened to have it with him and now it's coming in handy.'

Ralph Armitage thought that was a hell of a way to describe fifty thousand dollars.

'You know what they're saying?' breathed Gabe Uhlein cautiously.

Marian Knightley had lost her friendly detachment. 'I know. Teenage boys,' she lashed back. 'And I don't believe it for a minute.'

Everybody had his own explanation. It might be an unpalatable explanation, but soon even that dubious comfort would be stripped away. They were about to move into the realm of the unexplainable. The first sign of the deluge came on Monday.

Elliot Patterson was completely exonerated of the massacre in Putnam County.

At lunchtime on the day of his disappearance, he had sold his car, obtaining the $2,700 purchase price in cash in accordance with a previous understanding. That evening the car had been left in a shop by its new owner to have seat covers installed. The delay in title transfer had sent the police haring after the wrong car.

Further information emerged. The alert purchaser reported that Elliot had been carrying an overnight case at their noon-time meeting. Investigation revealed that pyjamas, underwear and toilet articles were missing from the house in Rye. It was clear that Elliot Patterson had intended to go somewhere and, wherever that was, he wanted several thousand dollars with him.

John Thatcher absorbed these details as they came to light, listened politely to endless speculation and finally asked a question.

'You said his bank account was normal, but what about his other property?'

'He didn't sell anything,' Lancer replied immediately. 'One of the first people Gabe Uhlein checked with was Patterson's broker.'

'That's not what I meant. Listen, George . . .'

And so, by Tuesday, an additional fact had come to light. Over the preceding year, Elliot Patterson had had title on everything he owned transferred into his wife's name.

It would be small solace to her. Sally Patterson was accustomed to financial security. Now she would have to come to grips with the realization that her husband had been planning to leave, planning for at least a year.

'In its way, this makes things simpler,' Thatcher pointed out. 'We can ignore accidents and concentrate on essentials.'

'Yes,' said a new Lancer. He was eager to trade in a queen-size fairy for a red-blooded wife deserter. 'All this nonsense about his interest in boys is just that – nonsense. We have nothing to worry about except the bearer bond. Unfortunate, but there it is. What do you say, John?'

John Thatcher was not making the same lightning ascent from ocean depths to clear sunshine. First, because he never had been in the depths. He had sensibly decided that if, over the course of life, he had learned to take in stride psychoanalysis, the Depression, modern woman and an affluent society, then he was not going to boggle at a little sexual perversion. Second, because he was by nature suspicious of suddenly clearing skies.

He looked deep into his brandy snifter, reviewed events and then said, 'I say, wait for the other shoe to fall, George.'

It fell the next morning with the news that Elliot Patterson had not, after all, confined his light fingers to a mere $50,000. He had also taken from the Brunswick Club files the College Board results for every single applicant for admission to the college.

The uproar was immediate.

It was also surprising. There was, after all, a grab bag of possibilities. The conventional could mourn the loss of a father and husband; the legal precisionist could seize on a $50,000 theft; the speculative could ponder Patterson's strange frugality in larceny; the prurient could see Elliot carousing with golden nymphs.

But, if the newspapers, magazines, television stations and radio networks were any guide, the American public was neither conventional, precisionist, speculative nor even – incredible as it might appear – prurient. Given an even chance, the great American public viewed the world scene in its guise of Parent.

Elliot Patterson's latest theft forced Brunswick College to send out a letter asking three hundred and twenty high-school students in the New York area to resubmit application data. This unleashed a storm of adverse publicity which could scarcely have been equalled by the discovery that the entire faculty consisted of debauchees insatiably corrupting the young, pausing only to recharge their unnatural energies with hallucinogens.

Worse was to come. All college-admissions tests were number-coded to preserve anonymity. It was possible to go from number to name, but not vice versa. No useful purpose would be served, Brunswick learned, by submission of a list of names and a request for scores. Grimly the college sent a further communication to the select three hundred and twenty. They had better unfurl their mechanical pencils and prepare for another round of multiple-choice questions.

By the time the third letter went out, announcing that Brunswick would not be able to mail admissions results until two weeks after its Ivy League rivals, the entire East Coast was up in arms.

Embattled mothers paraded with placards: WHY MUST OUR CHILDREN PAY FOR THE CRIMES OF ELLIOT PATTERSON? Irate fathers could not believe Brunswick expected their sons to turn down perfectly good colleges in favour of problematic acceptance by Brunswick. Particularly, they said hoarsely, when the alternative to college admission was the draft. A psychologist with a daily news column spoke tellingly of the trauma caused by the effort to get into college. A sociologist, spread over a Sunday supplement, said all this would merely confirm youth's lack of faith in the older generation. Preserving that faith was a parent's most sacred duty. To that end the parent must be unfailingly reasonable, totally unbiased, open to cultural innovation and undismayed by personal hostility. The sociologist did not explain how this was supposed to prepare the young for a world that could be relied upon to display none of these characteristics.

Outside the boundaries of the printed word – and the laws of libel – opinions were aired with even greater freedom.

In the office of the Dean of Admissions of Cremona College (Cremona, New York) there was, sad to say, nothing but satisfaction.

'I have always maintained,' Dean Flayer told his crony from the Endowment Fund Office, 'I have always maintained that there was more to these committees than meets the eye. I deplore the way these so-called prestige colleges . . .'

The crony, who knew that Flayer would gladly give his eye teeth to be removed from the backwater of Cremona, interrupted to ask what he thought lay behind Elliot Patterson's disappearance. Flayer told him. It was an explanation being echoed in many admission offices, many prep-school faculty lounges.

Had any doting parent heard it, his blood would have run cold.

A variant reading was being aired in the offices of a testing service. A Mark IV was whirring gently in the background; two statisticians, in the foreground, were whirring less gently.

'You can see where this crap about all-round boys and interviews leads,' said one irately. 'If a kid has brains, it shows up in his test scores, and that's that. To hell with these letters of recommendation and school transcripts. Give him the test, then let him in or slam the door.' His two-month-old son showed unmistakable signs of genius.

His companion's seventeen-year-old son had found it necessary to complete his secondary education at a military academy.

'Well, having brains isn't everything.'

He was interrupted.

'Oh, come on! Look at this creep who's run off. Probably somebody paid him plenty to get some dumb boob into college to keep the draft off his neck. One thing for Susie here' – he looked affectionately at the giant computer – 'nobody can buy her off.'

In nonspecialist circles, the particular supplanted the general. The conversation taking place in a graceful colonial home in Mineola was typical.

'I don't like it,' said Mrs Hughes. 'Why have they let this man run off with your records?'

Her son Jonathan, like his father, had perfected a technique of colloquy with his mother in which the outward form was maintained without inner substance.

'Listen, Mom, I'm taking Lila to dinner tonight. We might take in a movie afterwards.'

'I wish you wouldn't date on a school night,' his mother commented unheatedly. 'You know you have to bring up your grades this semester if you want to get into Brunswick. Although I don't know that I really like the idea. After all, something funny must be going on there. Your father said so this morning at breakfast.'

Jonathan was carefully knotting a tie while his mother dithered on. He completed the operation to his satisfaction, and straightened.

'Mom, will you tell Dad to watch how he pulls into the

garage tonight?' he remarked pleasantly. 'I had to leave my car outside last night. I just had it washed, and it looks as if we might get rain.'

Mrs Hughes promised to bring the matter to Jonathan's father's attention.

'You met this man, didn't you?' she continued, picking up the discarded shirt.

Direct questions sometimes flushed answers.

'Patterson?' asked Jonathan, giving his hair a final caress. 'He's on the committee. He wasn't outstanding.'

This flat judgement did not surprise Mrs Hughes. Most of Jonathan's world was not outstanding. She reverted to an earlier theme.

'I still don't know why you want to go to Brunswick. Your father was happy at Fordham. Your cousin Frank likes Columbia.'

Jonathan dropped a kiss on his mother's cheek and departed. He did not particularly burn to go to Brunswick College, but, with quiet determination, he insisted on putting a couple of hundred miles between himself and his home.

Home offered him endless care, respect and indulgence – an array of durable goods from Mustang to electric guitar. Jonathan enjoyed unlimited access to ready cash, a congenial circle of youthful familiars. Home also contained a mother, a father and three siblings. With a fervour that would have surprised all who knew him, Jonathan Hughes, aged seventeen and a half, yearned to escape from all this into freedom and self-fulfilment.

Unaware of this *angst*, Mrs Hughes promised Jonathan's younger sister to shorten a dress, made arrangements to transport Byron and Quentin from the dentist to the riding academy, with her thoughts still circling monotonously around Jonathan. Finally her need to talk sent her to the telephone.

The result was that at 5:07, a commuting hour when listening housewives were joined by carborne husbands, Radio Station WPDQ – 'We cover Manhattan, Connecticut and New Jersey like a blanket!' – in the person of Paul Handratty, a talkmaster, transmitted a dialogue as follows:

Caller: Paul, Paul . . . wait just a minute until I turn my radio down.

Paul: Ha! Ha! Let's hope it's not a big living room. Back yet, Mrs H?

Caller: Hi, Paul? I'm just a little nervous.

Paul: There, there, Mrs H. We're all your friends here. Now, what was it you wanted to talk about?

Caller: Well, I don't know just how . . . I mean that it's complicated . . . Paul, did you read that article about the man who disappeared with the test scores for Brunswick College?

For three minutes Mrs Hughes made lavish use of illustration and reference to 'my son'. Talkmaster Handratty, vulnerable to gentility, asked kind questions. The son who emerged bore little resemblance to Jonathan; the inconvenience of duplicating data was treated like one of the tragedies of youth; the repetition of an examination like a refinement of Oriental brainwashing. Mrs Hughes's unfocused worry was transformed into the passionate anxiety of a pioneer mother.

Paul: That sure is terrible. No wonder you're worried. And your son, too. Let's see if our listeners have any information to add.

Caller: You've made me feel better already.

Paul: That's what we're here for. Remember, call us again some time, now that you've broken the ice.

There followed, in rapid succession, calls from: a Brunswick alumnus currently operating a small law practice in Massapequa, Long Island; a lady from Astoria who had inside information proving that the Communist Conspiracy was Taking Over the American Campus; a mother whose son had blossomed into acne with Brunswick's third letter; a drunk with an ingenious explanation for Elliot Patterson's behaviour that really should not have been publicly disseminated; two ladies from Scarsdale who saw anti-Semitic forces at play; a precocious youth from Bronxville who pointed out reasoning flaws in the statements of his predecessors.

Paul Handratty signed off at 6:00. The next day, he and his radio station moved on to other problems, namely the leash law in Mamaroneck.

But by then the damage had been done. Over 1,857,987 people heard this discussion. George C. Lancer, chauffeur-driven, had not. Rose Theresa Corsa, subway commuter, had not. John Putnam Thatcher, who disliked prattling, had not.

But, it rapidly developed, almost everybody else had.

10. The Department Must Approve

Beset on all sides by the radio-listening public, warned of a forthcoming television documentary on college admissions which might feature one of the three hundred and twenty, receiving withdrawals of application in every mail, Brunswick College had no reserves to meet a commando raid.

Mrs Curtis, aged eighty-nine, had unequivocally thrown in her lot with the older generation. In her opinion, youth could take care of itself. She was worried about her $50,000.

'It's not the money,' she said, baring litigious teeth. 'It's the principle. This was to be in memory of my husband.'

Representatives of the Alumni Association hastened to assure her that, in the eyes of Brunswick College, the gift had been made and the memory of Warren V. Curtis would remain forever green.

His relict responded with an ultimatum. Either Brunswick stopped pussyfooting around and put some muscle into its call for a police investigation or she would sue. No one acquainted with Mrs Curtis's courtroom history could doubt her sincerity.

Reaction was mixed. The college authorities in Coburg, New Hampshire, one eye on the budget, were all for placating substantial donors at any cost – otherwise contributions would fall off. The Brunswick Admission Committee in New York, fearing police interrogation of the four boys who had last seen Elliot Patterson, were all for protecting their youthful protégés. Applications for admission were already at an all-time low.

It was George Lancer's unenviable lot to act as mediator. He reported to Thatcher that up in Coburg they seemed to feel that in a pinch they could run the college without students, but without money – never.

'It might be an improvement,' said Thatcher unsympathetically. 'Somebody should tell those Regents in California about it. Firing presidents is no solution. But eliminating the student body could end the rioting and effect real cost reductions at the same time.'

Lancer dismissed California with an impatient grunt. 'Anyway, I've insisted that Lyman Todd be present at the interrogation. It's the least he can do. And he has to come down to talk to Mrs Curtis anyway.'

'Todd? Oh, the new president.'

'It's to reassure the parents,' Lancer explained. 'Furthermore, I've promised them that we'll have a lawyer there to look out for the boys' interests.' He frowned suddenly. 'Carruthers was needlessly obstructionist at first, but thank God, he's come around.'

Thatcher was amused. 'I'm sure it will be an experience for him,' he said politely.

Stanton Carruthers was one of Wall Street's leading trust-and-estate lawyers. Few were his equal in dealing with the Internal Revenue Service. As a result, he knew no more about criminal law than any layman who reads the papers, which is to say that he was rapidly qualifying as an expert on the subject of involuntary confessions.

But Police Headquarters is not composed of imbeciles. Already the Elliot Patterson disappearance had been labelled as a tiresome case, requiring great efforts, littered with false scents and fraught with tender toes. Carruthers's voice on the telephone was enough to alert Centre Street to the status of the four boys. They had money and interest behind them. The officer in charge of the case became markedly cooperative.

Certainly, the interview could be held at the Ivy League Club. Certainly, Mr Todd and Mr Carruthers could be present throughout. Perhaps it would be best if the Department sent an officer who specialized in youth problems?

Carruthers, reflecting that those were not the problems involved, austerely said it would not be necessary.

Accordingly, at the appointed hour, the Ivy League Club was the scene of yet another meeting, Lyman Todd, still an athletic man in his mid-thirties, contrived to look worldly and avuncular. The police captain spoke in slow, soothing tones. Stanton Carruthers was silent and watchful.

The boys showed less concern than their elders. Since each had applied to four different colleges, each was resigned to unending interviews, smokers, tests, guidance pep-talks and informal get-togethers. They had arrived early and split into two pairs, flanking Carruthers, as they waited for the other participants.

On one side Jonathan Hughes described customizing his Mustang while Carter Sprague interjected comments about the Grand Prix. On the other side two pleasant-faced nondescript boys discussed football versus rugby.

The entrance of Lyman Todd and Captain Litton brought everybody to their feet. Todd headed straight for one of the nondescript boys.

'Well, I'm glad to see you again, Pete. I hope your father isn't too disturbed about all this.'

Pete looked amused. 'Mother hasn't told him about it yet.'

'Splendid, splendid! There's really no need to worry him. I know he has a full schedule already. He was telling me about his recording sessions when we met at the Brunswick benefit night. You'll be sure to give him my regards, won't you?'

Todd's eagerness made it plain that this last was no mere civility. Not until the introductions did Stanton Carruthers absorb the fact that Pete was Pier Luigi Fursano, son of the great Arturo Fursano, maestro for the ages.

Pete's companion was Douglas Younger, and there were no cordial inquiries about his parents. Captain Litton had no difficulty in ranking the boys by importance.

'Now, boys,' he said, 'this shouldn't take long. But first I want to get the geography straight.'

With practised speed the police captain established the few

relevant facts. The elevator on the second floor of the Ivy League Club opened directly on to a corridor. The corridor contained two doors, one on the right leading to an ample conference room, and one on the left leading to a small waiting-room. Beyond the waiting-room was the office with its file cabinets and clerical personnel. The office had no independent access to the corridor. The Admission Committee on that memorable afternoon had started with a meeting in the conference room, making periodic forays through the waiting-room into the office.

'Yes, yes,' said Todd impatiently. 'That was when they were reviewing contributions. The boys here know nothing about that.'

'Except that they kept us waiting,' said Carter Sprague petulantly. 'They weren't even here when we arrived.'

Was he commenting unfavourably on Todd's and Litton's tardiness today?

'Mr Armitage was here,' interrupted Douglas Younger with painstaking accuracy.

Carter looked at him with dislike, but young Fursano broke in: 'Sure. And Mr Patterson came in right after. We didn't wait so long, Carter.'

Younger seemed to have a catalogue mind. 'We didn't have to wait long *then*,' he said. 'But, after Mr Dunlop and Mr Marsden got here, they took care of something else before they got to us.'

Carter Sprague was not the only teenager who kept a running tally of his elders' derelictions. It was with an effort that Captain Litton produced a smile and pushed on.

'Right. Now I want you boys to think carefully. Let's go over your movements after the meeting became concerned with your admission.'

The boys agreed they had first been herded across the corridor en masse for a speech about Brunswick College.

'You know the sort of thing,' Sprague explained. 'A rather tedious description of traditions and past great men. The pines of Brunswick and some Vice President or other.'

'It wasn't so bad,' Douglas Younger objected. 'They told us

where Brunswick placed in the Ivy League last year and who they played against.'

Sprague had no sympathy with juvenilia. 'They also emphasized its rural surroundings,' he said as one delivering a knockout punch. He still envied his classmates from St Mark's who were going to set up cosmopolitan apartments in Cambridge.

But Pete Fursano was stirred to life. 'It sounded pleasant,' he said simply, out of a lifetime on the symphony circuit. 'I like the country.'

Sprague subsided instantly. Stanton Carruthers, who liked to get the power hierarchy straight, now saw why Carter Sprague had chosen to sit next to Jonathan Hughes. He knew better than to pass himself off as an experienced Continental to young Fursano, who probably spoke at least five languages and had been to school everywhere.

Captain Litton was noticeably uninterested in these asides.

'Okay,' he said heavily. 'And after the joint talk, you were called in one by one. Now I want to know what happened to the rest of you during these single interviews. Did you wander off? Did you stay in the waiting room?'

A confused jumble of recollection was now surfaced. There had been visits to the men's room, attempts to use the phone in the office, one mad dash down to the cigar stand in the lobby (Jonathan Hughes supplying himself with the latest issue of *Hot Rod*). Prolonged debate was necessary before a conclusion could be reached. The conclusion was that at no time had the waiting-room been vacant.

'All right. Now we come to the end of the interviews. How did that take place?'

It had been quite simple. Mr Armitage had stuck his head in the door and said they were no longer needed. They had proceeded to collect their belongings. Jonathan Hughes had left immediately, taking the elevator before the conference-room door opened. The other three boys had still been present when the Committee surged into the corridor. They could testify that Elliot Patterson had been carrying an attaché case.

'But they all were,' contributed Douglas Younger. 'I went

down in the elevator with them. I noticed it because I wondered what kind of jobs they had.'

Only Pete Fursano had heard Carter Sprague ask Elliot Patterson to stay behind. He confirmed Sprague's description of the incident.

'Yes. Mr Patterson said Carter could only have a few minutes because he was in a hurry. They were both sitting down on opposite sides of that little coffee table when I left.'

So far, so good. Captain Litton then took Carter Sprague over the incident of the falling briefcase.

'That's right,' said Carter, unutterably bored. 'He was telling me he had to go and shoving everything into his briefcase, when it slipped and everything was spilled.'

'Why was the briefcase open? Was it open when he joined you in the waiting room?'

Carter had to abandon nonchalance. It was only after a moment's thought that he could reply.

'No, it wasn't. I'd mentioned my maths marks to him and he opened some folder and checked it. I think it may have been these College Board scores there's been such a commotion about.'

'But you didn't see it?'

'No, I didn't,' Carter agreed.

'You say you helped pick up his things?'

'Naturally,' said Carter with dignified reproof. 'He was an older man.' The explanation conjured up a white-haired cripple.

Captain Litton was untouched by the rebuke. 'Tell me what you saw, what you helped pick up.'

'Folders,' snapped Sprague. 'File folders.'

'How many were there?'

Carter looked suspiciously at the detective. A question hovered on his lips, but he decided it was best left unspoken. Finally he answered tentatively as if afraid of giving the wrong response, 'There must have been five or six.'

'Are you sure there weren't more?'

Carter was stung. 'There could not possibly have been more than six. Seven at the most!'

Litton retired into private calculations. Todd and Carruthers did not intervene. The boys, including Carter Sprague, looked bewildered.

'What colour were the folders?' Litton demanded.

Carter Sprague had learned a lesson. 'They were just folders, ordinary folders! Buff or white or something!'

And from this position he would not be budged.

After that, Litton seemed to lose interest. He formally asked Sprague if Elliot Patterson had displayed any emotion other than a desire to hurry off. He did not pretend to be very interested in Sprague's opinions on the matter. Even his questions about the joint stroll toward Fifth Avenue where the man and boy had parted company were casual. Stanton Carruthers, who had heard George Lancer's misgivings on this subject, was prepared to protest, but there was no need. By the time all four boys had been dismissed with appropriate thanks, Carruthers had not once opened his mouth.

However, when he brought Lancer up to date, he was not overly reassuring.

'I didn't like it,' he confessed. 'Litton just slid away from the whole subject of Sprague and Patterson leaving together. Obviously the police have decided to go into that on their own. They aren't going to take a chance having us put in an oar.'

Lancer was inclined toward a more cheerful view. Two whole days without seeing one prospective entrant to the college of his choice (or his parents) was having a beneficial effect on his spirits.

'Maybe they have something else to get their teeth into. Did you ever find out what all that business about the folders meant?'

'Yes. Apparently the police have figured out why Patterson took those College Board scores with him. Or they think they have. They went through all the Brunswick files together with the clerical staff. Admissions folders are buff with a green label. The alumni and donor folders are white with a red label. There was one strange white folder. The contents were in Elliot Patterson's handwriting. One of the clerks remembers finding it in the waiting room after Patterson and that boy were there.'

'So?'

'The assumption is that Patterson intended to leave the test scores behind, but didn't have time to take the file into the office. He left the wrong one, that's all, a white instead of a buff.'

Lancer, in line with his new policy, did not point out that knowing why Patterson had taken the scores did not undo the damage caused by their absence. Instead he rubbed his hands together cheerfully and said, 'Well, things are beginning to clear up. By the way, what was in the folder he left behind?'

'Nothing that explains anything. Just some notes he made on four of his classmates. I suppose he thought they might be good for contributions to the college.'

Lancer stopped rubbing his hands suddenly.

'Let's hope he isn't lining up prospects for a few more thefts. If it wasn't for Mrs Curtis, I'd be willing to forget the first round. But he can't get any ideas about making a career out of this!'

If any humour was intended in Lancer's mock-bitter lament, it went right over Stanton Carruthers's head. A life in trusts and estates does not encourage lightheartedness in matters of personal property.

'No, I don't think it can be that, George,' he said stolidly. 'None of these men sounds good for $50,000.'

Lancer was swift to pounce. 'Then he certainly wasn't thinking in terms of donations. Who are they, anyway?'

'Wesley Stubbins of Peoria, Illinois. Christopher Taine of McKeesport, Pennsylvania. Alec Baxter of New York City. Henry Perkins of Bethesda, Maryland. Ever heard of any of them?'

Lancer shook his head. He did not remind Carruthers that the men with less than $50,000 whom he knew could be numbered on one hand. He didn't have to.

'And that's all?' he asked.

'By no means. There's a lot of biographical information about each one. Here, look at this one. Alec Baxter, thirty-six years old, born in Forest Hills, Long Island. Son of Reverend Allen Baxter, Episcopalian clergyman. Went to Episcopalian day school in Garden City, then to Brunswick. Majored in art, then went to Chicago for two years' further study. Scholarship to Paris for two years. There's a list of prizes and scholarships. Taught art at Brunswick for three years. Had a one-man show in Boston eight years ago. Then, there's work as a commercial artist and now he seems to be a freelance. There's a physical description too.'

Lancer rubbed his jaw. 'And he's got the same sort of material for all of them?'

'That's right. Stubbins is a professor in a small college. Taine runs an employment agency, and Perkins works for the Department of Commerce in Washington. There doesn't seem to be any connection among them, except that they're all from Patterson's class. Then, if you can make head or tail of it, there was a small index card clipped to the whole batch that just says "Father Martin" on it.'

'I'll bet he isn't an old Brunsie!'

Carruthers shook his head dubiously. 'You never can tell. But we could check it. Not that it seems to make much difference.'

'None of it makes any difference. It just proves Patterson was up to lots of things we don't know about. And we've already had that hammered home. But I don't like the sound of it. Not one single bit!'

11. Numerical Grades Are Not Given

A full report of these developments speedily reached the Brunswick Admission Committee; it added to the prevailing difficulties. Already publicity, compounded by Mrs Curtis's martial trumpetings, had made it impossible for them to meet in their usual quarters in the Ivy League Club. There, the ceaseless clamour of the telephone, the periodic appearance of anxious adolescents accompanied by indignant mothers, and the routine descents of the police had put an end to all comfort to the unconcealed fury of those affiliated with the other colleges sharing quarters with Brunswick.

'I know you want to talk to someone in authority, madam,' said a venerable graduate of Tiverton College, Tiverton, Massachusetts. 'But, I, thank God, have nothing to do with Brunswick!'

Madam did not believe a word of this, but the Brunswick offices certainly bore him out. Three harassed girls, shanghaied from the Armitage Insurance Brokerage and the Sloan Guaranty Trust, were manning desks squeezed between the filing cabinets. They were typing on improvised surfaces, slitting open letters and creating a paper storm. The waiting-room had been designed for graciousness, but an ungainly switchboard had been installed to relieve the bottleneck at the Ivy League Club communication centre; two more girls were endlessly repeating the same message:

'No, I'm afraid there's no one in the office. If you will kindly leave your name . . .'

Even the lobby, consecrated to the comfort of the adult male, swarmed with suburban housewives and their offspring.

'Where exactly is the Brunswick Admission Committee?' somebody snarled.

The manager of the Ivy League Club was stampeded into truth. 'I only wish I knew!'

The Brunswick Admission Committee, in emergency session, was meeting in a seminar room of the Gary Museum of Contemporary Art. None of the members had asked what the emergency was. Nobody had to.

Nevertheless, Neil Marsden saw Jim Dunlop gazing at his surroundings with frank fascination as he strode up the ramp. To look at him, no one would think that Mrs Curtis had worked everybody into an impossible corner, that the police were grilling Brunswick applicants, that all hell had broken loose.

Well, Marsden had a devastating all-purpose retort to philistinism.

Fortunately, Armitage joined them before the exchange could commence. He, Marsden decided, was aesthetically blinkered, since he remained oblivious to the Gary, merely congratulating Marsden for suggesting this change of venue.

'Good God, yes,' Marsden replied. 'I've never liked the Club, but now it's absolutely impossible. Do you know that some woman called me up – here! – yesterday ! Kept me on the phone for forty minutes about her little Willy.' He closed his eyes, then consciously resumed the chair. 'And now this new business about Elliot's little private list of classmates pops up. What the hell was he up to?'

Since it had already been agreed that nobody knew or cared to guess, Ralph Armitage simply ignored this.

'You know, I had an idea,' he said. 'Elliot must be bonded.'

'Say, you're right!' Dunlop exclaimed. 'Professional fund raisers must be bonded. But Ralph, would the bond that covers Target Associates do us any good? Elliot wasn't raising funds for Target.'

Neil Marsden respected money but found money-making rather vulgar. Impatiently he pointed out that it looked as if Elliot Patterson had been raising funds for Elliot Patterson. Armitage shook his head slightly but explained that no matter what Elliot had been doing, a bonding company might quiet Mrs Curtis.

'I repeat, what good will a bond do?' Marsden said. 'We've got a lion by the tail. The whole world thinks that something very peculiar is going on at Brunswick. And for all *I* know, they may be right.'

These sentiments were still bouncing off the aggressively unpainted concrete walls when George Lancer entered. Lancer looked pained but determined.

Armitage greeted him and said, 'George, I thought of approaching Gabe Uhlein. We might be able to get some coverage from Elliot's bond. That way we could get Mrs Curtis off our neck.'

Before Lancer could reply, Marsden again objected. 'What good will that do with the police?' he demanded. 'They're the ones who are after the boys.'

Ralph Armitage was not easily shaken. 'That won't do any harm,' he said reasonably. 'We all knew Elliot better than those boys. And there was absolutely nothing out of the ordinary about him that last day, as we all told the police!'

There was a confused murmur of assent. Neil Marsden again waded in.

'Unless Carter Sprague knows more than he's telling. I'd like to know what the police know, or suspect, about that kid.'

The distasteful implications of this made Lancer plunge ahead more abruptly than he had intended.

'Do any of you know anything about Alec Baxter, Wesley Stubbins, Christopher Taine? Or Henry Perkins?'

'Who? Oh, Elliot's classmates,' said Armitage. 'Hell, I don't know why everybody has gotten so nervous about that list. Elliot might have planned to raise money from them. Maybe they were just friends he wanted to look up during reunion.'

Dunlop nodded. 'Probably that's what the police are assuming. They'll check them out as a formality. But since none of us can think of any reason for Elliot to make that detailed list, well...'

Suddenly Neil Marsden snapped his fingers.

They looked at him inquiringly.

'I thought I recalled one name. Baxter. Alec Baxter. He's an artist. I'm pretty sure I've seen watercolours.'

With a grin, Armitage pointed out that that knocked out any theory about potential donors. This was the last smile of the meeting.

'I think it would be wise to see what we can find out about these men. Baxter, of course, is our best hope since he's in New York,' said Lancer with a frown. 'Should we uncover anything of importance we'll inform the authorities, but with any luck, we'll simply be able to clear away red herrings.'

With rare unanimity, the committee agreed with him.

Ralph Armitage strolled out of the Gary Museum, refused a ride and bade farewell to George Lancer, who was clambering into a waiting limousine. Preoccupied, he checked his watch. A quick lunch and he could get back to his own desk. Brunswick and Elliot Patterson were taking too much time and attention from the insurance business.

Still, he had agreed to discharge a number of tasks. Characteristically, he decided to get things over. Ten minutes later he was in the utilitarian offices of Target Associates. Although he was not consciously aware of it, they were a more congenial background for him than the Gary.

Gabe Uhlein was on a business trip to Utica. Mrs Knightley was still at her desk. It was she who came into the waiting-room to greet him.

'It's about Elliot Patterson,' Armitage felt obliged to explain.

'I thought it must be,' she replied. 'I recognized your name, Mr Armitage. Come in, won't you?'

Usually Armitage found businesswomen either irritating or embarrassing. Marian Knightley was neither. She had a calm air of repose that discouraged superfluities.

In less time than usual, Ralph Armitage was broaching the subject of Elliot Patterson's bond.

'Yes, of course,' said Mrs Knightley. 'And if we could convince the bonding company that this is a legitimate claim, it would help solve some of your problems, wouldn't it? I understand that Mrs Curtis insists on police action.'

Armitage admitted as much. With rather grim amusement, he countered by suggesting that it would do Target Associates no harm. Unpleasant speculation about Elliot Patterson's fund raising was doing his firm no good. Unruffled, Mrs Knightley agreed and promised to put the matter to Uhlein when he returned. Without in any way committing herself, she left Armitage feeling that she was favourably inclined towards his suggestion.

Armitage was not unduly impressionable but he registered something else as their conversation continued. Mrs Knightley was not interested in discussing the mystery of Elliot Patterson's disappearance. She was perfectly friendly but firm. Not until the end of his visit did he reveal his second reason for approaching Target Associates.

'Well, let's hope we can work something out. By the way, Mrs Knightley . . .'

'Yes?'

The monosyllable was pleasant and somehow daunting.

'A little problem has come up. The police have found a short list of classmates that Elliot kept. Probably nothing special, but we can't quite understand what it's for. Somebody suggested that they might have something to do with his work here.'

'Who were they?'

She listened as he read his list, then replied, 'No, I don't think so. Leave their names and I'll check, but I don't think any of them are Target accounts. We do have a Harold Perkins who is treasurer of the Maslow Fund, but he's far too old to be a classmate of Elliot's.'

Armitage jotted four names on a business card, put it on her desk and rose to leave. 'So you don't know any of them, hmm?'

Possibly Mrs Knightley did not like being inaccurately paraphrased. At any rate, she raised her eyebrows slightly.

'Not Stubbins or Taine,' she said. 'Alec Baxter, though, is an acquaintance of ours.' Quite deliberately she added, 'My husband is an architect.'

Armitage never knew why he felt impelled to say, 'Oh sure, Baxter's the artist, isn't he? Well, thank you again.'

As he rode down in the elevator, Ralph Armitage reflected that a woman like Marian Knightley could only deal with a very strong man – or a very weak man.

Which was, it suddenly occurred to him, a new light on Elliot Patterson.

Jim Dunlop would have been the first to admit frankly that he was ill at ease later that afternoon. He sat at his desk staring at his telephone with dislike.

'I've got Mrs Patterson on the line for you,' the receptionist announced.

Beating down an impulse to bolt, Dunlop grasped the phone.

'Sally? How are you? Yes ... No ... Yes ... Well, I'm sorry to hear that. No, I'm afraid I don't have any news ... no. Oh, I wouldn't pay any attention ... You know what newspapers are like ... Yes. Your brother-in-law is one hundred per cent right ...'

He was perspiring freely.

'What I called for was this, Sally. Did ... does ... Elliot know a Wesley Stubbins, Christopher Taine, Henry Perkins or Alec Baxter?'

Mrs Patterson countered question with question.

Dunlop cleared his throat.

'Well, one reason the names might be familiar is that they're classmates of Elliot's. We were just wondering if Elliot has kept in touch. No! Sally, we just ... er ... came across their names. Oh, you don't think so ...?'

He mopped his brow. Sally Patterson was no longer the woman of two weeks ago. Sweet cooperation was no longer her line. Nevertheless she gave him something to think about.

'What was that? ... Oh, I see. Well, thanks, Sally. We'll be getting good news ...'

After incoherent adieux, he turned his attention to her last remarks. Was there any significance in the fact that Elliot Patterson had been eagerly planning to attend his class reunion at Brunswick the forthcoming week-end?

Sally Patterson hung up the phone and turned a white-lipped face to her sister and brother-in-law.

'I can't stand it!' she said flatly. 'Everybody is making a mystery of everything. They find little pieces of paper in Elliot's files and they act as if he'd been planning a bank robbery. And none of them pay any attention when I tell them it isn't possible. Who do they think they are? Have they been married to Elliot for fourteen years?'

Bill Consett shuffled his feet restively. He had been continuously on duty for over a week now, and he was getting sick of it. Never at his best when faced with feminine sensibilities, he felt that this much of a workout was an indulgence a man granted his wife but no one else. For years he had been telling himself that Sally and Elliot were good sorts. The patent falsity of this contention was becoming apparent.

'Sally,' he said in a tired voice, 'people can't help thinking Elliot is up to some sort of funny business, the way he's acting.'

He wasn't the only one who was tired. For fourteen years Sally had been conscientiously reasonable, prepared to discuss any difference and thrash out a workable compromise, ready with an elaborately patronizing explanation to repress her daughters' small mutinies. She had taken intelligent interest in all the problems of her family, from mud pies to religious awakenings. Insofar as was humanly possible, the Patterson household had been modelled on the Mother of Parliaments under an exceptionally able prime minister.

And now look! What thanks did she get for this endless discipline? One betrayal after another. Elliot leading some kind of underground life for months. Saving pennies and dimes like a ten-year-old planning to run off to sea. The discovery of a fifteen-dollar-a-week savings account had hurt more than anything else. As if she were the kind of wife who went through her husband's pockets!

'Something happened to Elliot this last year. He never would have done anything like this before. I tell you, I knew Elliot. I knew his every mood, his every thought. Good God, we planned everything together, we were close to each other. I knew what he was going to say before he did himself.'

'Maybe you knew too much about him,' Karen Consett suggested. She knew what had happened to Elliot – an uncomplicated twenty-year-old armful of fluff who left him a little mental privacy. Poor old Elliot would have been a pushover.

Balefully Sally glared at her sister.

'That's what marriage is,' she said defiantly, nailing her colours to the sinking mast. For years she had been warning Karen that it wasn't enough to feed a husband and take care of his laundry. You had to work at being a wife. Why, Karen and Bill had as much communication as a pair of amoebas!

And what made it all so unfair was her sure conviction that if only Elliot had told her his troubles, they could have worked something out.

In sharp contrast, Neil Marsden was feeling the first purr of contentment to come his way for several days. First, a series of long telephone calls to well-placed friends had established one thing, certainly in his mind. Stubbins, Taine and Perkins were nobodies; this meant roughly that they did not publish in certain periodicals, live at certain addresses, or have certain incomes.

But at the Capricorn Gallery he struck pay dirt. A husky voice pinned down the elusive echo raised by the name Alec Baxter. Neil listened carefully until the first deep disappointment.

'A commercial artist! You mean one of those advertising hacks?'

'No, no!' said the telephone.

Alec supported himself with commercial work on and off. But he did watercolours. Rather nice. Stronger than most. Lots of shadow.

After this discussion had continued for what most people would think was too long, Marsden was startled again.

Capricorn Gallery repeated that it had even sold some Baxters a few years back. One had been purchased for some college. Capricorn forgot which. Another . . .

Another was now in the collection of George C. Lancer.

After effusive thanks, Neil Marsden remained deep in thought. He was generally reckoned a very wily young man with a sure touch for the ladies who sat on boards. And Lucy Lancer was an important patroness of the Gary. Normally Neil Marsden would have jumped at the opportunity to approach her.

Today, however, it was a full twenty minutes before he automatically straightened his tie, adopted a smile rarely seen by his assistant, and reached for the telephone.

George C. Lancer was neither intimidated nor contented. He was uncomfortable. On the whole, he enjoyed the world of affairs, of arrangements, of committees and public appearances. He preferred to have this activity sparked by something congenial to him, like mergers, international loans or currency crises. Nevertheless, he was willing to cooperate with the functionaires of Brunswick College.

Now, however, they were intruding on his domestic comfort.

'John,' he said the next day, 'I hope you won't mind lunching upstairs.'

'Certainly not. Lucy all right?' Thatcher asked civilly.

It was one of Lancer's small pleasures to dine at home when he chose to bring business to the luncheon table. Theoretically this was to introduce privacy and relaxation to the frenzy of big business. Actually it was to exploit Matthilde to the fullest.

'No, Lucy's fine,' said Lancer. 'But she's having a guest for lunch today.'

'Oh yes,' said Thatcher who had frequently dined *à quatre* with the Lancers and another patroness.

'Marsden. That little twerp on the Brunswick Committee,' Lancer amplified. 'We could join them . . . but frankly I'm tired of this thing . . .'

Nevertheless, it remained the topic of his conversation over roast beef and potatoes in the President's Dining Room of the Sloan. Lancer summarized the findings to date, as reported by Armitage, Dunlop and Marsden. Tactfully Thatcher agreed that they were indecisive. If he thought differently, he kept the opinion to himself.

'And I can assure you, John, that I did not know that Lucy bought a picture by this Baxter – whoever he is!'

Thatcher grinned.

'Oh, come on, George. This lunch isn't that bad.'

George acknowledged the truth of this. 'You're right. Fact is, I don't like the way things are going. I'm pinning my hopes on clearing this up soon. Maybe when Todd calls from Brunswick this afternoon, the news will be good.'

Thatcher did not offer odds.

Sometimes sympathy from friends outruns prudence. By the time Thatcher regained his own office after lunch, he was encumbered with a chore for Brunswick, namely identification of a name in Elliot Patterson's papers.

'A Father Martin?' Miss Corsa asked, making a note. 'What church?'

Thatcher was on his way to his own desk. He answered that he did not know and, without thinking, suggested a rundown of the Martins in the telephone book. After that she could call it a day.

He reckoned without Miss Corsa's passion for thoroughness.

'Mr Thatcher, most parishes don't list telephones in their priests' names.'

'Try East Village. That's where these artists are. And Baxter's the only one who lives in New York. There may be a connection.'

Miss Corsa brushed this aside. 'That is, if Father Martin is a Catholic. He may be in the Episcopalian Church. Or Orthodox . . .'

'Now Miss Corsa, let's just stick with statistical probabilities!'

Miss Corsa disapproved of light dismissals.

'Or he might be in orders, rather than in a parish . . .'

'Miss Corsa . . .'

She was implacable.

'For that matter, Mr Thatcher, Martin could be either a first or a last name.'

Thatcher fled.

Miss Corsa, having shown him the vast complexity of the task he had assigned her, would now deploy her enormous reserves of patience and expertise and unearth a Father Martin who knew something about Elliot Patterson. If anybody could do it, she could.

And what would Father Martin know?

Thatcher ran down a list of possibilities. There was nothing in any of them to relieve the much-tried Lancer. Or Brunswick and Mrs Patterson for that matter. Everything remained indecisive, to choose a word Thatcher had used before. What four schoolboys had seen, what four fellow committeemen had seen, what Elliot had said and done, even what four classmates might know . . .

Nothing yet altered the basic fact that, unless Elliot Patterson turned up on the doorstep clutching $50,000 in one hand and a file of test scores in the other, things were going to get worse.

His phone rang.

'John? George here . . .'

John Putnam Thatcher did not have to ask. The news from Brunswick had been bad.

12. Commencement Address

Probably the most active irritant in the news from Brunswick was the disruption of Lyman Todd's schedule.

The president of Brunswick College had been a public figure before rising to his present eminence. His doctoral thesis, suitably modified, had become a paperback bestseller in undergraduate circles, where it was viewed as a significant and cogent commentary on the role of man in urban society. While a professor at a large East Coast university he had vigorously championed the liberal arts as preparation for involvement. (Subsequently his lectures on Greek patterns of personal involvement were barred to freshmen.) When Brunswick's ageing president approached retirement, Todd became Academic Dean and made plans for his own reign. His maiden speech unveiled a two-pronged attack. Students must be educated to take their place in society; their elders must be educated to value a bigger, a better and a wealthier Brunswick.

Now businessmen will contribute, but only on a businesslike basis. So Lyman Todd entered every office armed with graphs, statistical charts and financial statements. Self-made men coughing up a cool million knew where their money was going. Corporations underwriting new laboratories could solace themselves with Dr Todd's figures on the projected shortage of physicists in 1985.

Todd was equally successful with loftier elements. Foundations and governmental agencies were startled to find Brunswick hurling itself into every public-service project going. Poverty, racial attitudes, urban renewal, mass transit, juvenile delinquency, air and water pollution – all found a home in Coburg, New Hampshire.

Within six months *The Wall Street Journal* reported that here was a bona fide scholar running circles around the business-school specialists currently employed by educational institutions with low endowments. After a respectful review of recent donations to Brunswick, the *Journal* turned to Todd, the man:

He travels an average of four or five days a week, criss-crossing the country in the private plane reserved for his use. A tireless public speaker, he is capable of communicating his own enthusiasm for modern education – sometimes to unlikely audiences. Again and again contributors have been impressed by his encyclopaedic knowledge and his ability to back up his theories with concrete data.

'Lyman is a human dynamo,' commented a close associate. 'Nineteen hours is his idea of a normal working day.'

In due course Lyman Todd read this article, as he read everything likely to be of use. Nothing if not conscientious, he accordingly embarked on a schedule featuring nineteen-hour working days, five of them including jet trips, with disastrous consequences to his renal function.

But these homeric endeavours left him virtually no time for the pedestrian chores of daily administration. Mrs Warren V. Curtis, unimpressed by proof that 95 per cent of all thefts over $25,000 dollars are committed by college graduates, was bad enough. Parents wanting reassurance for nebulous fears were worse.

Indeed, only one interruption of Lyman Todd's circuit riding was truly welcome. In alternate years, Brunswick played its traditional football rival on home ground. This mid-October week-end always saw the foliage of the surrounding mountainside reaching a melodramatic climax. A light dusting of frost could be seen early in the morning, the smell of burning leaves was everywhere, and the air was like wine.

Wily college fathers, decades past, had realized that it would be flying in the face of providence to waste this powerful atmospheric stimulant to nostalgic generosity. A major reunion week had been grafted on to the festivities and was now a time-honoured part of the ritual. The arrangements for this week-end were receiving Todd's personal attention; as a result, his secretary was busy arranging audiences and denying access to the Presence.

Among the first to be admitted was, naturally enough, the permanent secretary of the Alumni Association.

'It's a shame that Elliot Patterson's class is having its fifteenth this year,' he said. 'There's sure to be a big turnout.'

'The fifteenth, eh?' mused Todd, his thoughts elsewhere. 'Not much leeway for donations with them, is there?'

The secretary was prepared to look on the bright side.

'The bachelors and the doctors do very nicely by us,' he explained. 'And speaking of bachelors, I've got the files on the four men you wanted. The ones in Patterson's class.'

'*I* don't want them. It's those people in New York.'

Here in the safety of Coburg, Lyman Todd was inclined to lump together Mrs Warren V. Curtis, George Lancer, Elliot Patterson's Admission Committee, Carter Sprague and the New York City Police Department.

'I suppose they have some reason for it,' he continued. 'But what do you mean about bachelors?'

'That's what they all are. I didn't catch it when Elliot asked for this material the last time he was up here. He just went through the records and then asked for everything we had on these four men – formal files, press clippings, everything. You're getting exactly what we gave him.' He tapped the folder lightly. 'Now that I've caught on to the bachelor bit, I think Elliot may have been trying a new fund-raising scheme. Or planning one. But I can't imagine why he left out the fifth man.'

'Fifth man?'

'There are five bachelors recorded in Elliot's class. He asked for material on all of them except Francis Riley.'

'Territorial problems?' Todd hazarded. He knew there were continual screams about poaching from the regional associations.

The secretary permitted himself a smile. 'That didn't seem to bother him with the others. Alec Baxter was the only one who lived in New York. Of course, as I said, Elliot may have been working on some scheme he was going to present to the national board. Anyway, two of them are going to be here for the weekend if Mr Lancer wants to speak with them.'

'We'll let Lancer worry about that. What I'm worried about is the press. There's certain to be some coverage of the weekend. And someone may try to tie it with this Patterson disappearance. Is there anybody in his class who could make a nice impressive statement about having every confidence in Elliot and being unwilling to judge a man prematurely?'

'I've thought of that.' The secretary congratulated himself. 'And I think I've got just the man for you. A junior congressman who was elected last year.'

'A congressman,' Todd murmured approvingly. 'That always makes a good impression, especially if he's a young one.'

So, in a comparatively relaxed frame of mind, he greeted his next visitors. They were a motley trio, comprising the manager of the largest hotel in Coburg, the head of the campus police and a representative of the college public-relations office.

'Naturally we want to cooperate with the college,' said the manager of the Coburg Inn perfunctorily. 'We're very anxious to avoid a repetition of last time.'

'We appreciate your cooperation,' said Todd gravely.

His briefing for the forthcoming week-end included newspaper accounts of the riot which had nearly wrecked the Inn two years ago. Brunswick had won a rare victory over its rival, and exuberant Old Grads, recapturing their youth with a vengeance, had gone on a spree necessitating reinforcements from the state police.

The PR man decided that the courtesies had gone on long enough. It was time to get down to business.

'We've taken precautions,' he announced. 'First of all, the alumni won't be arriving until Friday night.' Diplomatically he avoided the outright reminder that, last time, the loyal sons of Brunswick had had three clear days in which to get tanked up before the game. 'Then, we've made a careful selection of the classes staying at the Inn. I think you'll find that your guests this week-end will represent the older, more responsible graduates.'

The manager controlled his enthusiasm. He retained a lively recollection from the last holocaust of a white-haired corporate executive mounted on top of the bar with a bottle in either hand, merrily challenging all comers. But all he said was, 'It doesn't matter who's assigned to our rooms. They all end up using our bar.'

'There's not much we can do about that.' Lyman Todd let the

velvet glove slip a little as he continued smoothly, 'Even putting the Inn off limits wouldn't affect the alumni.'

The manager, who knew he was being reminded of the substantial revenues derived from the college by the Inn, agreed the plan was impractical.

The PR man was pained by the hint of the mailed fist. He rushed into the breach. 'But our real reliance is on Ed, here. His campus police will be out in full force.'

Ed Webster, a craggy New Englander now drawing a pension from the Berlin (New Hampshire) police force, took the floor.

'I guess we all want the same thing,' he drawled. 'There's bound to be some high spirits, but if we nip them in the bud, there'll be no call for outsiders. My men will be posted at all the likely trouble spots. Their orders are a little different from last time. If any party gets too rough, they'll encourage it to break up. But if friendly talk doesn't work, they'll get the town cops to give them a hand.'

Everybody nodded. An extended post mortem after the last event blamed failure to call in local authorities until the riot had mushroomed beyond the control of anything less than the military.

'I hope,' said the Inn manager, 'that the town force isn't going to be too much in evidence.' He had a vague picture of his bar lined with blue-coated minions.

Ed Webster's easy speech did not falter. He was paid to deal with people who insisted that potential rioters be handled with care, whether they were eighteen or eighty. 'They're being as helpful as they can. My men are sworn in as deputies, and the town boys will stay out of sight as much as possible. Some of them have to be around, though. They've got this alert for Elliot Patterson, for one thing.'

'Patterson again! We never seem to stay away from him very long. What do the town police have to do with him?' the president demanded.

'The New York Department thinks there's an outside chance he may turn up here. Seems he was talking about it. They've sent up a teletype and an official request for cooperation.'

'They must be out of their minds,' said Lyman Todd with more frankness than he usually permitted himself. 'Why, there are at least a hundred people who could recognize him. You take it from me, this is the last place he'd show his face!'

An inexorable fate seemed determined that Todd's day should centre around the alumnus Brunswick could best spare. His final visitor for the morning was Gabriel Uhlein.

'I can't tell you how distressed we are by this situation,' Uhlein proclaimed piously as he took his seat. He was fresh from an interview with his lawyer, in which he learned that Target Associates had absolutely no responsibility for the misdeeds of employees committed outside the scope of their employment. 'Of course we have every confidence in Elliot.'

'So do we.'

Both men now formally recognized that they were committed to public defense of Patterson.

'But it would have made a much more comfortable situation if Elliot's bond covered his activities for Brunswick.'

'It certainly would have!' retorted Todd, still smarting from an interview with Mrs Curtis. The return of $50,000 no longer appealed to her; now she wanted blood.

Uhlein, bringing his ship into harbour very nicely, leaned back expansively. He was holding his overcoat on his lap as a sign that he did not intend to make extensive inroads on the presidential time. Nonetheless, he seemed to be settling down for a leisurely, congenial conversation.

'It's almost always awkward when fund-raising activities are undertaken on an amateur basis. So many difficulties can be avoided when the situation is put into a professional context. Not that we don't admire the dedication and energy of community groups.' He raised a large, beautifully manicured hand to dispel the illusion. 'Alumni groups and church workers have always been noted for their wholehearted generosity with time and effort. But in crude dollars-and-cents terms, the results can be frankly disappointing.'

Lyman Todd stared at his visitor. It was being rapidly borne in upon him that Gabriel Uhlein, far from paying a courtesy visit to announce the bonding company's position and proffer condolences, was actually touting for business. His first reaction was incredulity. In his opinion the employer of Elliot Patterson should be hiding underground, not puffing his firm. His second and overriding reaction, however, was the pique of a gifted amateur patronized by a professional.

'In crude dollars-and-cents terms, Brunswick has been doing remarkably well,' he said bluntly.

'Yes, I saw that article in the *Journal*. Let me congratulate you on it. These are happy times in which we're living. There's nothing like an expanding economy, is there? And,' Uhlein continued dreamily, 'the big-money institutions are at last realizing they have a stake in higher education. That realization, of course, should be reinforced. So much could be done by the full-time efforts of a trained staff. It's difficult to see any limiting factors.'

'I fail to see how any professional efforts could preserve us from our two major embarrassments. The first is the publicity attendant on Patterson's disappearance. The second is the imbroglio caused by the disappearance of the New York test scores.' Todd was deeply affronted. Good God! What did the man mean by full-time efforts? Did he realize he was talking to someone who put in a nineteen-hour working day? Consciously he steadied himself and searched for a light note.

'We're even having some of the New York applicants up for our football week-end to make up for their inconvenience. No, I'm afraid I don't think having this in the hands of professionals would help us one single bit. But I'm grateful that you dropped by to tell us about the bond. I hope you didn't take such a long trip just for this.'

Because you're not getting anything else out of it, was the unspoken addendum clearly underlining his words. As he spoke, he rose, bringing the interview to a close.

Professional fund raisers are used to rebuffs, and never more so than when selling their services. Uhlein also rose.

'Oh, no,' he said, quite unruffled. 'I thought I'd stay over and take in the big game. It should be a very interesting week-end.'

13. Indoor and Outdoor Sports

The only thing to be said for luncheon at the Faculty Club of Brunswick College immediately prior to the football game, John Putnam Thatcher decided, was that it would have been a good deal worse without Lucy Lancer. He said as much when they emerged from the dining-room into the maelstrom of Old Brunsies, giving happy yelps of recognition and making plans for after-game festivities.

'That's why I came, John,' Lucy answered placidly.

When George Lancer had asked him to the Board of Trustees meeting in Coburg, Thatcher had not been surprised to learn that Mrs Lancer would be in their party. Lucy's principle of providing support to her husband was not unique. But seldom is it carried into operation so successfully. Inevitably her husband's colleagues benefited. Many a banking convention had been made endurable to members of the Sloan Guaranty Trust by Lucy Lancer's calm good nature and easy acceptance of social burdens. Now she put these gifts into practice once again.

'There's Neil Marsden bearing down on us. And I see he's got that man who collects Manets in tow. You might want to slip away for a few minutes.'

There was nothing Thatcher wanted more. Unobtrusively he allowed himself to be engulfed by some departing football players. When he came up for air, he was safe on the other side of the room and could take stock of his surroundings.

They had arrived that morning, and Lancer and Thatcher had gone straight to the Board meeting. There Thatcher, in his role of consultant, had counselled prompt restitution of Mrs Curtis's $50,000. She would be effectively neutralized by this manoeuvre, and the resultant publicity would be all to the good.

Thatcher and Lancer had expected opposition. They were dismayed, however, to be met with indifference. As bankers, they were undeniably biased towards financial solution of problems. More important, perhaps, as men with adult children, they had not fully appreciated the perils raised by the monkey wrench in Brunswick's admission procedures.

Did they realize, demanded an oil magnate with alarming eyebrows, that by being late with its acceptances, Brunswick was going to get the culls of this year's crop? 'My God!' he thundered, 'I'm not going to stand by and see us take Amherst's leavings!'

And what about the agony to Brunswick alumni? asked a small balding man. Could a Brunswick father conscientiously advise his son to turn down Wesleyan? As so often these days, the conversation ultimately turned to the young people themselves. Could a boy enter Brunswick with a positive attitude after these ghastly preliminaries? Would his entire first year be marred by unconscious hostility?

On the whole, Thatcher had been quite grateful when the next item on the trustees' agenda had ended his usefulness and dismissed him to the society of Lucy. Now he was deprived even of that. He looked around with growing resentment. So far, Coburg could have been duplicated in any other New England college town with a reunion in the works. There were the peripheral motels taken over by the Fifth, Tenth and Fifteenth. There were the downtown inns bearing handmade banners: 'Welcome Twenty-fivers,' strung between the pillars of the veranda. There were the dormitories ruthlessly emptied of undergraduates for the Fiftieth and its attendant medical personnel. There were the station wagons from New Jersey, driven by balding young men, and filled with wives, children, picnic hampers, thermos bottles, blankets and more banners. There were aged members of the faculty doing first-rate Mr Chipses, managing by sheer virtuosity to shed charm and humour over incidents they had long since forgotten, involving students whose names they had never known. There were junior members of the faculty making ironic comments of broad sociological content. There were the underpaid custodial members of the staff, frequently Irish, who evinced no offence at being greeted as 'Old Tom' and simply worked harder, untroubled by the increase in a population forever and fundamentally alien to them.

There were also those concerned with the problem of Elliot Patterson.

'Hello, Thatcher. Do you know if the Board has come up with anything?'

The speaker was Ralph Armitage. Introduction revealed his companion as Gabriel Uhlein. Mildly Thatcher replied that the Board was going to concentrate its fire on the educational testing service and try for examination results early enough to meet the Ivy League deadline.

'They don't seem to be very interested in Patterson or his $50,000,' he said with great forbearance.

Armitage was amused. 'Then they're the only ones who aren't. Everybody else is buzzing with it.'

'The Board's quite right,' said Uhlein unexpectedly. 'This admission mess is a godsend, in some ways. Everybody will forget about Elliot, given half a chance.'

'Very convenient, from your point of view,' Armitage retorted.

Uhlein's composure was unshaken.

'From everybody's point of view,' he said firmly. 'Marian tells me you tried to get Sally Patterson up here for the weekend. That was a mistake. It would just stir things up.'

'Christ! I didn't want her to come.' Armitage was nettled. 'I was out to see her about the insurance. I'm Elliot's broker, you know. Then she started talking about how Elliot had been planning to come to reunion and how he'd been taking more interest in his classmates recently. She was working herself up, saying other people knew more about his plans than she did. It sounded as if she was thinking of coming up herself. So what could I do?'

'Tell her not to be silly!'

'I'd like to see you pulling that!' Armitage ran a finger inside his collar. 'I told her if she was set on coming, I'd be happy to escort her. The minute I agreed with her, she changed her mind. She wasn't making much sense. I know she's got troubles, but I don't know what's come over Sally Patterson.'

'Mortification, that's what,' a new voice announced patly.

Neil Marsden was being actively malicious. Unmarried, he had not yet acquired proper respect for female temperament. His eyes were brightly interested as he blandly expanded his remarks.

'The self-satisfaction of a lifetime has been shattered. That's what's wrong with Sally Patterson. She's so used to being a great white mother, deciding what's best for everyone, she doesn't have any defences.'

Armitage grunted annoyance while Uhlein looked openly censorious. The party line was that Sally was a victim, to be sympathized with and avoided whenever possible. Even if they had agreed with Marsden, they would have condemned his frankness. As a matter of fact they did not. Neither of them pretended to have his analytic interest, but they had a lot more field experience.

'I hear that we're supposed to help out with the New York applicants,' said Armitage with an abrupt change of subject. 'Does anyone know who's with them now?'

'Dunlop and his wife are doing their turn. And I helped settle them in,' Marsden added.

Thatcher could think of nothing more uncomfortable for a high-school boy than being settled in by Neil Marsden. Then, remembering Carter Sprague, he decided his ideas were old-fashioned.

'So it's up to me. I'll take over for the game. Anybody else going down to the stadium?' Armitage turned to pick up the hat and coat lying ready on a chair.

'Not me!' said Marsden with a distinct snap. 'They couldn't make me go when they had me here, and they're not going to now!'

Uhlein muttered something evasive about joining another party, and Thatcher, about to disclaim any interest in football games, found that other plans had been made for him.

Lucy Lancer was reclaiming him, her serenity unruffled by her grim tidings.

'George is here. It seems that we're expected to sit with the trustees in the president's box.'

Lucy might be unruffled, but her husband, emerging from the

throng, was not. The walk to the stadium was enlivened by his indignation.

'Football games!' he sputtered. 'We come two hundred miles for serious business, and this is what they have in mind!'

'Perhaps it's what they had in mind when they made you a trustee,' Lucy said.

'They made me a trustee because of my money,' her disgruntled husband said crushingly. 'And in three years this has been the first mention of football.'

Thatcher wasn't feeling any too cheerful himself.

'Elliot Patterson has much to answer for,' he pronounced. 'I'm beginning to want a half-hour with that young man.'

Instead he was to get three cold hours in a stadium. From ahead muted roars could be heard: Brunswick, Brunswick, Rah! Rah! Rah! The band struck up:

> Bold bad men of Brunswick!
> Rolling down the field!
> Honour to her banners!
> The Brunsies never yield!

From even farther away, a small contingent took up the challenge and hurled it back:

> Ten thousand men of Harvard
> Want victory today!

Thatcher followed Lancer and Lucy down to their choice seats amid a fusillade of greetings from middle-aged men who seemed to enjoy the opportunity to shout. Fortunately, the fuller-throated students were somewhat removed.

'George! Hey, George!'

'Say, look over there! There's Bill Cotton! Bill! Oh, Bill!'

'No, no, plenty of room – hey, squeeze down, everybody!'

'ROLL YOU MIGHTY BLUE LINE, ROLL!'

The Homecoming Game commenced. It continued interminably and finally ended. It featured three fumbles by the opposition, but four fumbles by the Blues. At half time the band presented a concert, its vigour almost compensating for its lack of precision. Throughout, the temperature dropped steadily. There was a good deal of flask movement along the long grey lines of the alumni (and, reprehensibly, among the young gentlemen of the student body). Hundreds of men, women and children simultaneously discovered the need for hot dogs and fell on the student vendors like a ravening horde.

'ROLL YOU MIGHTY BLUE LINE, ROLL!'

'Good kick!'

'Petenuski's got the ball!'

'Ohhhhh!' (Petenuski dropped the ball.)

'Brunswick! Brunswick! Rah! Rah! Rah!'

Final score: Harvard 28, Brunswick 7.

The chill sun had disappeared by the time a stiff and cold Thatcher clambered to his feet and let the vast throng propel him slowly to the exit. It was twenty minutes before he could make himself heard, but this did not matter. His mind was deliberately blank and it would require some time to restore operational conditions.

'And now, George?' he asked, trying unsuccessfully to sound receptive to the delights in store.

Lancer stepped out of the way of a phalanx of upperclassmen.

'Now, we look for some information about Patterson. Everybody's giving parties tonight. I've got a list of the ones that might be useful.'

'And do you really think we're going to find out anything?' Thatcher inquired politely.

'Of course I don't!' George Lancer was indignant. 'But it's that or a ceremonial banquet with the trustees after a major football defeat.' He peered at his companions, ready to quell mutiny. 'We'll try to drop in on the Deke house. Patterson was a Deke, and they always have open house. Then, we'll stop by Franklin House. He roomed there . . .'

'Doesn't that sound nice?' Lucy Lancer said to no one in particular.

They mounted narrow stairs to a party given by an associate professor of astronomy who had once roomed with Elliot Patterson. Straight Scotch in none-too-clean glasses and water hard to come by. Voices rising, more smoke, distant sounds of convulsive frenzy from a student gathering down the hall.

'Elliot? We see each other, oh, say, every other year or so. We don't have much in common any more. I guess I saw him when he was checking out some people in Alumni Records.'

Thatcher, trying to retain some interest in life, scrupulously asked about Stubbins, Taine, Baxter, and Perkins, the mysterious quartet immortalized by Elliot Patterson.

'Don't remember any of them,' said his host cheerfully. 'Another Scotch?'

Gloomily Thatcher accepted and prowled around the crowded room, continuing his self-appointed task. Elliot Patterson's Four Horsemen had not made a lasting impression on anybody.

'Not Big Men on Campus,' someone concluded.

George Lancer was signalling from beyond the sofa. Beside him Lucy engaged a distinguished looking man with a beard – the Commander Whitehead variety, not the hippie variety.

'Yes,' he said wearily when Thatcher arrived. 'Yes, I know both Patterson and Baxter in New York. All I seem to do these days is explain to people that I know them.'

There was a murmur of sympathy. Life was hard now on anyone sucked into Elliot Patterson's orbit, no matter how casually.

'I had lunch with Patterson about six weeks ago. He didn't say he planned to steal a packet.' This was delivered with fine irony. 'Alec Baxter I haven't seen since last spring. He's gone crazy.'

Everybody brightened. Incoherent sounds of encouragement were offered.

'I'm the art director at Funston Advertising,' the beard continued. 'We were planning a big magazine campaign for one of our clients. Very slick. We needed some high-class watercolours, formalized but vigorous. I thought of Alec. It was a chance in a million. And do you know what he said?'

'What?' Lucy asked dutifully.

'He said he didn't want to tie himself down to that big a commitment. Now, I ask you!'

There was no need to pursue further inquiries. That had been Alec Baxter's last free lunch on this particular expense account. The beard could be ruthless.

Soon the threat of distinguished visitors from Oxford propelled them into departure. Hasty withdrawal down the stairways, past youthful couples, past revelry, past noise.

'Night!' said Thatcher, drawing a deep breath. The campus lights were confetti'd along the paths, shadowed by the pines; the lights from dormitories, clubs, from gymnasiums and faculty houses, looked warm and inviting.

'Here's the Deke house,' George announced, leading the way up to a sinister Victorian mansion. Reluctantly Lucy and Thatcher followed.

Dekes of earlier days were present. They were accepting drinks, looking fondly at battered furniture in the shabby living-room and congregating around the fireplace, telling other past Dekes about the exploits of their sons. Current Dekes bustled about, projecting deference to their elders and waiting impatiently for them to remove themselves so the party could begin. Some hotheads could not wait; from an ominously darkened dining-room came catatonic rhythms and female giggles.

'I wish,' said Lucy Lancer, 'I wish I were the kind of woman who could get away with fainting. But what good would it do? George would just revive me and we'd have to go on.'

George looked as if he were going to launch into a catalogue of the horrors that had been the alternative to this way of passing the evening.

'Good God!' murmured Thatcher, catching sight of something worse than that which had gone before. This party also included future Dekes. Carter Sprague, presumably escaped from some sort of chaperonage, was grandly gesturing with an amber glass and doing the man-among-men routine.

'Yes, I saw Patterson,' he said with grave intentness. 'It was after you left.' He nodded towards Armitage and Jim Dunlop, who formed part of the circle around him. Here in the Deke house, everybody was fascinated by Elliot Patterson's fall from grace.

'He was the dullest man we pledged in over twenty years,' someone confided to Thatcher.

'We sat together for ten minutes. I'd say, after the kids cleared out.' Carter seemed to feel that his narrative lacked dramatic tension. Lowering his voice, he continued, 'You could tell he was nervous, on edge. Oh, he tried to hide it, but it was the little things that gave him away. At one point he dropped his briefcase and everything spilled – '

'That's Elliot for you,' said an irreverent voice. 'A butterfingers to the end.'

The circle started to break up. Carter made a last bid for attention. 'I picked his things up for him. He couldn't have done it himself. His fingers were literally out of control.'

A murmur of doubt greeted this announcement. Thatcher had already registered the fact that Carter Sprague was gingering up his official version of Patterson's last public moments.

'Did *you* notice any of this concealed tension?' someone asked Armitage with open scepticism.

'Well . . .' Armitage evaded tactfully.

Thatcher's confidant saw the opportunity for some baiting. 'You boys aren't the noticing kind, I guess. After all, even if he wasn't trembling like a leaf, he was sitting across the table from you with fifty thousand he'd just pocketed. All that time before you started to interview the kids, he must have been a little nervous. And the way I remember it, when Elliot was nervous, it showed.'

'No, no, you've got it all wrong,' Jim Dunlop protested. 'He hadn't taken it yet. We put all the Curtis stuff back in the files together. Elliot took it after we left. And,' he said looking defiantly around the room, 'I still don't think Elliot stole it. I think he was just keeping it for Kitchener when something else caught up with him.'

This provoked a division of sentiment from the slightly muzzy onlookers. One faction derisively reminded Dunlop of the Patterson preparations for a skip. The other group, equally

115

derisive, maintained that Elliot was too wet to have pulled off anything like this.

There was yet a third reaction. Carter Sprague, seeing his one claim to adult prominence slipping away, was moved to object.

'But that couldn't be right.'

Jim Dunlop made the mistake of speaking as a man to a boy. Clapping a friendly hand on Carter Sprague's shoulder, he said, 'Now, now. You don't understand. Everybody really likes Elliot a lot. You'll understand these things better when you're a fraternity man yourself.'

Resentment was his only thanks. Carter leaned back against the wall in a posture meant to appear airily casual. Thatcher was willing to bet that he could no longer remain upright without swaying. It soon became apparent, however, that others were either taken in or felt no responsibility to interfere with Sprague's social education.

Someone about to forage at the bar took orders. 'Three Old Grand-Dads, a John Jamieson, and two Red Labels, okay?'

Carter pushed himself erect and thrust his jaw forward.

'No, not two Red Labels,' he said clearly.

The drink-bearer shrugged his shoulders.

'Okay, son. Three Red Labels. Will that satisfy you?'

But Carter was back against the wall, his moment of clearness over. He giggled slightly as he answered, 'Just one Red Label, tha'sall.'

Armitage and Jim Dunlop exchanged looks. But Armitage contented himself with a grimace. It was not the habit at the Deke house to control drinking among the young and innocent. *Au contraire.*

Dunlop, in search of support, edged towards Lucy Lancer.

'He's really had enough,' he said sounding quite young himself.

'Isn't anybody supposed to keep an eye on him?' Lucy demanded. 'He's just a boy.'

Thatcher pointed out that this boy would soon be very sick. Happily, before Lucy's crusading instincts could lead her to forget that they were guests, and unwelcome ones at that, George finished his low-voiced conferrings and announced it was time to go over to Franklin House.

The reception at Franklin House featured an underpatronized buffet boasting baked ham, a salad and edible bread. Thatcher and Lucy attacked with enthusiasm. This was not difficult, since the bar, at the other end of the room, was still doing most of the going business. Here, too, liquor was flowing like water. Evidence was provided by a glassy-eyed Neil Marsden, muttering thickly and incoherently in a corner. But at Franklin House, feelings were running high as well.

'Look,' said a stocky man backing into Thatcher as Lancer stalked him, 'I'm getting fed up with these questions about Elliot Patterson!'

Thatcher carefully removed from his sleeve traces of potato salad. Lancer opened his mouth, but his victim was implacable.

'First, it's some clown of a dean. Then those damned police. Now you! I didn't come here from South Dakota to spend my time getting grilled!'

A general growl of support rose from the bystanders. Another man, equipped with a full glass, took up the refrain.

'We've all told everybody what little we knew about Elliot. Hell, most of us don't even remember him. He wasn't a big man.'

From behind a hostile file, a mocking voice yodelled, 'Don't forget the Chapel Association!'

Lancer tried to soothe ruffled feelings. 'It's all very unfortunate,' he said. Interestedly Lucy looked on while busily filling her paper plate with a third helping. Thatcher reached for a cup of coffee. 'But you understand how serious this is. These questions about Elliot are necessary.'

'I'm fed up with Elliot!' said the class spokesman again.

Carefully putting down cup and saucer Thatcher advanced to Lancer's side.

'George,' he said quietly, 'the natives are getting restless.'

'All right,' Lancer conceded. 'We'll forget about Patterson.' Rather unfortunately he then went on to ask about the elusive quartet in tones suggesting they were out to better the Brink's caper.

This time there was a howl of unadulterated rage.

'*I'm* Hank Perkins.' A goaded little man rose pugnaciously from a chair. 'Look. I haven't heard of Patterson in fifteen years. I don't know anything about the other three. I don't know why the hell Elliot had *my* name, unless he thought he was going to start some con games and was lining up suckers. But if this goes on, I'm going to sue somebody about something!'

Thereafter it seemed wisest to abandon further inquiries. The entrance of Ralph Armitage, travelling the same circuit as they, provided a welcome diversion. The hours flowed by and the Scotch flowed by.

Then the proceedings were enlivened by the collapse of Neil Marsden, whose incoherence had not been quite comprehensive enough to conceal the offensive tenor of his remarks. There he lay, a shocking spectacle in his dishevelment, a surprisingly heavy beard appearing on his pallid cheeks. The frequenters of Franklin House reunion parties were hardened to such sights, however, and they peered owlishly down at the fallen figure. Then, with boozy good nature, Ralph Armitage and two others hoisted the slight burden and disappeared up the stairway.

'Bodies, bodies everywhere tonight!' commented an unknown with collegiate pride.

Thereafter nothing of interest happened except that one civic-minded citizen asked Lucy to lend her Cézanne for a museum exhibition at Purdue, and an equally large-minded colleague tried to proposition her.

When she was telling George about this latter event on their way home to the president's house, she confided that, at fifty-five, this sort of thing really bucked one up.

'It's what you should expect,' said her husband severely, 'when you run around looking fifteen years younger than you are.'

This reply was naturally satisfactory to Lucy. What's more, it went a long way towards restoring Lancer himself to a good mood. The three proceeded to the big white house under the clear star-spangled sky wrapped in a mantle of quiet contentment.

Even John Thatcher, retiring to bed, felt rather tired, appropriately drunk, and very happy.

14. Chapel Is Required

Ideally, Sunday breakfast should be a leisurely affair, allowing time for extended consideration of a bulky newspaper. For one brief moment, when John Thatcher awoke the next morning, he anticipated this ritual with lazy pleasure. Then he realized where he was. It was God and Country at Brunswick College. Sunday breakfast at eight o'clock; chapel at ten.

But the amenities of the president's house were sybaritic enough to sustain Thatcher's general and undeserved sense of well-being, a hard head being one of his happier possessions. By the time he had showered, he decided that an ancient and beautiful campus, wooded mountains, and tonic New England air provided a salutary departure from his city-bound routine.

He was even hungry, he noted, leaving his room and heading downstairs. More to the point, after chapel and luncheon, Thatcher and the Lancers were returning to the city. It was all very satisfactory and Thatcher was quite content to tread the stately measure of academic procession in the meantime.

The faint strains of *Gaudeamus Igitur* were dispelled almost immediately. George and Lucy Lancer were down already, with Lucy as bright-eyed as if yesterday had never been.

'Morning, John,' said Lancer over a noble stack of flapjacks. 'Lyman asked us to go ahead. He'll try to join us later. He had to go over to his office.'

Belatedly, Thatcher grew aware that in the distance a telephone was ringing. Furthermore, barely visible in the corridor, serious young men bustled about with papers, pencils and other evidence of endeavour.

'Ah yes,' he said, setting himself down before a large glass of orange juice. It was not his place to advance criticism about Brunswick but, in all honesty, this early-morning activity did not impress him favourably. After all, he and George ran the third largest bank in the world, a bigger proposition than Brunswick on virtually all fronts, without wrecking Sunday mornings. At least, not their own.

Something along these lines must have struck Lancer, for he commented, 'Lyman impresses me as a very capable fellow. Old Chaffee was fine, but toward the end, there's no doubt he wasn't able to give Brunswick the attention it demands.'

Lucy took up the conversation, unerringly replying to what her husband had left unsaid.

'But what attention does Brunswick require at this hour on Sunday morning?'

The answer to this reasonable question was not slow in coming.

'Oh, isn't Mr Todd here?' A hornrimmed young man peered blearily around the dining-room. Upon learning that the president was in his office, he apologized for the interruption and explained, 'It's the telephone company. They insist that the college guarantee payment.'

Observing that this did not clarify matters, he meticulously added an explanatory footnote.

'Three seniors – and their dates – smashed into a telephone pole on Route 46 last night. Took the pole right down. Knocked out a lot of service, too. That's why the company is being sticky about everything.'

His calm recital startled Lucy into inquiry about injuries.

Without visible emotion, the young man rapidly ran down an appalling list of broken legs, scalp lacerations, concussions and possible internal injuries, checked his watch and set off for Todd's office.

'There you are,' said Lancer. 'That kind of emergency obviously explains why Lyman has been called upon to deal with things personally.'

Another outburst from the distant telephone suggested to Thatcher that this might be a gross oversimplification. And before breakfast was over, the bankers had been presented with a persuasive sample of what keeps college presidents busy. It was transmitted by young men who hurried in and out of the dining room, and by Lyman Todd himself, arriving with his guests' second cup of coffee. He was rosy-cheeked from the cold, buoyant with energy and manifestly on top of things.

'Sorry to be late,' he announced cheerfully. 'And Mrs Todd can't be here because she's presiding over the Family Breakfast down at Wiswall.'

'The accident?' Lucy asked conscientiously.

'Which accident?' Lyman Todd replied, proceeding to give his guests an astonishing bird's-eye view of higher education in America. There had been four separate accidents involving Brunswick personnel during the night, one of them destined to deprive the English department of a Yeats expert for six weeks. No fatalities as yet, but parents and other loved ones were speeding to Coburg. A small fire in one of the freshman dormitories had caused some anxiety, seven hundred dollars' worth of smoke damage and a visit from the town fire department. Two young women had been discovered at a compromising time in circumstances all too clearly proscribed by the parietal rules and Brunswick's honour system. One member of the class of 1902 had suffered an attack 'of some sort' that necessitated his removal to the county hospital in an ambulance.

'Then there are the usual losts,' said Lyman Todd, digging into his flapjacks.

'Losts?' asked Lucy Lancer with a fascination that Thatcher shared, even though he was tiring of this motif in Brunswick's affairs.

'We always have losts during Homecoming,' said Todd. 'This time two husbands – class of 1959 – didn't turn up in their motel rooms, according to their wives. Three sophomores from Franklin – no, I forgot. They found them sleeping in their cars. A couple of those schoolboys from New York didn't end up in their own beds, according to Von Beyer. They'll turn up somewhere. They always do!'

On the whole, Thatcher was pleased that he had been spared this insight into academic administration until his own sons had put college behind them.

'Are there any other ... er ... Homecoming characteristics?' he inquired with interest.

With fork arrested, Todd thought for a moment. He was not

intellectually given to theory, the way assistant deans are.

'Liquor,' he finally decided. 'People who rarely drink apparently find it impossible to spend two days here without soaking it up steadily.'

His guests were in no position to contradict him.

'And chapel,' Todd continued judicially. 'People who never attend chapel, who aren't regular churchgoers, always turn out for chapel here. Makes quite a jam ... That reminds me. Do you know what else happened this morning?'

They were afraid to ask.

'Somebody called my office,' Todd said. 'Said that Elliot Patterson had walked into Franklin House in the early hours!'

He savoured their surprise, then, with a practiced chuckle, added, 'That's another characteristic of Homecomings, Mr Thatcher. Practical jokes! You would not believe the number of times we have had to get a VW out of the second storey of the Science building. Well, I think perhaps we'd better get going.'

As they rose, Lancer cleared his throat and suggested that dismissing Elliot Patterson's possible reappearance as a prank might not, all things considered, be wise.

Lyman Todd projected complete agreement. 'Oh, that hasn't escaped me,' he reassured Lancer. 'I sent Billings over to check the minute I heard about it. But nobody at Franklin knew anything. And nobody admits making the call. Still, George, if Elliot Patterson has turned up ... well! But don't worry. I've put Ed Webster on to it.'

Lucy and Thatcher led the way out into the brilliant cold morning. The great carillon was ringing a summons to worship. But snatches of surrounding conversation proved that things of this world were weighing heavily at the moment. The disappearance of Elliot Patterson had caused Brunswick College nothing but trouble. Perhaps this was why some of its sons did not regard his return as an unmixed blessing.

> Once to–o every ma–an and na–a–tion,
> Comes the–e–e mo–o–ment to–oo decide!

This ancient hymn, unsingable and virtually unmusical, is for reasons known only to initiates the staple of college chapels throughout New England. Thatcher took refuge in a craven sustained note and admired his psalter-mate. Without a quiver Lucy Lancer raised a firm no-nonsense baritone and intimidated surrounding pews.

The chapel was a simple, beautiful structure in which Brunswick had worshipped God since 1814. It was, as Lyman Todd had predicted, filled to overflowing. Many worshippers, Thatcher was forced to conclude from the confused search for the morning's psalms, were not devout churchgoers. On the other hand, he fairmindedly admitted to himself, there was something admirable about them; despite the excesses of the night before, a goodly number of Old Brunsies had brought circled eyes, pallid complexions and twitching fingers to chapel.

The Sloan Guaranty Trust, of course, was holding its own. George Lancer was himself: well-tailored, healthy, radiating the slightly impatient intelligence that is the hallmark of the high-level executive. Lucy was simply Lucy, enough to cause heart-burning wherever she went. He himself had rarely felt better.

'Let us pray,' said the cleric.

This signalled a lecture to the Almighty about the socio-economic problems of our time. Thatcher felt that piety required him to withdraw his attention and let it roam. Two pews over he sighted Ralph Armitage, heavy-lidded, but otherwise holding his own quite well. Perhaps it was not the Sloan, but New York in general that deserved congratulations.

Idly he tried to locate the rest of the Admission Committee. Neil Marsden was nowhere about. Without censure, Thatcher recalled that Marsden had been last seen dead drunk at Franklin House. It was probably technically impossible for him to present himself in the tabernacles of the anointed.

Since Lyman Todd had already informed his guests that the cleric – 'Give us, O Lord!, the power to discern inequities and the strength to combat injustice!' – was married to a Miss Rockefeller and since Lucy Lancer was gracing the scene, Thatcher could only conclude that Neil Marsden had been boobytrapped by Demon Rum.

The Dunlops were also among those absent.

The cleric was now strongly counselling God to force his

creatures to examine their hearts for seeds of antisocial bias. Thatcher decided that age might be the critical factor. He looked over to the student body. No, it was not age. A large number of undergraduates were present.

Some of them, he realized, had simply ignored yesterday's bacchanalia. Thin and intense, they prayed with a fervour that underlined the absence of incense and candles. This group had probably spent yesterday in the library.

Then there were the boys from Groton and its ilk. With the accuracy of experience, Thatcher singled out their vacant faces. This Christianity was muscular. Thatcher suspected that these stalwarts had not been to bed. But Brunswick being Brunswick (and Groton being Groton), standards were maintained; all attire was correct in an extreme.

The first rows of the student section had been reserved for the thirty-five visitors from New York. Even making due allowance for Roman Catholics, Jews, agnostics and other bona fide absentees, the turnout was meagre. The assistant dean in charge looked, even during prayer, quite wild.

Several of the young visitors, Thatcher recalled from Todd's summary, were still AWOL.

'. . . let us, therefore, O Lord!, praise Thy ways while working to bring Thy Kingdom to pass on earth. Amen!'

There was a confused shuffle as Miss Rockefeller's husband came to an end. The anthem returned them to normality.

> His blood red banner streams afar.
> Who follows in His train?

As they left, Thatcher was relieved to discover that the proconsular presence of the public Lyman Todd was to be removed.

Todd had gone into one of his fluent apologies about official duties and had pressed on. Thatcher watched him hurry off, stopping to greet someone, smiling anonymously into the crowd, simultaneously exhibiting warm appreciation of people and pre-occupation with larger issues. He did it very well. Thatcher only wished he could admire him for it.

'And now?' he asked Lucy as they moved slowly through the

crowd to the famous Brunswick Green. ('Lest we forget *thy* Green, O Brunswick, Lest we forget thy sheltering pines ...')

'God knows, John,' said Lucy smiling brilliantly at a dim suburban matron.

George Lancer disentangled himself from a group of friends and supplied the requisite information. Luncheon at the Coburg Inn.

'I reserved a table,' said Lancer. 'Just the three of us. Then we can get going back to New York.'

What volumes that spoke, Thatcher reflected.

The Coburg Inn was a typical blend of colonial quaintness spiced by a liquor licence. The influx of churchgoers introduced a genteel din, punctuated by hearty hails from Old Brunsies. In the dining-room, late risers were finishing even later breakfasts, despite the sullenness around them. The staff, like all New England dining-room personnel, was devoted to the setting up of tables and indifferent to food and comfort. Large bowls of foliage flanked the fireplace; there were innumerable conversations filled with promises to keep in touch, with plans to get together. It was busy, colourful, cheerful, exuberant.

And, abruptly, it was shattered.

From somewhere upstairs came a long, drawn-out scream.

For one frozen moment, the Coburg Inn was paralysed.

Then, as Thatcher and the Lancers involuntarily swivelled to look up at the balcony, the first shrill keening crescendoed. There were shouts, the pounding of feet, and wild cries.

'Good God!' said Lucy, clutching George's arm. 'What can ...?'

'Shh!'

A red-faced man, his shirt still unbuttoned, had appeared at the balcony railing. Blindly he stared down into a sea of shocked upturned faces.

'She opened the door ...' he began.

The lobby was still.

He took a deep breath. 'The maid opened the door. And there's a body on the bed!'

Before anybody could respond, he gulped and went on: 'My God! There's a knife sticking out of his back.'

15. Student Body

It was Carter Sprague who lay dead on a bed, skewered through the heart with a carving knife.

But it took ten minutes before this information became generally known. In the first stampede a bottleneck formed in the doorway of the bedroom, composed of two men supporting the gasping maid who still clutched a passkey in one hand and clean towels in the other. Behind them pressed the latecomers. Only the nearest and tallest could see anything, but their observations eddied along the corridor and down the stairs.

The manager did what he could, sending a clerk to the phone, summoning the housekeeper to console the maid, pleading with his guests to remove themselves. But real order was not restored until the arrival of Ed Webster. He instantly ordered everyone downstairs, sent word to the town authorities and posted himself before the locked door.

John Thatcher and the Lancers, who had removed to the sunlit dining-room, listened to the first flurry of shocked comment:

'It's only a kid up there! Can you believe it?'

'There's blood everywhere. The whole bed is soaked with it.'

'Murder! With a knife, for Chrissake!'

But as those upstairs were hustled into the dining-room, the news became more specific.

'It's that kid who was at the Dekes last night. You know, the one still in high school,' announced a burly man with ex-football-player written all over him. He had been the first to reach the maid's side.

Thatcher and Lancer stared at each other in consternation.

'You don't think he can possibly mean Carter Sprague?' Lancer was almost whispering.

Thatcher tried to summon up details of the night before.

'I don't remember anyone else his age at the Dekes. In fact, I seem to remember Sprague saying that he had played hookey from the high-school group.'

'That poor boy,' Lucy Lancer murmured.

Her husband was startled. Then he flushed.

'I should be ashamed of myself. It's a tragedy, a boy that age. And all I can think of is that he was such a miserable little pest.'

'Somebody seems to have rated his nuisance value a good deal higher than that,' Thatcher said tartly. He appreciated Lucy's distress, but if her husband was going to be required to rally to Brunswick's support, and it seemed all too likely, then he should know how badly that support would be needed.

Lancer took the point instantly. 'Good God, you don't think this has anything to do with Elliot Patterson?'

'I don't know,' Thatcher admitted, 'but I do know that a lot of people are going to leap to that conclusion.'

As usual, Lucy's good sense was to the fore. She pushed aside her plate.

'I don't want to be a defeatist, George, but remember, someone saw Elliot Patterson here in Coburg.'

George scowled irritably. 'For heaven's sake, Lucy, that was some sort of crazy rumour! And it was probably inevitable with all the publicity about Patterson. But I don't believe it for a minute!'

'You're probably right,' his wife said pacifically. 'But that just bears John out. Everybody is thinking about Elliot Patterson. After all, you can scarcely blame them. And that means that whether he was here or not, when people hear about a murder they are going to think of Elliot Patterson.'

There was no need for anybody to dwell on the fact that Carter Sprague had been the last person to see Elliot Patterson. In New York, at any rate.

Humanitarianism forgotten, Lancer stirred his coffee viciously.

'Offhand I can think of ten reasons for young Sprague to have gotten himself killed,' he said defiantly.

'I'm not sure that I can,' Thatcher replied.

'Good God, John!' Lancer exploded. 'I know he's dead. But you can't claim that he was one of the world's sunflowers.'

'Certainly not.'

'And there's no telling what fun and games he was up to last night.'

Thatcher knew there were times when real kindness takes the form of firmness.

'Now, George. He spent last evening in a crowded room on public view. When we last saw him he wasn't up to anything more than an extended session in the bathroom.'

Ten years earlier, Lucy Lancer had been dealing with the physical well-being of teenage sons.

'That's right, George.' She nodded. 'That boy was very drunk.'

Thatcher continued his lesson. 'As soon as this murder hits the papers, one aspect is going to capture everyone's attention. All the personnel of the first Brunswick fiasco are present, possibly including the mysterious Patterson.'

He swept an arm around the dining-room in illustration, and obediently Lancer followed his gesture. All the tables were crowded now, and at each of them, the name Carter Sprague was freely used. There seemed to be no doubt. The body that lay upstairs on a blood-soaked bed was Carter Sprague.

'I see what you mean,' Lancer muttered.

At a large centre table, Ralph Armitage sat with six or seven classmates who were probably fraternity brothers as well. Heads were together in heated discussion. Were they talking about the Deke house, Thatcher wondered?

Over in the corner Jim Dunlop listened seriously to an older man. Even across the room it was apparent that he was feeling unwell. His companion, however, looked robust. Who was he? Thatcher wondered.

A movement in the doorway attracted his attention. It was the manager, looking ill himself. He relayed police requests that everybody stay put, then scurried away. A hum of protest and speculation rose.

'God, you don't think Elliot knifed that kid, do you?'

The speaker, an acquaintance of George's, had left his own table to wander over.

'Why should it be Elliot?' George demanded with a fine show of indignation.

The acquaintance shrugged. 'That's what everybody's saying. Of course, I don't believe it for a moment. Probably a tramp or something. Still, it's odd. All this business about the New York Committee and Elliot – and now murder.'

He drifted off before Lancer could retort. Lucy's repressive eye kept George from giving vent to his emotions and allowed Thatcher to muse aloud.

'I wonder who has actually seen Patterson,' he said. 'Certainly everybody seems sure that someone has. But there's a fine distinction, isn't there?'

With conspicuous self-control, Lancer said that murder simply loosed a good many irresponsible tongues.

'Of course it does, George,' said Thatcher. 'But it's what they're saying that interests me. And the police as well, I suspect.'

Fortunately, before Lancer could reply, the dining-room door was flung open again. This time it was a booted state police officer.

He quelled the first spate of questions with a raised arm. 'Sorry, you'll have to wait a little longer, folks. The captain wants to talk to you, one by one. Just stay where you are. And will Mr' – here he consulted a small notebook – 'Mr Neil Marsden step across the hall?'

Involuntarily Thatcher's eye raked the room. No, his first impression had been quite correct. Neil Marsden was not present.

Thatcher was not alone in his curiosity. As the trooper called for the next witness, a Mr Willoughby, who rose immediately and was speeded on his way with derisive encouragement, the endless talk took a new turn. Only fragments were intelligible.

'The Tenth's right here in the Inn and . . .'

'Say, Marsden's on that New York Committee, isn't he?'

'. . . Willoughby and Marsden didn't see much of each other . . .'

'. . . doesn't look good for an undertaker, does it?'

George Lancer was too distracted to heed the gossip swirling about them. 'You were right, John,' he groaned. 'They're going for the Committee, all right.'

'Oh, no, they're not,' said a grim voice.

Startled, they looked up to find Jim Dunlop and his companion at their side. Without waiting for an invitation the two men sat down. Dunlop spoke in a doomed voice.

'They're saying Sprague's body is in Marsden's room. And it's been there for at least eight hours.'

'Good God!' Lancer exclaimed. 'What does Marsden have to say about it?'

'Marsden doesn't seem to be around,' the young man said tightly. 'The cops are talking to the people who had adjoining rooms. But I don't think they'll get anything. It was – it was a madhouse here last night.'

He sounded despondent and fell into bemused silence. His companion was forced to introduce himself.

'I thought I recognized you, Mr Barnett,' said Lucy Lancer graciously. 'You're running for election on the East Side, aren't you?'

'I was,' said Barnett. 'I may be out of the race entirely by now.'

Thatcher was taken aback by this pessimism. Barnett had received a good deal of publicity for his modern campaign tactics. Data processing, image projection and sociological surveys had played a prominent role in his strategy. So had avoidance of the issues.

Dully, Dunlop explained. 'The fund raising was being handled by Elliot Patterson.'

'That was bad enough,' Barnett amplified. 'It's hard to get people to give in the first place. Once they get the idea that they're just contributing to a Brazilian vacation for someone, it's impossible. Not that Uhlein hasn't been damned good at keeping this under wraps. Target Associates has barely been mentioned in connection with Patterson's disappearance.'

'Uhlein's done a great job,' Lancer agreed sourly. 'He's left all the bad publicity to Brunswick.'

'Well, it was Brunswick money Patterson took off with,' Barnett pointed out. 'But keeping anything under wraps is impossible now. The press will have a field day. And just yesterday Uhlein was saying we were over the hump.'

Jim Dunlop was emotionless. 'What is Uhlein doing up here, anyway? He's not a Brunsie. Maybe he had some kind of rendezvous with Patterson.'

An odd suggestion, Thatcher thought, particularly from the impressionable young man who had accompanied them to Rye.

'I can tell you what he was doing,' said Lancer, keeping to the subject. 'Incredible as it seems, he was trying to sell Todd on using professional fund raisers.'

Barnett grinned, but Dunlop was not listening.

'I believe,' Lancer continued austerely, 'that his theory was that none of this mess would have happened if Patterson had been acting for Target Associates.'

'Well, Uhlein doesn't seem to be around any more,' Barnett said. No politician was going to waste comment on Uhlein's gall. 'I was looking for him this morning and – '

He broke off as there was a stir from the doorway. For a moment the room tensed, expecting another summons from across the hall. But the trooper was admitting someone through the door he had earlier closed. Lyman Todd was joining the afflicted Brunsies.

In the carrying voice of a public speaker he addressed the room:

'This tragic event is still too close to us to permit a formal statement. But I do want to thank you now for that fine public-spirited cooperation which I know that Brunswick College and I can rely on.'

A subdued congratulatory murmur followed and the president, with bowed head, strode toward the Lancer table. With one accord, Andrew Barnett and Dunlop effaced themselves. Presumably neither felt capable of rising to the president's conversational heights.

George Lancer did not even try. In a whisper, he tried to relay the latest developments. But Todd overrode him.

'This is a sad occasion,' he announced. 'A sad occasion.'

Which gave him, Thatcher reflected disagreeably, no marks for originality. But Todd, if not a creative thinker, was an organizer to his fingertips.

'I've been in touch with the Governor,' he reported in a lowered voice. 'He says that Captain Nivelle is a first-rate officer. And he'll give us every consideration.'

Inconsequentially Thatcher wondered precisely what constituted consideration when the Brunswick campus was littered with one bloody corpse, seventy-eight disgruntled witnesses and possibly one fine family man running amok.

'Not that we can hope to escape disagreeableness,' Lyman Todd acknowledged, letting his eyes roam briefly over the dining room filled with men who, so shortly before, could have been described as potential benefactors. 'The police have to trace young Sprague's movements last night.'

Involuntarily Thatcher glanced at Lucy. Lyman Todd was probably the only man in the room who did not know that Carter Sprague had spent a large part of his Saturday at Brunswick disgracefully drunk in a fraternity house. Oh well, he would learn soon enough.

'Although they assured me that they will be very careful in questioning the boys from New York,' Todd continued.

Lancer merely looked at him. The great uproar about misplaced test scores, even about misplaced $50,000 bonds, seemed very far away.

'But Ed Webster is going to sit in,' Todd continued. 'We'll hope that that will help.'

'Yes,' said Lucy faintly. Her instincts were kindly, but intelligence prevented expansion.

'Still, it is unfortunate,' Todd continued. 'The police are asking everybody to stay for a few hours until the questioning is complete. That means . . .'

That meant more Brunswick than Thatcher cared to contemplate. He repressed a sigh.

Before their eyes, Lyman Todd steeled himself. 'I don't mind saying that I'm not altogether happy with some of the things that are being said. Elliot Patterson, for example.'

This time, nobody could hearten him.

'Of course, that isn't so,' said Lyman Todd firmly. 'Elliot Patterson is not a murderer. There must be some other explanation for this tragedy.'

Possibly it occurred to him that any other explanation of the murder of a young boy, a guest of the college, following a football game on the campus might not be preferable. At any rate, he became preoccupied.

Suddenly, there was a buzz loud enough to interrupt.

'Well, will you look . . .!'

'Hey!'

In the doorway was Neil Marsden. He was very unlike the picture of sartorial elegance he presented on Fifth Avenue. His clothes were rumpled and stained. The greenish pallor of his skin was emphasized by shadowed, staring eyes. As he stood in the doorway, shudder after shudder wracked his lean body.

'They took me up to my room,' he said, staring sightlessly ahead. 'There's blood everywhere and this kid . . . My God, there's a knife sticking out of him. In my room!' On the last phrase his voice lost its automaton quality and rose in horror.

It was Ralph Armitage who went to his side.

'We've been waiting for you, Neil,' he said, placing a steady hand on Marsden's shaking shoulder. 'We all wondered where you were.'

The quality of silent accusation came home to Marsden. Incredulously he looked at the banks of faces, instantly reserved and cautious.

'Wondering where I was?' he echoed. 'You mean you thought . . .?'

'No, no, Neil,' Armitage said. 'We were worried about you.'

'Worried!' Marsden stared back at the room defiantly. Unconscious of what he was doing, he wiped the back of his hand across dry, cracked lips. 'So you want to know where I was, do you? All right! I was drunk, passed out cold. You know that. I just got up, I tell you! Are you satisfied?'

Still that incredible silence. Marsden had always been a loner.

Rapidly his confidence, which could only have been sustained by a furious discharge of nervous energy, was ebbing. Now he spoke more slowly.

'But I was. Lots of people know it. I've got witnesses, damn you! Put to bed like a teenager. With the pack of you gloating. But that doesn't make any difference now. Over at Franklin House, they know. They were still laughing themselves sick this morning. Ralph! You know. You were there. Tell them you were there!'

There had been an internal meter to Marsden's defence. If Ralph Armitage had fallen in with that meter he would have answered the appeal on time. But he let one beat pass, then two, then three . . .

Then:

'Sure! Sure, I did, Neil. Now come on in and get some coffee into you . . .'

As if on signal, the dining-room resumed its various hums of conversation.

But John Putnam Thatcher knew that he was not alone in wondering. It is normal to feel distaste when a man breaks down pitiably and revealingly in public.

But had there been something more in Ralph Armitage's voice?

16. Midterm Examination

Meanwhile, across the hall, the police were moving with an efficiency hitherto unknown at the Coburg Inn. Upstairs, specialists photographed, measured and ultimately removed the late Carter Sprague, then subjected Neil Marsden's room to the same professional scrutiny; they were not moved by the pathos of a young boy's untimely death, but then they were not moved by the Coburg Inn's housekeeping, either. Two uniformed officers rounded up the entire staff of the Inn, herded them into the large kitchen and began taking down names, addresses and statements. Nothing of interest emerged, except for one aged maid's hysterical insistence that she had seen a villainous brigand, blood dripping down his arm, lurch down the stairway at dawn. From his long black beard and golden earrings she knew it was Elliot Patterson.

Outside, squad cars barricaded the Coburg Inn from the crowd which was ready to invest catastrophe with a carnival atmosphere. Unknown to the police, however, the enterprising editor of *The Daily Brunsie* had infiltrated their defences, and together with two reporters was assembling a quote-studded story that was to be the envy of most metropolitan papers. At the same time, state policemen, Coburg policemen and campus policemen were fanning out over the campus with questions aimed at pin-pointing Carter Sprague's every move, conversation and thought since New York.

The intelligence guiding this activity belonged to Captain Joseph Nivelle of the state police, and he was presently occupying the manager's office behind the reception desk. With him, to help handle incoming information and act as liaison with Brunswick College, was Ed Webster. They were not slow to arrive at the very conclusion George Lancer had feared.

'Bad business. Especially this New York connection,' said Captain Nivelle, a large nerveless man capable of quelling motorcycle riots at lakeside resorts virtually singlehanded. Like his subordinates, he was not reacting to the poignancy of Carter Sprague's murder; another difficulty beset him. Scarcely two hours had passed since Vivian, the maid (now recovering at the Coburg Community Hospital), had discovered the corpse, but already the telephone lines had been busy and Captain Nivelle had been reminded how important Brunswick College was, how many important and impatient men the dining-room currently contained.

Ed Webster grunted.

'Yup, it's bad business,' Captain Nivelle continued. He sighed and dismissed a wistful recollection of his last murder, which had involved three mill hands, a dispute about cards and endless quantities of low-grade gin. 'Well, let's get on with it. Either somebody killed this kid for the hell of it' – a euphemism covering a wide range of aberrant behaviour – 'or this must be connected with the Patterson disappearance.'

Webster cleared his throat to report that it had been rumoured Elliot Patterson was at Brunswick.

'I know,' said Joseph Nivelle. He did not have to add that

every police force in the state was trying to verify this. Elliot Patterson, in fact, held the promise of a sane reason for the insane murder of a seventeen-year-old boy. Patterson had stolen $50,000. Somehow Carter Sprague had endangered him. So, Elliot Patterson crept out of the woods, found a sturdy carving knife in the kitchen and killed Carter Sprague.

There was an attractive simplicity about this theory, but it depended heavily on Elliot Patterson's presence in the vicinity. And this remained highly problematical.

Nivelle sighed again and fell back on routine. 'No use wasting time figuring out why somebody killed this kid,' he decided. 'The thing to do is try and get a picture of what went on here yesterday.'

Webster rubbed his chin. 'That's going to be harder than you think, Joe. Marsden's a pretty good example. He says that he passed out over at Franklin House last night. Didn't get back here until today. Well, a lot of people will swear they saw him put to bed, I'll bet. But can anybody swear that he didn't get up in the middle of the night and come over here to the Inn? He could have killed the kid, then gone right back to Franklin House. Hell, people could have passed him on the street, and they wouldn't remember it today!'

Joe Nivelle was not given to idle questions, but, for once, his patience with the frailty of others wore thin. 'You know, Ed, I don't understand. Will you tell me why a lot of grown men – important men too, according to the Governor's office – come up here and make damned fools of themselves every chance they get?'

Ed Webster grinned.

'College spirit,' he said. 'Same thing that makes the senior class smash store windows on Front Street every spring. Myself, I never got to college. So I used to call it something else when we had to clean up a lot of property damage, or when a bunch of fraternity boys got beered up and started swinging. But they explained it to me. It's just college spirit!'

Nivelle growled and announced that before he was through he would know exactly what Carter Sprague, and everybody else, had been up to on Saturday, college spirit or not.

To a point, this was easy. As time passed, information funnelling into the manager's office began to shed light on at least part of Carter Sprague's last day on earth.

Together with his fellow aspirants, he had arrived at Brunswick College shortly before lunch time on Saturday. Driver Tony Micolli (of the Abelson Charter Service) kept detailed records. 'Eleven-thirty,' he said. 'Right on the button!'

'Do you remember this kid Sprague?' asked Nivelle.

Micolli openly pitied such ignorance. 'Listen, two things I do. I drive and I count. Take thirty-two kids from Manhattan to Coburg, they say. So whenever we stop I count thirty-two when we get back in the bus. That's all. For all I care, they could be thirty-two midgets.'

'All right, all right!'

Micolli, however, was an enthusiast.

'Now,' he explained earnestly, 'now, I subtract one! I count thirty-one!'

'Charlie, get this guy out of here!'

From arrival at Brunswick, through lunch and the football game, Carter Sprague was an open book.

'No, he was *not* a particularly cooperative boy,' said Assistant Dean Von Beyer. 'In fact, none of them was particularly cooperative.'

Assistant Dean Von Beyer's week-end of chaperoning the New York contingent, crowned by murder, had destroyed, perhaps permanently, his conviction that our good young people outnumber juvenile delinquents by a large margin.

'But he was with us at lunch,' he continued listlessly. 'And he was at the football game. It was after the football game that we got separated. That was the last I saw of Sprague. I reported to the president's office when he wasn't in the dormitory this morning. I don't know what more I could have done. I couldn't put them on leashes, could I?'

Nivelle interrupted this self-pity. 'When he was with you, did you see Sprague show any particular interest in anybody he met? Or, did you see anybody who was unusually interested in him?'

Dean Von Beyer passed a trembling hand over his eyes. He

dredged up a pep talk given by Lyman Todd, together with personal greetings to each boy. And at lunch Carter Sprague may have conversed with almost anybody. Dean Von Beyer did not remember. Dean Von Beyer was feeling very, very unwell.

Carter's contemporaries were made of sterner stuff although this brush with death had visibly shaken them. Nivelle and Webster confronted three unnaturally solemn youngsters.

'Now you were the boys who spent the afternoon with Carter,' Nivelle said sternly. 'Did you notice anything out of the ordinary?'

After an exchange of glances, Douglas Younger emerged as spokesman.

'We didn't really know Carter very well, sir,' he said.

Ed Webster put his recent exposure to the young to use.

'Tell us everything,' he directed.

The picture of Carter Sprague's afternoon that finally developed was lacking in surprise. Airily Carter had explained that he was submitting to Brunswick's outmoded notions of entertainment only because of parental pressure. He had deprecated football as a sport and a spectacle. He had commented, without approval but without suspicious intensity, about the appearance of Brunswick alumni and their families. He had said that he certainly wasn't going to spend his evening being treated like a child. He had even invited them to join him.

Carter Sprague had not endeared himself to his companions, although wild horses could not get them to admit it now.

With a troubled look, Pete Fursano spoke up:

'The only thing Doug left out is that we spent a lot of time chewing over that meeting in New York. You know, when he – Carter – stayed behind to talk to Mr Patterson.' Fursano seemed to feel that justification was necessary. 'Well, you know, everybody has been so excited about those folders. I mean, why Mr Patterson took our test scores.'

Douglas Younger seconded him. 'It kind of made him' – he gulped slightly – 'I think it made Carter feel important. The police and everybody wanted to know what he saw Mr Patterson taking with him. Then the other day they called up and asked some more questions. The rest of us were pretty fed up with the whole thing but he – Carter – wasn't.'

They all looked ashamed of themselves.

This was where things began to get complicated. After he set out on his own, Carter Sprague became more difficult to trace. Indeed, the picture became a collage of many accounts – including brief statements by John Thatcher and the Lancers. By the time the long day was finished, however, Nivelle had pieced together a bird's-eye view of Carter Sprague's path from football stadium to death in a bed at the Coburg Inn. Not every minute was accounted for, but most of the hours were.

From a junior at Pierce House:

'So, I was throwing a party right after the game, and this kid turns up. Hell, I'm not going to pour good beer into a complete stranger, so I told him to beat it. Yes, it was just about twenty minutes after the game. No, I never saw him before.'

From a faculty wife, proceeding from library to home with one infant and one book-bag:

'Yes, officer, I am quite sure. It was exactly five-fifteen. People were still pouring out of the stadium. I was hurrying home to cook dinner early, and I had to get things defrosted. He stopped me and asked me where the Deke house was. No, I knew he wasn't a student. He was too polite.'

From the president of the Dekes:

'No, I don't know when he got there but it must have been pretty early because he was already tanked up by nine, let me tell you. Guess I shouldn't say that now ... Well, I can tell you one thing – I'm recommending we forget this Homecoming Open House ... What? No, I didn't see when Sprague left. But he was hanging around for a long time. Look, the general idea is for the grads to drop by for a quick one, then scram. We've got girls up for the week-end and better things to do than sit around listening to the class of 1949 gas about the old days. But this bunch! We couldn't really get the party going until after midnight.'

Nivelle knew that the party had still been in process when the police arrived on the doorstep Sunday. Furthermore, he sensed rightly, that it was going to prove difficult to keep Carter Sprague in focus at the Deke house and after. But this was the critical point. What had taken Carter Sprague from the Deke house?

Unfortunately, reminiscences of Saturday evening grew cloudier with each passing hour. A great many people, including Thatcher and the Lancers, were convincing when they reported that Carter Sprague was alive, if regrettably drunk, during the early part of the evening. Inevitably the reliable witnesses had departed; those who had remained at the Deke house showed a tendency to stare blearily at Nivelle and claim that a curtain of oblivion had fallen.

'Still, when I had to report that I had seen Neil Marsden drunk at Franklin House,' Lucy Lancer reported after her siege in the manager's office, 'I thought I had lost ground as one of the reliables.'

Thatcher, extremely tired of the smoke-filled dining-room, of George's continuing conferences with fellow inmates, and of Brunswick College in general, agreed that everything sounded deplorable.

'Who is breaking the news to the Westerveldts?' asked someone gravely.

'Lyman, thank God!' said Lancer.

Thatcher repressed a shudder and resolutely directed his attention to the line of inquiry being pursued, without apparent result, by Captain Nivelle. A steady stream of winesses averred that they had been able to place Carter Sprague, quite alive, at the Deke house. But what had happened to him next?

For that matter, what had happened to him before that?

Had he spent time threatening Elliot Patterson? Had he pursued some dark diabolical plot of his own? Had he simply been cadging drinks in places not yet uncovered?

Surprisingly enough, Jim Dunlop provided a partial answer. Grey-faced, he was slumped at a nearby table. Next to him, not speaking, was his wife, Lou, who had been admitted some hours earlier. She had not contributed to any recovery on her husband's part.

'Dunlop is the picture of guilt,' Thatcher remarked in an undertone to Lucy.

Lucy was distressed. 'And, John, he sounded so strange!'

Ralph Armitage extricated himself from a protracted discussion with Lancer to give a rather painful smile. 'It's no time for humour,' he said, 'but it was funny at the time.'

Jim Dunlop's story, first presented to Captain Nivelle, swiftly percolated among the interested parties. He had, indeed, fallen from grace. Exhilarated by the football game, he had deposited Lou with friends and dropped in on the Dekes for a quick one. But the quick one had been transformed by nostalgia into one more, then one more.

'I got pretty drunk,' he admitted tragically. Nivelle remained expressionless at this refrain. 'But I knew the Dekes wanted to get rid of us. Nothing cools a party more than a bunch of middle-aged men sitting around boozing. The girls don't like it. Then I saw Carter Sprague. No, I don't remember what time it was. It must have been after midnight. He was pretty far gone, so I thought that was no place for him. You know. Anyway, I promoted a move for us older guys to come on over here to the Inn and leave the Dekes . . .' Dunlop shook his head.

Nivelle leaned forward at this, as Thatcher did later at the second reading. The party, including Carter Sprague, had been duly assembled, and a great confused move to the cars commenced. Ralph Armitage, returning to pick up his own car, had been enlisted to aid Dunlop in handling the sodden Carter Sprague and transporting him to the Coburg Inn. The whole variegated, inebriated party arrived at the bar, safely and ready to join the conviviality.

'No, I must have lost sight of him,' said poor Dunlop. 'I remember helping him in . . .'

But Ralph Armitage, Andrew Barnett, two brokers from Springfield, Massachusetts, and other old Brunsies confirmed this. Even the bartender contributed a vivid piece of corroboration.

'So I close the bar at two,' he said truculently. 'No, I don't serve kids, and I didn't serve this one! But these guys had brought their own liquor. They were passing out on the sofa. They were singing. Two guys in the corner were crying.'

'College spirit,' said Captain Nivelle, depressed. No trustworthy account of Carter Sprague's sojourn in the Coburg Inn would be culled from this group of sinners. He spent forty minutes finding this out:

'Yes . . . I think I remember . . . No, I wasn't feeling so well . . . Well, there were a lot of people here . . .'

One man even claimed that he had spent the evening in silent meditation in his room.

But an interesting fact did come to light.

Jim Dunlop may have forgotten his wife. His wife had not forgotten him. She went to an early dinner with friends, then fears began to assail her. Could Jim have met with an accident? Where was he?

Instead of returning to their motel room and waiting with uxorious patience, Lou had been propelled – at a very late hour – to follow her husband's trail. It led her to a now darkened Deke house, where soulful music echoed through rooms mercifully rid of the embarrassment of adults. Then to the Coburg Inn. Where, at three in the morning, she finally found her husband. He had completely forgotten about Lou's existence.

What had followed between husband and wife had amused older Brunsies. But today Lou was betrayed, not betraying.

'It was sickening,' she said with a small girl's quaver in her voice. 'People were passing out. I had to help J – Jim out to our car. But' – she regarded Captain Nivelle like a martyr at the stake – 'Carter Sprague was alive then. I saw him! He looked dreadful. I thought he was going to be sick. He was going upstairs.'

'Was he going upstairs alone?' Captain Nivelle barked.

Lou Dunlop looked at him piteously. Then she took a deep breath.

'Yes, he was alone,' she said. And burst into tears.

It was very late when the Lancers and Thatcher were freed from the Coburg Inn, and they were not the last to leave. Neil Marsden, the Dunlops, two Dekes and Armitage were gloomily awaiting renewed calls from Captain Nivelle, whose show of stamina, at least, was impressive.

The long, slow transformation of Sunday afternoon into Sunday evening had taken on a nightmare quality of smoky air, of unanswered questions, of impassioned outbursts from businessmen with urgent appointments elsewhere, of a white-lipped argument between Neil Marsden and somebody named Frank.

Cold sandwiches produced by an embittered kitchen did nothing to make the situation better.

George C. Lancer sounded hesitant. 'I told Lyman we'd drop in before we leave,' he said, stretching the stiffness out.

Lucy and Thatcher both regarded him thoughtfully. They were standing in the cool darkness outside the Coburg Inn. The crowd had finally dispersed. The state troopers had not.

John Putnam Thatcher felt constrained to repeat an earlier sentiment:

'George, you're a sucker for punishment!'

17. Bachelor of Arts

Inside the president's house, Thatcher found no reason to change his mind. Only an arrant optimist could have prophesied anything but ruin and despair for Brunswick College. Thatcher could easily sketch in the outline of its coming public image. Brunswick cajoled millionaires into donating considerable sums and what happened? Enterprising members of the Alumni Association made off with the funds. Brunswick demanded that applicants take admission tests and what happened? The Admission Committee lost the scores. Brunswick invited high-school seniors up for a football week-end and what happened? They got murdered.

Nor were the police inquiries of a nature to comfort the college's dwindling band of adherents. The police, it soon became clear, did not like the rumours that Elliot Patterson had been abroad in Coburg on the fatal night. They did not like Neil

Marsden's story, corroborated so reluctantly by Ralph Armitage; they did not like Jim Dunlop's story, corroborated with such suspicious haste by his wife. In fact, there was only one thing that did please the police, and that was the list of Elliot Patterson's four classmates.

'Bolt holes!' Nivelle decided. 'That's why he hasn't been picked up. He had a bolt hole ready with one of these four. And you say two of them are here?'

No matter how you sliced it, the old grads of Brunswick were not going to come out of this smelling like roses. And Lyman Todd, Thatcher noted approvingly, was not an arrant optimist. He was in his office with Lancer and Thatcher, a resentful Lucy having been delivered into the hands of Mrs Todd. There, with a steadily sagging face, Todd received police emissaries, delivered a statement to the press and telephoned the United States Senator from New Hampshire. The Senator was too busy thanking his lucky stars he went to the University of New Hampshire to be of much help.

But there was yet another blow in store.

Todd's grasp of events did not disintegrate entirely until two of his assistants burst into the room, progressing in a series of swooping sideward bows as they made way for a visitor. The three men sprang to their feet at the intimations of royalty. It was a moment before the swirling throng clarified enough for Thatcher to see. At the centre of the whirlpool a small man stood erect, his slight figure vibrating with a controlled spare virility. The face was familiar from millions of record jackets, from television, from *Time* magazine, from the podium itself. Maestro Arturo Fursano had flown to his son's side.

'I must see my son,' he hissed. 'My Pier Luigi, he is still alive?'

'Certainly, certainly, Maestro,' Todd babbled. 'We'll send for him at once.'

A chair was produced and was waved away. Arturo Fursano had not come to New Hampshire to sit. He had come to rescue his only son from assassins.

'Child murderers! Monsters!' he proclaimed as he prowled the room.

The entrance of Pete Fursano did not noticeably lower the emotional temperature. Father and son embraced, the son overtopping the father by a clear eight inches.

'Well, Dad,' said Pete affectionately.

'My son!' cried the Maestro in thanksgiving.

Cautiously Lyman Todd tried to steer them into calmer waters. 'I'm sorry you had to come up yourself. I was on the point of calling Mrs Fursano.'

'No!' It was a rebuke. Imperious black eyes flashed; the slight figure strutted forward on cat feet. 'When there is violence, it is not a matter for women!'

Within minutes he was to be proven wrong. In some families it was the women who flew to meet danger. Mrs Jonathan Hughes arrived under police escort.

'Mrs Hughes, here, has a theory,' said Captain Nivelle.

'I told Jonathan's father we should never let him come up here,' she said tearfully. 'It's all a plot, I know it is. Someone wants to kill all the boys!'

Todd immediately launched a flood of soothing phrases. Carter Sprague had been alone with Elliot Patterson. The other boys had not. Therefore they were in an entirely different category.

The tone, more than the words, had its effect. Doubtfully Mrs Hughes dried her eyes and admitted that she might be leaping to conclusions. Then, in a flash, the good work was undone.

'So!' Arturo Fursano inhaled sharply. He stroked his moustache with delicate ferocity. 'Someone wishes to kill Pier Luigi. Well, let them try!'

Daredevil challenge was not for Mrs Hughes. Instantly the handkerchief was out again. 'Jonathan must have police protection! Until that awful Patterson man is caught.'

Helplessly Todd looked at the police officer. There was no reassurance there.

'She might be right,' said Nivelle. 'We don't know what happened with Patterson. I think I'll put it to the police down in the city.'

'But there were three other men present when Patterson

talked to these boys,' Lyman Todd protested. 'We do know what happened.'

The captain's silence was eloquent. It would be a long time before any police force believed a word uttered by a member of the Brunswick Admission Committee.

'And now' – Fursano resumed the floor – 'I remove my son. There shall be no further question of Brunswick College, Pier Luigi.'

'I don't mind,' said Pete equably. 'Any place in the country is all right with me. I'm down for Williams, too.'

Todd was stung. 'Williams has no musician-in-residence programme.'

An involuntary look of contempt was politely banished from Fursano's face. 'Bah!' he exclaimed. 'There is no question of that. Pier Luigi is not a musician.'

Thatcher was lost in admiration at this trenchant realism. He was willing to bet that Pete's performance would have had any other parent hiring Town Hall. And he was right. (He did not know that the Maestro could afford realism. The musical hopes of the house rested on one Flavia Fursano. Only eleven, she still had long pigtails that bounced when she ran, but already she had very grave doubts about current interpretations of Mahler.)

To be lost in any emotion was not safe when George Lancer was at the mercy of Lyman Todd, Thatcher learned on the way home.

'He's in such a mess,' Lancer excused himself.

'His mess, not yours, George,' said Lucy.

'I know that. But when I turned him down on everything else he wanted, this seemed like such a small thing.'

Thatcher was stern. 'Just what did you agree to do?'

'I said we'd try to find this Alec Baxter. If Patterson is hiding with him, it would be a help for Brunswick to get there first.'

'Oh, well,' Lucy breathed a sigh of relief. 'There can't be any harm in that.'

Banks have their own way of doing things. While the New Hampshire police sent out fliers about three Brunswick alumni, while the New York police made the interesting discovery that

Alec Baxter did not own a car, was not listed in the telephone directory and patronized neither the gas nor the electricity company, George Lancer's secretary undertook her own inquiries.

Thus, within a surprisingly short time, Lancer was once again enabled to interrupt John Thatcher's working day.

'Until last June, Baxter had a checking account with the First National City. His address then was on West Twenty-fourth Street,' he announced without preamble.

Thatcher was resigned.

'I suppose we have to go and look at it, but it stands to reason that if he closed the account, he moved.'

'Yes, I'm hoping they can tell us where he went.'

There was no argument from the Sloan's vice-president. Thatcher was just as glad to go. Miss Corsa, still tirelessly canvassing every far-flung outpost of the Roman Catholic Empire, had filed an interim report. Within the metropolitan area there was no Father Martin – admitting any connection with one of Elliot Patterson's four names – who had a parish of his own, who was cloistered in monastic orders, or who was engaged in mission work among the Indians on Long Island.

For one giddy moment Thatcher thought it might all have been too much for Miss Corsa. But secret research with the door locked proved she was right. By God, there is an Indian reservation on Long Island! He didn't want to be around when she learned that one of Elliot Patterson's accounts was the Armenian Apostolic Diocese. It would turn out that they were being regularly massacred by Turks up in the Bronx.

During the taxi ride Thatcher reverted to Baxter's bank account.

'If we don't find anything at West Twenty-fourth Street, will the First National go through their records for us? His last cheque could probably tell us a great deal – if he made it out to himself and used it to open an account someplace else.'

Gloomily Lancer shook his head. 'That won't do any good. I've already tried. They remember how he closed out – it made quite an impression on the teller. He drew out the balance in

147

cash – $4,200. The teller said Baxter had never taken more than a hundred in cash before.'

Thatcher's gloom matched Lancer's. 'Another Patterson,' he predicted. 'We're probably heading straight to some woman who's keeping everything the way Alec loved it.'

'Baxter isn't married.'

Thatcher did not disturb the innocence of Lancer's thoughts. But he reminded himself that Baxter moved in less conventional circles than Rye.

In the event, however, nothing more alarming than a surly janitor awaited them at West Twenty-fourth Street. It was a shabby brownstone converted into furnished apartments.

'What's all the fuss about Baxter?' the janitor grumbled. 'You're the second lot after him.'

His surliness was dispelled by the grandeur of Lancer's ideas about tipping. 'Yeah, Baxter had the top floor front, the one with the skylight,' he continued, mellowed. 'But it's been rented to other people for months now.'

They asked about a forwarding address.

'No, nothing like that. Just gave notice, packed his bags and left.'

'He may have left word with the post office,' Thatcher speculated. 'If so, the police will be able to get it.'

'Hey! What's this about the police?'

They soothed the janitor. It was not Baxter himself who was of interest to the police, they explained. Merely a friend who might be staying with him.

The janitor was immediately knowing. 'Not Baxter!' he said. 'Oh, maybe overnight sometimes. But he wasn't shacked up with anybody, if that's what you mean.'

Lancer tried to turn the subject. 'That isn't what—'

'If he did any helling around, it wasn't here,' the janitor continued half-regretfully. 'Of course, he was away weekends a lot. Especially in the summer.'

Thatcher stirred slightly. This was the first Baxter characteristic to emerge. 'What was he like?' he asked. 'As a tenant?'

Alec Baxter had been an ideal tenant. Quiet himself, he had not been unduly critical of noise from others. 'Some of these old biddies, Christ! They call out the riot squad if somebody has a party on Saturday night!' Not that the old biddies didn't have a point. It was the kids who were the problem. They moved in with nothing but their clothes and a fifty-watt hi-fi set.

'Folk music?' Thatcher suggested sympathetically.

'At fifty watts, it doesn't make any difference what it is,' the janitor replied darkly.

Under prodding, a picture developed. Baxter had been a propertyless transient in a world of the same. But he had been adult, hard-working, respectable. He was a familiar figure on the street, going down to the corner in an old tweed jacket and chinos for cigarettes, for a pound of coffee, for beer. He had made no friendships with the other tenants. They were mostly old residents or kids. It was not an artistic neighbourhood. 'Thank God!' breathed the janitor.

It had just been another dead end, Lancer summed up as they made their way toward Eighth Avenue. Thatcher was agreeing absently when suddenly he interrupted himself to stretch out a detaining arm.

'Did you see that, George?

'See what?'

'That store we just passed. The artists' supply place.'

Lancer looked back at the modest sign and shop front. 'What about it? Oh, you mean they might know something about Baxter?'

'Somebody else seems to have that idea. That's Ralph Armitage in there.'

Without a word they retraced their steps and descended to the below-grade entrance. Through the glass front they had a clear view. It was indeed Ralph Armitage deep in conversation with the shopkeeper.

They went inside.

'Hello, Armitage,' Lancer greeted him. 'Are you looking for Baxter too? We've just come from his old apartment.'

'I don't seem to be getting anywhere,' Armitage said sourly. 'He seems to have disappeared off the face of the earth last June.'

The shopkeeper tut-tutted. Alec Baxter had simply moved,

that's all there was to it. He wasn't the kind to advertise his movements.

'He certainly isn't,' Thatcher agreed. 'By the way, Armitage, you must be the other patty the janitor mentioned. I suppose the police haven't gotten this far yet.'

Armitage snorted his opinion of the police.

'Oh, they'll get here. Slow but sure. We tried a short cut through bank accounts. How did you manage it?'

'Marsden knew a gallery that sells some of Baxter's stuff. They dug out this address for him.'

Thatcher nodded. He had found out what he wanted to know. Both Neil Marsden and Ralph Armitage thought it worthwhile to track the elusive Baxter. An unlikely alliance, but police suspicion might be cementing the bonds of the Brunswick Admission Committee.

The shopkeeper was interested by the mention of a gallery.

'That'll be the Capricorn,' he commented. 'They were doing nicely by Baxter. Have you seen his seascapes? Beautiful control. He's got a real future, if you ask me.'

'He doesn't seem to have much of a present,' Armitage said with a glance at the street outside. 'And I thought the real artist lived over in East Village.'

It was the shopkeeper's turn to be contemptuous. 'East Village! Beards and hippies! Alec is too old for that sort of thing. And he was coming along. I don't suppose he had a suit to his name, but he had to take less and less commercial work.'

Fine, thought Thatcher irritably. More commercial work would have made it necessary for Alec Baxter to have a fixed location. But apparently he was free as air.

'He must have some friends,' he persisted. 'Apparently he kept in touch with people. There was that advertising man we met in Coburg. We're working from the wrong end.'

'Oh, Alec has friends. There are those people he goes to in the summer. I remember sending some supplies up to him there.' The shopkeeper had constituted himself Alec Baxter's champion.

'You mailed things to him?' Thatcher was alert.

'Sure. I was getting in some brushes he wanted, but he was going out of town for a couple of weeks. Let's see.' He frowned in thought.

'Yes?' Armitage prompted.

'Now, don't rush me. It's coming.'

'Maybe you've got a record –'

A minatory hand was raised. 'Don't push. I can hear it. It wasn't Quigley ... Kentley ... no, but almost ... Knightley. Knightley! That's it! Mr and Mrs Stephen Knightley. Somewhere up in New Hampshire.' The shopkeeper ended in a flourish of triumph.

'Well! Can you beat that?' Armitage asked the world at large. 'Mrs Knightley.'

His companions looked surprised that he had fastened on the person rather than the place.

'Mrs Knightley is Gabe Uhlein's partner,' Armitage told them. 'And now it turns out she's got a place in New Hampshire.'

Lancer was skeptical. 'What makes you think it's the same Mrs Knightley? There must be hundreds.'

'Hell! She told me Baxter was a friend of her husband's. She told me so herself. But she didn't say he was a resident in the house.'

Thatcher cut in. 'That seems to settle it. The next step is a talk with Mrs Knightley.'

'We could go there right now.' Armitage was bristling with energy.

Behind his back Lancer and Thatcher exchanged speaking looks. They were not particularly anxious to join forces with Armitage.

'Why don't I call her and see if she's free?' Thatcher temporized. 'It would be more courteous to make an appointment.'

The shopkeeper offered his phone. Within minutes fate had handed Thatcher the means with which to shed Armitage.

'Neither Mrs Knightley nor Gabe Uhlein is in the office. I'm afraid we'll have to defer our talk with her. The receptionist doesn't know when they'll be back. In the meantime, you two

Old Brunsies will want to look at the papers. The first stories about the murder have just hit.'

18. Classes Will Not Meet

The temporary unavailability of Uhlein and Mrs Knightley had beneficial effects over and above sending Ralph Armitage after the latest editions.

'At the moment, George, there doesn't seem to be anything to stop our returning to the bank,' Thatcher pointed out.

And a fine thing it was, he reflected, when George C. Lancer, Chairman of the Board, and John Putnam Thatcher, Senior Vice-President, drifted into the Sloan Guaranty Trust only as a last resort.

In the taxi, Lancer projected tempered restlessness. 'I'd like to talk to this Mrs Knightley. You must admit, John, that it is odd. There seems to be a link between Elliot Patterson, Baxter and Mrs Knightley. And if Baxter is staying up in New Hampshire . . .'

Thatcher would admit that it was odd, but he was not looking forward to another interview. He had already been present at too many. George was splendidly ignoring the screaming headlines about Carter Sprague and Brunswick. This he approved. The publicity department of the Sloan Guaranty Trust could do just so much. Let the Brunswick College information office carry some of the load. It would make a nice departure from their usual round of complacent press releases about the million disappointed applicants who stood behind each Brunswick freshman.

More or less idly he said, 'Uhlein was up at Brunswick at Homecoming, wasn't he?'

'Ye-es,' said Lancer, thinking hard. 'Yes, he was. Left right after the football game, I understand. The car-rental agency told the police he checked out of Coburg at six-thirty on Saturday.'

When they reached the Sloan, Lancer decided to stop at

Thatcher's office to see if Miss Corsa had tracked down the elusive Father Martin. There, comfortable as few people managed to be in Miss Corsa's domain, was Mrs George C. Lancer.

'Lucy!' said George. Because he liked things in their place, he sounded more surprised than pleased.

'Well, Lucy,' said Thatcher with amused suspicion, 'I'm delighted to see you, of course. But what are you doing here?'

He did not miss the conspiratorial glance passed across the desk. Clearly a very good understanding existed between Miss Corsa and Mrs Lancer. This was a credit to them both, but Thatcher saw in this praiseworthy alliance a threat to his well-being, in the form of social obligation or worse.

'I dropped in to talk about what you want me to do about Carter Sprague's funeral,' Lucy said. 'Then I got fascinated by these calls Miss Corsa is making to locate your Father Martin.'

George regarded interest in clerics, together with concern about a highly publicized funeral, as feminine frivolity. He looked inquiringly at Miss Corsa. Composedly she reported that she had not found Father Martin.

George made an indeterminate noise.

'I can see you're busy,' his wife said, gathering up her furs. This time she carefully did not glance at Miss Corsa or Thatcher. 'Too busy to tell me what you want me to do about the funeral?'

George fell into the trap and, in some detail, favoured her with a well-organized summary of the mysterious connections between Elliot Patterson, Alec Baxter, Gabriel Uhlein, Marian Knightley, country places in New Hampshire and the murder of Carter Sprague. 'So, we're busy trying to get in touch with Target,' he concluded, hinting at an afternoon with Miss Corsa and his own Miss Evans dropping everything to pursue the hunt. He then glanced at his watch.

'I see, dear,' said Lucy sweetly. Including them all in a brilliant smile, she said, 'Well, I won't make you take me to lunch, then. John, do drop by for drinks this evening.'

And she swept out.

Was Miss Corsa regarding her superiors with undisguised disapproval?

'Hmm,' said John Putnam Thatcher.

Just as he suspected, Lucy knew more than she was telling. She knew exactly where Gabe Uhlein was. He was at the grand ballroom of the Waldorf-Astoria, helping supervise the dress rehearsal of the Junior League's fall fashion show for the benefit of the Manhattan Home for Little Wanderers.

Lucy Lancer had long since left the Junior League behind her, but there was not much along Little Wanderer lines that escaped her. There had been the usual disappointment with the proceeds from last year's benefit, the usual committee quarrels, the usual resignations and, unusually, a decision to deliver the Junior League into the professional hands of Target Associates. So far, announcements, tickets and the programmes showed marked improvement. It remained to be seen if Target Associates could do anything with a fall fashion show that insisted on using member models.

'Mrs Lancer!' The scrawny young woman, her arms full of carelessly heaped designer gowns, was awed.

Lucy searched a capacious memory, dredged up one of the Asbury stepdaughters who had married and turned fashionable. 'Hello, Amanda,' she said crisply. 'I thought I'd drop by to see how things are coming.'

Amanda launched into a recital of hardship and duress but, after looking around, Lucy said, 'Why, that's Mr Uhlein!'

Amanda continued about the selfless devotion required by the Junior League, but was sent back to her duties. Lucy made her way across the ballroom floor, undeflected by crowds of dishevelled young men and scurrying young matrons. On the improvised stage at the bandstand a woman with athletic contours pivoted in a mustard-green pant suit designed for another figure.

Foursquare in the middle of the floor stood a middle-aged woman, watching angrily and occasionally pushing a hand through untidy hair. Then, in accents boroughs removed from the Junior League, she shouted up to the stage:

'Mrs Morse! You gotta wiggle a little, dearie! You're stiff!'

At a small ringside table, Gabe Uhlein sat with a companion. Rising as Lucy approached, he breathed pleasure at seeing her and introduced Mrs Knightley. Mrs Knightley's tawny silk suit, Lucy noted instantly, compared favourably to the creations being sported by the young ladies rushing around. And Mrs Knightley knew how to wear her clothes.

Lucy joined them. 'I was passing and stopped on an impulse,' she said with a twinkle.

She saw no need to add that the impulse was the wicked instinct to discomfit George. Fortunately, neither Gabe Uhlein nor Marian Knightley was disposed to look too closely at this; their eyes strayed back to the stage and to Helene still busy hectoring Mrs Morse. And it had been a long time since anybody challenged Lucy Lancer's right of entry to such functions as this.

'Look, honey,' Helene was pleading. 'Can't you loosen up? I know! Why don't you pretend . . .?'

'Helene!' Uhlein barked, jumping to his feet. 'I'm sure Mrs Morse is trying.'

He bounded out to Helene's side and was engulfed by a bevy of highly articulate women.

Marian Knightley smiled. 'Helene is one of our function co-ordinators,' she explained, 'but she usually works with professionals. It was easy enough to line up the clothes, but the models aren't her usual kind.'

Uhlein was back, beaming impersonally in all directions. But in an undertone he said, 'Marian, the next time I get talked into handling anything at all where the amateurs insist on interfering – shoot me.'

'All right, I will.'

This was inspiration enough for Lucy. When peace returned to the bandstand, and Mrs Morse was succeeded by Mrs Olliphant (Oriental pants and a forced smile), she swiftly outlined ambitions of the Friends of the Aged Mariner.

Gabe Uhlein brightened. 'Certainly. Let's see. A banquet? A ball? A fashion show – no, no!'

Mrs Knightley told Lucy that Target Associates would be

happy to forward literature on the various ways that worthy causes could raise money. This was not what Lucy had in mind.

Mendaciously she launched into a recital concerning a late-afternoon committee meeting and members hostile to professional fund raising. This, she judged rightly, was enough for Gabriel Uhlein.

'Surprising in this day and age to find that sort of resistance,' he deplored, keeping an eye on Helene, who had turned from Mrs Olliphant to a weary-looking band leader. 'Still, it exists. Now Marian and I really should stay to see this final run-through . . .'

So, as she had hoped, Lucy arranged to remain with Uhlein and Marian for the next hour, then to accompany them back to Target Associates. She was congratulating herself on her tactics when she felt, rather than saw, Marian Knightley's gaze. Was there wariness in the air?

Not on Gabriel Uhlein's part, at least. Between trips out to Helene, a conference about the arrival of 400,000 scented plastic roses, and consultations with Mrs Wainright Buell, programme chairman of the Junior League, who was getting closer to tears by the minute, he rattled off ways the Friends of the Aged Mariner could raise money.

'Of course,' he insinuated, 'a long-term programme, with follow-ups, will certainly get you more, dollar for dollar. In our experience . . .'

Firmly Mrs Lancer said that the Friends were going to take the plunge with a limited agenda. She was enjoying herself, and this would do the Aged Mariners no harm, but, she realized, extracting information, incriminating or otherwise, from this pair was not going to be easy. Gabe Uhlein's loquacity was as carefully controlled as Mrs Knightley's silence.

'All right!' Helene commanded. 'One last run-through! Now, yellow suit! Please swing it a little. And Olliphant – cut the grin!'

'She doesn't have the Junior League touch,' Gabe mourned. 'On Hadassah she's unbeatable.'

After preliminary cries, shouts and shushings, the overhead

lights dimmed, flattering pink spotlights glowed, and the five-piece band played 'A Pretty Girl is Like a Melody.' The dress rehearsal of the Junior League fall fashion show was in full swing.

To Lucy it was just like hundreds of similar affairs, but Uhlein was intense as he peered at the parade. Mrs Knightley was jotting notes.

'Beautiful!' Uhlein shouted at the interval, scooping up Marian's notes and hurrying off towards Helene, who looked like thunder.

Marian Knightley lit a cigarette.

'Has anything come up about Elliot?' she asked quietly. 'Gabe told me that you and your husband were up at Brunswick when . . .'

She did not need to continue. Obviously the murder of a young boy had no place in this world of harmless vanities and self-indulgence. Lucy Lancer came to a swift conclusion. Marian Knightley had formidable reserve; Marian Knightley might not be trustworthy. But Marian Knightley was not negligible.

'As far as I know,' Lucy said, 'nothing has come up about Elliot Patterson. And as for this appalling tragedy of Carter Sprague, there seems to be only suspicion.'

Mrs Knightley looked up. 'But the police let everyone leave Brunswick,' she remarked. 'That must mean something.'

Lucy thought back to the endless discussions at Brunswick and after. 'It may, but I think that the police are as much at sea as the rest of us,' she said.

For a moment neither woman spoke. Bubbles of laughter and clarinets, of suggestions and commands, danced around them. Lucy examined her emerald cocktail ring.

'From what George says, everybody feels that the key may be the list of names Elliot left behind. One of the men has disappeared, but some sort of lead has turned up.'

A frown shadowed Mrs Knightley's smooth brow. 'Oh?'

'I remember,' said Lucy who was in the enviable position of lying, of knowing that her companion knew she lied, and of still being able to continue. 'I remember because we bought one of his watercolours.'

'Alec Baxter,' Mrs Knightley said. Was it resignation or defeat?

Lucy nodded. 'Apparently they think he might be staying with friends in New Hampshire.'

This time there was no doubt. Mrs Knightley was jolted. 'Friends in New Hampshire? Oh, for heaven's sake!'

Gabriel Uhlein, reappearing, misinterpreted this. 'I know, Marian, I know. But I told Helene that they really don't want a smooth professional show. They like the homemade look!'

Both ladies looked at him with exasperated incomprehension.

'Gabe,' said Marian with a half-smile, 'we've been talking about Elliot. And about the murder of that boy up at Brunswick.'

Uhlein's face fell into heavy solemnity. 'Terrible thing. We're sending flowers, of course. A gesture of respect.'

With an edge, Marian Knightley said, 'Now, it's Alec Baxter.'

'Who? Oh, that artist?'

'That's right,' she said steadily. 'That artist friend of mine and Steve's.'

'Sure, sure!'

'Now,' Mrs Knightley continued, 'somebody thinks that Alec may have been staying up at our cottage in New Hampshire last week-end, when Carter Sprague was murdered. You can see what they must be thinking, Gabe. We did have a guest last Saturday night. If it had been Alec – or somebody else – why, the police might start wondering.'

'Saturday night?' Gabe Uhlein asked hollowly.

She was implacable.

'Saturday night, Gabe. At our cottage. At Saxe – just twenty-seven miles from Brunswick. Where Carter Sprague was murdered.'

She was certainly leading her witness. And with success.

'Why should they think it was Baxter?' Uhlein demanded nervously. 'What difference . . . oh, all right. I'll tell them that I spent the week-end with you. That I went straight to your place from Coburg.'

'Oh really?' said Lucy Lancer, politely losing all interest. 'Look, I think they're ready to begin.'

The second half of the Junior League fall fashion show was unmarred by anything worse than a severe case of hysterics which proved conclusively that Mrs Morse could, after all, loosen up.

On the trip from the Waldorf-Astoria to Target Associates, Lucy Lancer could sense Gabe Uhlein's uneasiness. This was understandable. It had been generally assumed that when he left Brunswick before Carter Sprague's murder, he had returned directly to New York.

Now it appeared that he had been conveniently close to the campus.

Or had he?

He was certainly finding it hard to keep from sending small worried looks towards Marian Knightley.

She, on the other hand, was gripped by a more positive emotion. After a brief, uninformative admission that she and her husband had entertained Alec Baxter for week-ends, as part of a social schedule that featured guests during most week-ends, she had talked resolutely about the Friends of the Aged Mariner.

With some glee Lucy Lancer envisaged greeting George and John Thatcher over drinks with a rich haul of information and speculation. The best, she discovered as they entered the waiting-room at Target Associates, was still to come.

'Oh, Mr Uhlein! It's so exciting! I was looking for the Barteau estimates and found this. Just look!'

A shiny-faced girl brandished a piece of paper at Uhlein, Marian Knightley and Mrs Lancer impartially.

'Noreen!' Mrs Knightley snapped.

'Oh, but Mrs Knightley, it's a copy of a letter by Mr Patterson! I'll bet the police will want to know! I'll bet the reporters will want to talk to me. I'll bet . . .'

Uhlein plucked the flimsy from her hand and unashamedly

both Mrs Knightley and Lucy Lancer peered over his shoulder, even though he read aloud:

'To Father Paul Etienne. The Brothers of Silence. Gethsemane, Alabama.'

'The Brothers of Silence? That's a monastery!' Lucy exclaimed.

Uhlein plowed on.

Dear Reverend Father:
I am very happy to recommend that you consider for your late vocation programme my long-time friend, Alec Baxter. He has for many years impressed me with the spiritual content of his life. Now that he has resolved his doubts, I know that his commitment to dedication, contemplation and religious service will be an inspiration to us all.

Alec Baxter's search for personal self-realization in the world has always been marked by a strong probity, purity of mind and body, and seriousness of purpose. His moral depths have grown steadily. I am fully confident that he is, in all respects, ready and eager to embrace the religious vocation and serve God as a member of your Order.

Yours sincerely,
Elliot Patterson

'Sweet Jesus!' said Gabriel Uhlein.

Marian Knightley's dark eyes sparkled with an undecipherable emotion.

'So you see, the man we entertained last weekend couldn't have been Alec. Alec has become a Brother of Silence. And Elliot' – she choked slightly – 'Elliot helped him do it.'

19. Candidates for Degrees

When Ralph Armitage had paused at the news stand to anathematize the methods of Target Associates which could lose its two principals for unspecified periods, he forgot that the same standards currently prevailed at the Armitage Insurance Brokerage.

His secretary hailed his return with relief. According to her, most of Manhattan was demanding his services.

'And I didn't know where you were, or when you'd be back,' she reproached him.

'Couldn't you turn some of them off on to Jake?'

'Yes, but Mr Consett insisted that he had to speak to you personally.'

'Consett?' Armitage frowned, waiting for bells to ring.

'Yes, he called three times.' She did not provide any further identification. 'And Mrs Patterson was very persistent, too. She left a number where she can be reached until four o'clock.'

Now the bell did ring. Dimly Armitage recalled a figure from his trip to Rye – a harassed man whose temper was rapidly shredding into fragments. The brother-in-law, that was it! Shivers of premonition ran down Armitage's back.

'Get me Consett first,' he ordered.

When the connection was made, Bill Consett came on the line with a rush.

'Armitage? I've been trying to get you for hours. You remember me, don't you? I'm El Patterson's brother-in-law. Sally isn't with you, is she?'

'Not yet,' Armitage admitted cautiously. 'She's been calling the office while I was out.'

'Dammit! I was afraid of that. I don't know what she thinks she's doing. I found out – just by accident, mind you – that she's listing the house for sale. When you think of the time I've put in at Rye! Sally's going crazy, I tell you!'

'Great!' said Armitage briefly. 'Thanks for the warning.'

But this was not Bill Consett's goal.

'Now wait a minute!' he sputtered. 'You've got to try and talk some sense into her. I know it's not easy, but she's just gone off the tracks. Especially since this Sprague kid was knifed up at Brunswick.'

'Upset, is she?'

'Well, what do you think? She's had the police practically camping on the doorstep. Even Sally can't pass off murder as one of those things she and El don't discuss with outsiders.'

Brusquely Armitage cut off further lamentation by promising to do what he could. Sally, he told himself, was not the only one going to pieces under the mounting pressure. Consett sounded as if he couldn't take much more. It was probably all a tempest in a teapot. Sally simply wanted to get away from the house, and who could blame her? The police and the press between them were no doubt making it uninhabitable. And the woman had three children to think of.

This carefully reasoned calm was shattered when he returned Sally's call. And not by Sally, but by the way the phone was answered. A brisk voice identified one of New York's largest stockbrokers and volunteered the information that Mrs Patterson was closeted with a partner. Would he wait just one moment, please?

After that, it was no surprise to learn that Sally wanted to see him instantly. In fact, she was planning to grab a taxi and be with him in a matter of minutes.

Now no one spends a lifetime in insurance without learning about distraught women – women who have lost their husbands, women whose homes have been reduced to charred ruins, women waiting anxiously in hospitals. One of the lessons painfully acquired is that women on the brink of hysteria will reach down for some vestigial remnant of self-control in certain environments. The office milieu, alas, is not one of them.

Armitage was damned if he was going to meet Sally Patterson in private; he wanted her on her best behaviour. Almost automatically he produced a tale of a midtown appointment and suggested that they meet for drinks at the Biltmore.

When Sally arrived under the clock in a crowd of college boys and girls, men meeting business associates, and married couples foregathering for an evening on the town, she did not seem on the edge of a breakdown. On the other hand, there was no denying that she lacked the all-enveloping calm that characterized her in her own home. She dropped her bag while Armitage was pushing in her chair, then fiddled nervously with her gloves as he gave their order. Armitage was not a senstitive man but he realized that this was due, in part, to the absence of her normal background. In Rye she was monarch of all she surveyed; here, in a suit and hat, she was a stranger to him and probably to herself. And no woman can play the role of wife and mother when meeting a casual male acquaintance for a drink. Not the least of Sally's problems was a loss of familiarity with any other role.

Armitage suppressed a smile. He was not as innocent as Mrs Armitage about the delinquencies so thrillingly portrayed in the ladies' magazines. Sally Patterson was decorously interviewing her insurance broker. But from the next table she might well look like a suburban matron debating whether to plunge into her first affair. Well, he knew how to deal with that!

'Drink up, Sally. It will do you good and you probably need it. This isn't an easy time for you.' He restrained himself with an effort from patting her hand.

To his surprise, Sally downed half her glass at a gulp.

'I needed that,' she said tightly. 'I've been rushing around the city all day.'

'And you've probably had trouble with the police to boot,' he said, carefully sinking his talk with Consett. 'They've got some crazy idea that Elliot was up in Coburg over reunion weekend.'

Even narrow vigilance could discern nothing but impatience in Sally's response.

'Oh, never mind that,' she said with a flat, dismissive gesture. 'Sometimes I think the police are insane. Elliot didn't spend a year planning to leave me in order to go to a college reunion.'

The brittleness in Mrs Patterson's reference to her husband was new but, under the circumstances, scarcely surprising.

'I always said it was a lot of nonsense,' Armitage lied. He had been one of the first to pick up the rumour of Elliot's presence. Now was not the time to say so.

'Anyway, that isn't what I wanted to talk to you about.' Sally finished off her drink in two quick swallows, took a deep breath, and continued: 'It's about Elliot's insurance policies. I want to cash them in.'

'All of them?'

'That's right. You said Elliot arranged it so that I could,' Sally reminded him. 'Just six weeks before he left.'

Ralph Armitage did not need the reminder. Doubtfully he looked across the table. Sally's hands were clenched into tight fists; she had wrought herself up to this announcement. But he was damned if he was going to let it go by without a question. He decided to put his faith in the civilizing influence of the Biltmore.

'Now, Sally,' he said gently, 'you don't want to make hasty decisions. If it's a question of reinvestment, you need some time to look around and see if you can do better. But if you're in a bind for cash, there's no reason to think about converting. You can borrow on the policies, you know.'

'Oh, no, I'm afraid that wouldn't do,' she replied with a return to her usual manner. Either the drink or getting the question out in the open had restored the gentle certainty of Rye.

Kindly she turned aside his advice, kindly she rebuffed his questions, kindly she refused another drink. With growing firmness, she made her point.

She wanted the cash, and she wanted it at once.

After she left, Armitage stayed on, his mind a swirl of speculation. Over a second drink and then a third, he reviewed the situation. Sally had put the house up for sale, Sally had spent hours at her broker's, Sally knew what she wanted done with her insurance policies. Only a fool could miss the obvious. The Patterson assests were all being converted into cash. And then what?

Thoughtfully he paddled his swizzle stick around the glass. One logical conclusion was that Sally had known Elliot's whereabouts all the time. Now she was preparing to join him. Had her new brutality about Elliot been camouflage? Was she trying to dispel suspicion that the Pattersons had been united all along?

It sounded reasonable, but, in heaven's name, why? There had never been anything to prevent the Pattersons' packing their bags and taking off for Timbuktu together.

Armitage groaned. Everything brought him back to the same starting point. The Patterson behaviour could be explained so easily in terms of large-scale theft from Target Associates. It virtually defied rational explanation on any other level. For a full five minutes Armitage actually considered the possibility of a mistake. Elliot was just the man to mess up a piece of major larceny. He had, after all, confused two folders at the Brunswick Club, leaving a list of his bolt holes and taking college test scores instead. Was it conceivable he could have done the same thing at Target Associates? Leaving a million dollars he had planned to steal and taking some plan for a blood-bank drive instead? No! Things like that just don't happen. People don't disrupt their lives, turn their wives into accomplices, plan mysterious disappearances, and then casually mislay their ill-gotten gains.

Armitage's last drink brought thoughts even more unwelcome. Everybody had been sidetracked at the very beginning by that automobile accident up in Putnam County. But, after all, what could be more reasonable than that Elliot Patterson had returned to Rye on his usual train, had been picked up at the station by his wife, and then disappeared? The world was now filled with people finding it reasonable that Elliot should have skipped after an undiluted fourteen years of Sally.

But look at it the other way. Elliot couldn't have been any picnic either. And Armitage had just been amused at Sally's resemblance to a woman in her first brush with adult passion. Was it so impossible? Now that he came to think of it, only the missing $50,000 bond had prevented the immediate emergence of this view. And, of course, the bond could be nicely explained as a mere accident of timing. But . . .

But there was always Carter Sprague to be accounted for. The boy who noticed more than he should have. Armitage was still surprised about that. He could have sworn the kid was too wrapped up in narcissistic admiration to notice anything. Armitage shook his buzzing head. He was, he decided, not very good at predicting people. Maybe he needed help. But, one way or the other, he would have a last try at finding out what in hell Sally Patterson was up to.

'Ralph Armitage just called,' Louise Dunlop told her husband while he was taking the key out of the lock. 'He tried the office, but you'd already left.'

Jim Dunlop was not enthusiastic. 'What did he want?'

'He's worried about Sally Patterson. She's selling everything she owns, and he thinks she may be joining her husband somewhere.'

'Well, why ask me about it? Why not ask Sally?'

'He did. She won't tell him anything.' Lou hesitated for a second, then slid on smoothly: 'I might be able to get something out of her. She'd be more likely to talk with another woman or at least let something slip out. Oops! There's the timer on the oven.'

Dunlop followed his wife to the small kitchenette and leaned against the door post.

'Never mind what Sally is likely to tell you. Listen, Lou, I don't want you getting mixed up in this thing. It's bad enough that I'm in it up to my neck.'

Lou made a great business of donning padded mittens and removing a casserole to the counter. She did not look directly at her husband.

'I already am in it,' she reminded him.

Jim Dunlop's mouth became a horizontal line. 'You mean you've had to provide your husband with an alibi?' he demanded.

'That, among other things,' she said shortly.

'I don't know why you couldn't keep your mouth shut instead of blurting out that story about seeing Carter go upstairs.'

'One of us had to do something. And I seemed to be elected.'

'Not by me!'

'Oh, not you! You think it's undignified for your wife to meddle in a murder. Let me tell you, I think it's undignified to have a husband in jail!'

'Anybody would think you saw me sink the knife into that kid,' Jim challenged bluntly.

Finally Lou abandoned the casserole and let her eyes slide sideways toward her husband.

'I saw Carter Sprague go upstairs alive just before we got you to the car,' she said stubbornly. 'That's my story and I'm sticking with it.'

'The perfect little helpmate!' Jim mocked. 'You think I

should be falling all over myself with gratitude, I suppose.'

'Gratitude is the last thing in the world I'd expect from you!' she flashed.

Motionless, they glared at each other – two clenched jaws, two white faces, two pairs of blazing eyes.

Jim Dunlop saw a stranger on the other side of the little round table with its two ice-cream chairs. They were growing up, all right, he realized with a sudden sense of loss. Unfortunately they seemed to be growing up in opposite directions.

The hostile silence was broken by the sudden peal of the doorbell. They stood frozen; then, as if on signal, they relaxed.

Neither would have admitted it for a moment, but the interruption was welcome. Not because disagreements were a rarity. Far from it. They were frequent, violent and satisfying. But thus far their squabbles had been on the nursery level, in the warm, cosy atmosphere of children allied against the outside world. This was a grown-up argument and, as such, introduced them to that disquieting abyss across which adults stare at each other – the abyss which can be bridged, but never destroyed.

One of the things that bridges the abyss between intimates is the introduction of an unsympathetic third party.

No one could have filled this role more neatly than Neil Marsden. He had been born contemptuous of the little ice-cream-chair attempts to combine domesticity, aesthetic individuality and economy. His ideas on the subject called for Mies van der Rohe chairs.

Unconsciously Jim and Lou drew closer to each other.

'Hello, Neil,' said Jim.

'I know I'm interrupting your dinner,' Marsden apologized perfunctorily. 'But I'll only take a minute, Jim.'

Jim nodded coolly. 'That's all right. We haven't started yet.'

Neil looked at him sharply. Jim Dunlop, easily accepting the fact that the caller was an intrusion, making no apologies for a dinner that would not stretch, maintaining polite reserve until he found out what his visitor wanted, was a far cry from the deferential youngster who had graced the deliberations of the Brunswick Admission Committee. It was Marsden's bad luck to have come at a time when Jim Dunlop had more important things to worry about than his effect on a curator of the Gary Museum.

'I've been thinking about Carter Sprague's murder,' Neil said, living up to his promise of dispatch.

'We all have,' said his host evenly.

'Yes, but I mean I've been *thinking*, not just complaining,' retorted Marsden with vivid memories of a recent conversation with Armitage.

'Well?'

'Nobody killed that boy for the fun of it. He knew something.'

'I thought everybody agreed about that.'

Lou intervened in an attempt to moderate her husband's severity. 'Nothing else makes much sense.'

'But everybody thinks it's something that happened during Carter's ten-minute talk with Elliot Patterson,' Marsden persisted. 'But we know that Elliot was carrying a suitcase with plans to go somewhere. Is it likely that he wasted a lot of time? No! He probably listened to Carter and left as soon as he decently could.'

'Well, where does that take you?' Jim remained unforthcoming.

'I think that Carter picked up something that happened earlier, when all the boys were there.' Neil Marsden emphasized the last point.

'I suppose it's possible. But then, why haven't the boys spoken up?'

'You remember those boys, don't you?' None of the boys had made a hit with Marsden. Even Carter Sprague had not been quite as simpatico as he thought. 'Do you imagine for one moment that any of them, with the exception of Sprague, is likely to see the significance of anything?'

Dunlop, refusing to be intimidated by Marsden's waspishness, reviewed the boys in his own mind. Jonathan Hughes was putting in a solid twenty-four-hour working day being a modern adolescent; he scarcely had time for anything else. Basically, Douglas Younger was the same, but being old-fashioned he concentrated on football instead of consumer goods. And then there was the son of the Maestro. He paused in his review.

'Fursano?' he suggested.

It was possible, Marsden admitted, on a theoretical basis. But there was an objection.

'He didn't notice anything this time. He's not the kind who would sit on something.'

Dunlop was wary. 'Then what do you want to do about it?'

'I want to go and question these boys – on the assumption that they haven't recognized the importance of something they saw or heard.'

'And you think you'll get somewhere?' asked Dunlop sceptically.

'I don't know. But something's got to be done. This can't go on. And I want you to come with me.'

The rejection implicit in Dunlop's entire posture now took the form of words.

'Now, wait a minute. What good would that do? One's enough for the job,' Jim started to protest.

'Take my word for it,' Marsden said grimly. 'From now on, it's not a very good idea for any of us to go near the boys alone. Mrs Hughes would probably start screaming.'

Dunlop was startled at the other man's gravity. But then Neil Marsden had been very unlike himself ever since Carter Sprague's murder – and since before as well, if Armitage could be believed.

'You want both of us to tackle the Fursano boy?' He stalled for time.

'No. Douglas Younger is our best bet. He's got a photographic sort of mind, even if he never thinks about anything.'

Despite himself, Dunlop was tempted. It would be a relief to settle once and for all what the three remaining applicants might know. Not that he believed there was anything in all this.

Carter Sprague had taken with him whatever information he possessed.

'You don't think maybe you've got a bee in your bonnet about these boys?' he asked dubiously.

'Tell me one other lead,' Marsden invited.

'Well, Neil, there is one other incident you may not know about. Ralph Armitage just called' – Dunlop lowered his voice – 'with a surprising story. Apparently Sally Patterson is up to something . . .'

20. Seminar for Majors Only

If Americans took marriage as seriously as plumbing, the U.S. divorce rate would plummet. Neophyte husbands and wives could be apprenticed under masters. There are, after all, as many arts and skills required to build a successful marriage as to unclog a sewer pipe.

For example, it would have done both Dunlops a world of good to watch Lucy Lancer in action.

The officer who ordered his men to hold their fire until they saw the whites of the enemy's eyes had nothing on Lucy. She too was a great believer in getting the maximum strike from whatever ammunition the world was careless enough to make accessible.

A less experienced wife might have rushed home to crow about the fruits of her afternoon with Target Associates. A less competent wife might have seized the opportunity to urge her husband never to underestimate the power of a woman.

Lucy did neither. She bided her time until the next morning, when she again presented herself to Miss Corsa as an assistant in the search for Father Martin. John Thatcher, hurrying into his office to accomplish as much as possible before being submerged by the claims of Brunswick, accepted her presence with a grunt, then continued his assault on an overflowing 'In' box. The unholy alliance between his secretary and the chairman's wife was enough to make his blood run cold without further provocation. Since provocation was certainly forthcoming, his blood could wait.

It came at eleven-thirty with the arrival of George Lancer, gently steaming.

'You would think the New York police could take some interest in this murder!' he began.

'You mean the murder of ... er ... Carter Sprague?' Thatcher asked cautiously.

Lancer exploded. 'Of course I mean Carter Sprague! Who else am I likely to be talking about?'

Thatcher pointed out that Lancer's recent association with his alma mater had been just one felony after another. A whole flock of murders overnight would no longer be surprising.

'And the last time we spoke with Lyman Todd,' he went on, 'we were considering the possibility of the other boys being murdered. Either in series or in one grand massacre.'

'Nobody else has been murdered,' Lancer growled, as if this simple fact were an additional affront. 'But Todd just phoned with the latest news. The state police have been active. And guess what they've come up with? The Knightley place isn't by the seaside or anything. It seems it's quite near Coburg.'

His ace was immediately trumped.

'Twenty-seven miles,' Lucy supplied sweetly.

George wheeled in astonishment.

'In the town of Saxe, New Hampshire,' she continued. 'What's more, the Knightleys were up there for the week-end, and Gabe Uhlein says he joined them after he left Brunswick.'

'Uhlein?' Lancer was incredulous. 'Are you sure?'

'Lucy, you hellion,' said John Thatcher roundly. 'What have you been up to now?'

Lucy Lancer surveyed the débâcle with satisfaction. George was totally deflated; John Thatcher could barely conceal amusement with severity. In the background Rose Theresa Corsa sat ready to supply an approving chorus.

Sternly Lancer put down the temptation to recriminate.

'Lucy, are you sure about Uhlein?' he repeated.

Lucy sobered. 'No, I'm not sure at all, George. I ran into Target Associates at a charity function yesterday,' she said, skipping over details that would merely exacerbate her poor husband, 'and mentioned that the search for Alec Baxter had led to friends in New Hampshire. Mrs Knightley immediately spoke up and said that she and her husband had been up at Saxe over the reunion weekend, together with a guest. Then she kept dancing around the subject, until finally Mr Uhlein admitted that he had been the guest. But he wasn't happy about it at all. Really, you might even say that she dragged it out of him.'

'That's understandable,' Thatcher interjected. 'Uhlein doesn't want to be involved in a murder. Why is his presence such a body blow, George?'

'Because of what Todd told me. The police got to work very quickly. The Knightley place is one of those lakeside cottages and, at this season, their neighbours have closed down for the winter. They're almost completely isolated. But one of the locals was out on the lake, and he swears that he saw three people busy around the boathouse – the two Knightleys and a strange man. The state police, of course, want help from the New York police.'

Thatcher pondered the information.

'I see,' he said at length. 'If somebody on the lake saw the Knightleys, they probably saw him. So they would know that they'd have to account for an unidentified guest. You think Mrs Knightley put pressure on Uhlein to come to the rescue. That would explain his reluctance. But then, so would his desire to disassociate himself from Carter Sprague's murder. It doesn't help us much, does it? But why are you so surprised at this Uhlein business, George? Did the local give a description of the visitor?'

'Nothing like that.' Mournfully Lancer shook his head. 'It was already dusk, and there was some dim lighting at the boathouse. The local can't describe the man; he doesn't even think he could recognize him. No, what bothers me, John, is how we got on to the Knightley cottage. It was through following up Alec Baxter's trail. Then Baxter disappears at the beginning of the summer, there's no other explanation of where he could be, an extra man turns up at the Knightleys', everything fits into place. Until suddenly Uhlein steps forth.'

Lucy pulled the remaining arrow from her quiver and let fly for a second bull's-eye.

'I'm afraid, dear, that there is an explanation of what's happened to Alec Baxter.'

Almost apologetically, she retailed the history of Elliot Patterson's letter to the Brothers of Silence.

'A monastery!' Lancer was stunned. 'Lucy, are you sure you're not making this up as you go along?'

Lucy's look spoke volumes.

'I don't exactly mean making it up,' her husband retracted hastily, 'but are you certain you understood?'

'George, I saw the letter. Or rather,' said Lucy, the conscientious witness, 'I saw the carbon.'

Lancer was reluctant to abandon his theory of Baxter as the mysterious visitor. Doubtfully he turned to Thatcher.

'What do you think, John? After all, a carbon isn't the same as the letter itself. For all we know, these two precious fund raisers fixed up this letter overnight and slipped it into the files.'

Before Thatcher could reply, he was respectfully forestalled by Miss Corsa.

'I beg your pardon, Mr Lancer,' she said from her desk, 'but that would be impossible in any well-run office.'

Miss Corsa's tone was pleasantly informative. She was genuinely tolerant of the ignorance of office mechanics sometimes displayed by her superiors. Nonetheless, it was perfectly clear what would happen to the expectations of anyone foolhardy enough to insert a superfluous carbon into Miss Corsa's files. 'There are letterbook numbers and file logs and stenographers' notebooks,' she amplified.

While George Lancer wasted time arguing that not all offices measured up to Miss Corsa's well-nigh impossible standards, Thatcher was pursuing another train of thought.

'George, don't you think we're in danger of overlooking the obvious? We started looking for Alec Baxter because he might have been concealing Elliot Patterson. There's no firm reason to suppose that the list of four names was ever intended for escape purposes. But one thing is certain. If Patterson is hiding with a friend, it has to be a close friend – not someone he saw only now and then. In fact, the most likely sort of intimate, outside of a relative, would be someone he saw practically daily, someone whose sympathies with him outweighed any obligation to Sally Patterson, or Brunswick College, or the police. Have you considered the possibility that the unidentified man in the Knightley cottage is Elliot Patterson himself?'

'You mean that Mrs Knightley has been hiding him all along?'

'Precisely.'

'Are you suggesting that there's something between those two?'

Scarcely a week ago, George Lancer would have sent up psalms of thanksgiving at this solution to their problem. Now he sounded censorious.

In a different way so did Lucy as she said firmly, 'No!'

Lancer's eyebrows went up. Lucy was the one who kept up with modern literature and was broadminded.

'Well, if she's hiding him, there obviously is something between them,' she conceded, 'but not what you mean. Not Marian Knightley! You haven't met her.'

Thatcher was interested.

'I notice you don't dismiss the situation, just the motive.'

Lucy nodded vigorously.

'You go meet her, then you'll understand. She's not a woman guided by conventional standards, that's not what I mean at all. I can see her doing all sorts of things that other people would shrink from. But she wouldn't do them for conventional reasons. You'll see.'

John Thatcher accepted both the judgement and the suggestion. 'You're probably right. After all, the husband seems to be part of the New Hampshire business, whatever it is. I confess I'm beginning to be curious to meet the lady. She does manage to keep herself in the background. George and I have been tripping over everybody else in this mess, but we could go on for months and never meet Mrs Knightley. What do you say, George? I'm in favour of phoning and making that appointment we didn't get yesterday.'

George Lancer's serious face was suddenly split by a grin.

'Yes, I agree. But look what happened yesterday when we didn't bring Lucy along. I can't take this sort of thing two days running. Are you planning more explosions, dear?'

'Now, George,' said Lucy indulgently, her seraphic expression a rebuke to such fantasy, 'you and John go and see Mrs Knightley for yourselves. I am going to be quite busy working on this list. Miss Corsa and I think that we're beginning to close in on Father Martin.'

If one calls for an appointment at eleven-thirty in New York, one ends up at the luncheon table.

Gabriel Uhlein beamed impartially on his two hosts. 'We've already had the pleasure of meeting Mrs Lancer, you know,' he said cheerfully. 'I don't think we'll have any trouble working out something for the Friends of the Aged Mariner.'

George Lancer blinked once, then expressed polite confidence in Target Associates. Under cover of his menu Thatcher reflected appreciatively on Lucy's tactics.

The first ten minutes passed in an exchange of commonplaces. They all deplored the trials of Target Associates and Brunswick College, although, as Lancer pointed out, Target hadn't lost a penny. They all extolled the talents of Lyman Todd, although, as Gabe Uhlein pointed out, he was a wee bit old-fashioned in his approach to fund raising. They all refused to believe that Elliot Patterson could have murdered Carter Sprague, although, as John Thatcher pointed out, this conclusion simply compounded the confusion.

Marian Knightley confined herself to short statements of agreement or disagreement, delivered calmly and concisely. But while Lancer and Thatcher were still searching for an opening, it was she who signalled the end of the first round.

'I expect your wife told you that Gabe spent last Saturday night at our cottage in Saxe, Mr Lancer,' she said coolly.

George Lancer, blandly buttering his breadstick, was equally cool. A lifetime of Lucy made other women child's play. 'Yes, she did. I understand the police heard you had someone there and thought it might be Alec Baxter.'

'They don't think so any more.' Was there a slight undertone of mockery in her voice? 'Gabe called them up this morning to explain.'

As if on cue, Uhlein took up the tale. 'It seemed advisable that there should be no misunderstanding. You can't be too careful in a murder investigation, and they might have gotten the idea that I drove straight to New York after the football game.'

'They might,' Thatcher said dryly.

'But now everything is cleared up.' Uhlein rubbed his hands together briskly. 'They were very understanding about the whole thing.'

Target Associates had wasted no time getting its story on record. But had they given the police all the facts?

'It must have been a relief to them to know they could cross off Alec Baxter. I suppose you told them about the carbon copy that came to light yesterday?' As he said this, Thatcher hoped that Lucy's familiarity with the letter had been gained by orthodox methods.

Apparently it had. No one reeled back in shock. On the contrary, Uhlein received the question in a welcoming spirit.

'Indeed, I did. Of course, they were suspicious at first. But they called Gethsemane right away, and that laid their doubts to rest.'

'You know what they found out?'

Uhlein became conspiratorial. 'I confess I was so intrigued by the situation, I asked them to call me back. If they hadn't, I think I would have called Gethsemane myself. But there was no need.'

'And Baxter is there?' asked George Lancer, a last-ditcher by nature.

'Everything was confirmed.' Uhlein's smile could not have been broader. 'Alec Baxter is there in residence, he's in the preliminary stages of entry to the order. And one of the references he supplied originally was from Elliot Patterson. Amazing, isn't it? Not the kind of thing you expect from artists.'

Marian Knightley demurred. 'It's not really what you expect from anyone, is it? I mean someone who has made an adult life in the outside world. It would be different if you were talking about a boy who went straight into a seminary.'

'But was it a surprise to you and your husband?' asked Thatcher. 'We heard that you had seen Baxter as late as May.'

'Yes, it was a complete surprise. He didn't say a word about this. But then, I imagine this is one of the decisions that people don't talk about. It must be too private for discussion. And – ' Mrs Knightley smiled slightly – 'he wouldn't expect me to be sympathetic.'

Thatcher could easily believe that Mrs Knightley would look on sudden retreat to the monastery as a confession of failure. He could not visualize her airing her views.

'Would you have tried to talk him out of it?' he asked with genuine interest.

Gabe Uhlein guffawed. 'Try talking one of these bohemian artists out of anything! They've had a lifetime of doing exactly what they want. I met Baxter through one of the advertising agencies we work with.' Uhlein paused for recollection. He had relaxed his manner, now that his disclosures to the police were no longer in the spotlight. 'He was the kind to pick and choose the work he'd do. And when he snaffled a grant from somewhere, he just packed up and went to Paris. Hell! He even insisted on living in some fleabag of a place so that he only had to do a minimum of work. Oh, I know, Marian, Steve says that he had a great future. But no one could have talked him out of doing anything. He wasn't in the habit of listening. So it would have been useless to try to talk him out of going into a monastery. And, if he ever decided he wants to leave, they won't be able to talk him out of that, either.'

Thatcher reflected that if Alec Baxter were only an acquaintance, he had sparked a disproportionate response in Uhlein. But maybe this was simply the standard reaction of conformity to any kind of deviation from the norm. Persistently Thatcher returned to his original question and to Marian Knightley.

'But would you try in a case like this?'

Mrs Knightley took a moment to reorient herself. Then she shook her head.

'I don't believe in interfering,' she said almost fiercely. 'Gabe makes it sound like a piece of self-indulgence, but I don't believe in that at all. A man must be terribly troubled to make that decision, more troubled than anyone realizes. He probably agonizes alone for months, maybe years, and those around him don't begin to understand what he's going through. It's not a time for gratuitous and clever interference from outsiders. Problems always look easy to people who don't understand them.'

'Oh, now, I didn't mean – ' Uhlein began to protest, but Mrs Knightley swept over him as she continued her defence of Alec Baxter:

'I don't begin to know what prompts a man to enter a monastery. I suppose it's some kind of idea of spiritual freedom. It's not my idea, but what difference does that make? Who am I to have ideas on the subject for someone else? I do know that, for a grown man who is committed to another way of life, the pressures that make him reverse in his tracks have to be so compelling that his whole existence must seem one long suffocation.'

'One long suffocation!' Uhlein's instinct to apologize had died aborning. 'He does what he wants, when he wants, how he wants. He should try the life some of us lead!'

Marian Knightley had lost her earlier heat. 'The trouble with you, Gabe,' she said lightly, 'is that if you don't understand something, you decide it doesn't exist.'

In the silence that followed, Thatcher lifted his coffee cup and toasted her:

'Alec Baxter is fortunate in his friends.'

Mrs Knightley's relaxation was complete. As she raised her cup in reply, there was a distinct twinkle in her eye:

'Alec Baxter deserves what he gets!'

21. Independent Work

In the taxi it developed that this inconclusive exchange had helped Lancer reach a conclusion.

'We're wasting time,' he decided, glancing at his watch. 'We have to get back to fundamentals.'

With instinctive caution, Thatcher agreed that this was sound procedure and invited elaboration. In his experience, getting back to fundamentals was easier in theory than in practice.

George complied. 'Just look at this list of names Elliot Patterson left behind. Including Baxter's. Or these reports of an unidentified man up at the Knightleys'. Now, what's come of them? Absolutely nothing. They've only obscured the major issue, which remains that Elliot Patterson has disappeared and has taken a $50,000 bond with him. That's what we should concentrate on. The rest ...' He broke off and shrugged, possibly in comment on their recent luncheon.

Thatcher sympathized. Gabe Uhlein and Mrs Knightley had provided him with considerable food for thought, but from the Brunswick point of view demanded of George, they had not, strictly speaking, been profitable. Nevertheless he felt obliged to enter an objection.

'You're not forgetting the murder of Carter Sprague, are you, George? I think that it should be included in the ... er ... fundamentals.'

'Of course, of course,' said Lancer with dissatisfaction. 'But, as I was saying, tracking down this Alec Baxter has merely wasted our time. What do we have? Baxter has turned religious. He has absolutely nothing to do with Elliot Patterson, with the theft, or with Carter Sprague's murder. This is simply an example of what I mean. Obviously, we can spend weeks finding answers to questions – and none of them will do us any good! We have to get back to the bare bones of the situation. Cut away the nonessentials!'

'I don't know that I agree with you,' said Thatcher. It would be unkind to add that cutting away the nonessentials left pitiably little information. Nor did he agree with George about the wastefulness of their forays. Marian Knightley's comments on Alec Baxter, like Patterson's abstraction of test scores, like Gabe Uhlein's visit to Brunswick College, were meaningless and irrelevant at the moment. But so was each individual piece of a jigsaw puzzle. Somewhere in the back of Thatcher's consciousness was the feeling that this whirlwind of isolated facts was beginning to take shape of some sort.

'Sorry, what was that, George?'

They had reached the Sloan. As Lancer paid off the driver and joined Thatcher, he repeated himself.

'I said, that's what I told Armitage. He called about Sally Patterson's selling off everything for cash. Seemed to feel it was important.'

He stood aside to let a substantial matron precede him into the Sloan's lobby, and Thatcher responded to the faint question in his voice.

'I suppose one could say it was suspicious,' he said. 'Mrs Patterson may be planning to join her husband. But if that's the case, we misinterpreted her completely. I admit that it's possible that we did, since I didn't pretend to understand her thought processes. Still, I'd be surprised...'

This was enough for George.

'Exactly,' he said with renewed assurance. 'I told Armitage that the police are the people to keep an eye on Mrs Patterson. After all, the poor woman has plenty of problems.'

Since Lancer was, at heart, surprisingly sentimental about such things as devoted wives, he dropped the subject and with some asperity said, 'I repeat, we should forget these detours. Get back to the essentials. Do you know what's happening up at Brunswick? Lyman called, and says that the situation is extremely bad. Says that the only thing keeping parents from withdrawing the students is the draft. If we don't get to the bottom of things, Brunswick may be irreparably harmed.'

Thatcher was leading the way to his own office. 'It's surprising what colleges can rise above,' he remarked.

But George was not listening to him. 'Good heavens! Lucy! Still here?'

There was no dissimulation about Lucy Lancer now. She and Miss Corsa, thick as thieves, were openly bubbling with triumph.

'Aha!' announced Lucy.

Miss Corsa was more informative.

'We found him, Mr Thatcher! We found him!'

George Lancer was bereft of speech. Thatcher hastened to enlighten him. 'No, George, not Elliot Patterson. Father Martin, I take it.'

Fortunately both Miss Corsa and Lucy were too pleased with themselves to register the tepidity of the response.

'I finally called the Cardinal's office,' Miss Corsa said with a militant gleam. 'And we finally discovered Father Jonas Martin. He's only been at St Patrick's for eight months . . .'

'And I was just waiting to see what your lunch was like,' said Lucy enigmatically.

'We decided,' Miss Corsa said with heavy significance, 'that it would be best if Mrs Lancer talked to Father Martin. Father Martin specializes in converts.'

Only, Thatcher reflected, a faithful Daughter of the Church could pack quite so much meaning into such a simple sentence.

'And so, George, I've just had a long talk with Father Martin. He was perfectly charming.'

George shook free from his initial disappointment and managed to sound receptive if not over-hopeful. 'Did he know anything about Elliot Patterson?'

'No,' Lucy told him. 'But he did know Alec Baxter. In fact . . .'

In fact, it had been Father Jonas Martin to whom Alex Baxter had first taken spiritual doubts, then religious uncertainties, and finally a profound new religious awareness that required a change of affiliation. There had been, Lucy reported, conferences, confessions, joint prayers, instruction.

Was that a smirk on Miss Corsa's face? Thatcher would never know. He turned his attention back to Lucy.

'And he knew all about the Brothers of Silence,' she was continuing. 'He said that as soon as he realized how sincere Alec

Baxter was, he urged him to consider a religious vocation. Father Martin admits that at first he was hesitant, because he thought Baxter might just be another one of the lawyers.'

'Lawyers?' asked Thatcher, fascinated.

Lucy lowered her voice. 'Apparently, John, Wall Street lawyers are notorious for being tempted to convert. Usually at lunchtime. Father Martin says that all the churches get them.'

While Thatcher was digesting this, Lucy continued: 'But Father Martin said that he was soon convinced that Alec Baxter had a soul in need of help. He said,' she quoted, with a telling look at Miss Corsa, 'he said he grew convinced that a monk's habit was more suitable garb for Alec Baxter than a business suit.'

This time there was no doubt. Miss Corsa – and probably the spiritual leader of her parish – may have shared the mansion with Father Martin, but they were in another room altogether.

Lucy had leaned back, waiting for the agreeable sensation of dispelling ignorance.

Thatcher tried to oblige. 'Yes, the police have confirmed that Baxter's at the monastery.'

Since this was an anticlimax, he cast back in memory. 'Baxter was originally an Episcopalian, wasn't he?'

'Yes,' said Lucy. 'His father was a minister.'

Thatcher persevered.

'I don't suppose Baxter mentioned Patterson?' he asked hastily, simply to give pleasure.

'Not once,' said Lucy promptly. 'I asked, of course. But Father Martin has never even heard of Elliot Patterson. He said he's too busy to read the papers.'

'All those lawyers,' Thatcher murmured.

But George was not deflected. 'Fine, fine!' he said absently. 'Now, I have an idea, Miss Corsa. Will you call Tolliver's department? Ask him to circularize our correspondent banks about any $50,000 bearer bonds that have been cashed or pledged as collateral in the last week.' Turning to Thatcher he said. 'It occurs to me that possibly alteration may be involved ...'

'George!'

Lancer, Thatcher saw with admiration, did not try to counterfeit incomprehension. Reasonably, he pointed out that since Alec Baxter was now a Brother of Silence and had left the world – including Elliot Patterson and missing bonds – behind him, he had ceased to be of interest. And so, too, had Father Martin. He remembered to thank Miss Corsa for her efforts. He only regretted that they had come to nothing.

Mrs Lancer spoke for both the ladies. Looking bitterly at her husband, she said, 'It's at moments like this that I have to remind myself that, under that expensive tailoring, George, you too have a soul worth saving.'

'Now Lucy,' said her much-tried husband. 'Stop that!'

If disappointment following upon disappointment was the lot of one Brunswick alumnus, two others were experiencing more positive rebuffs.

Jonathan Hughes sat on the sofa in his living-room, glaring at Jim Dunlop and Neil Marsden. In the wing chair by the fireplace, Mrs Hughes was upright, ready to fly to the defence of her young, summon the police or scream, as necessary.

'I don't know why you've come,' she said indignantly. 'Jonathan is certainly not going to attend Brunswick. No power on earth ...'

A trying week had eroded Neil Marsden's smoothness. 'We understand that, Mrs Hughes,' he said with a snap. 'As I told Mr Hughes ...'

Mrs Hughes turned tearful eyes on her son. 'I don't know why your father isn't here!'

Ignoring her, young Hughes confronted his inquisitors with a mixture of hostility and defensiveness. 'Look, I've told the police everything. Sure, I was with Carter Sprague all afternoon. But after he cut out, I don't know what he was up to.'

Before Marsden could retort, Dunlop said hastily, 'We're not asking about Carter Sprague, Jonathan. We want to talk about that last day at the Brunswick Club. About Mr Patterson ...'

'Christ!' It was an exaggerated show of patience worn thin.

'Listen, I'm fed to the gills with this crap! What was in the folders! What colour were they! What kind of labels did they have! Who the hell cares?'

Mrs Hughes was reactivated.

'Jonathan, I will not tolerate language like that! Your father...'

Defeated, Dunlop looked at Marsden. Drawn and pale though Neil was, his eyes glittered with purpose. But Jim Dunlop was by no means sure what that purpose was.

Nor was he sure when they left the Hughes home. But he was a good deal more tired. Moreover, he had serious troubles of his own.

'Look, Neil,' he said abruptly as they left the Long Island Railroad and emerged at Thirty-fourth Street, 'I don't know what good this tracking down of the kids is doing. What's the point of hammering at them about what Elliot Patterson had on the table? Hell, if we don't remember, what do you expect to get out of them?'

Marsden muttered something under his breath and without apology grasped Dunlop's arm and steered him into the bar they were passing.

'Look,' he said tautly after they had ordered. 'Don't you realize that we've got to get to the bottom of this thing, fast? There's already been one murder – because somebody saw something. We've got to find out if anybody else saw anything.'

Dunlop inspected him. Then, with care, he said, 'I'm keeping my nose clean.'

Marsden looked up so quickly that he spilled his drink.

'What precisely does that mean?' he asked with a venomous edge.

Dunlop looked at him steadily. 'Exactly what I said. I'm signing off. No more errands for Ralph. No more interviews with you. The best thing for me to do is get as far from Elliot Patterson and Carter Sprague and the whole mess as I can.'

For a moment they were silent. Then, with curious emptiness, Marsden said, 'I'm sorry, Jim. But you can't. You're in this up to your neck, just like the rest of us. And we've got to clear it up before it gets worse. Much worse! No, you can't quit now. I'll line up that Fursano kid, and when I track him down, I'm going to talk to him. And Jim, you be there. For your own sake!'

He was staring into his second drink.

Was Neil Marsden pleading or threatening? Without another word, Jim Dunlop tossed a bill on the table and left. He was reluctant to remain longer with Neil Marsden. But he was also reluctant to return to Sutton Place. He could remember when going home was the high point of the day, when he often forgot errands in his eagerness. Now he dragged, stopping for unnecessary cigarettes, almost stopping for another drink.

Marsden had been right about one thing, Dunlop thought. He was in it up to his neck.

Lou was in the kitchenette. She did not emerge when she heard him.

'I'm home!' he called unnecessarily. Only domestic sounds replied.

Dunlop tossed down the carton of cigarettes and proceeded into the tiny living-room. He was staring at the bar – a bottle of gin and a bottle of Scotch – when Lou appeared.

'I was thinking about having a drink,' he said.

She looked at him as if he were a stranger.

'Ralph Armitage called,' she said.

Elaborately Dunlop kept his attention on the bottles. 'I guess I will. Have one with me, Lou. It will do us both good.'

'He said that a friend of his in a bank up in Boston called. He thinks that Elliot Patterson's bond was cashed in Portsmouth, New Hamphire. Just before Homecomiing Weekend.'

Without reply, Dunlop poured two healthy drinks.

'Jim?'

'Drink up, honey,' he said with a sudden unconvincing grin.

She ignored this. 'Jim, Ralph wants you to go up to Portsmouth. To check this out.'

'Me? All by myself? Without tagging behind Armitage or Marsden?' Dunlop was mocking. 'Great! That's my first promotion.'

'He can't make it himself,' Lou said, averting her eyes.

With a show of indifference, Jim toasted her. 'Drink up!

Well, I'm not going. I'm through running around. To hell with them all! If Elliot Patterson's bond got cashed in Portsmouth, somebody else can go up and do the dirty work. Not Jim Dunlop. I've had it!'

She turned quickly, but not quickly enough to conceal tears.

Alone in the tiny, once-warm living-room, Jim looked at her untouched drink. First he was growing up. Now he was floating back in time to the little boy, alone, afraid of the dark, afraid. Out there, somewhere, terrible things were happening.

Suddenly Jim Dunlop put down his drink.

Out there, somewhere, a noose was tightening.

22. Visiting Lecturers

By now the Brunswick Admission Committee had ceased to exist for all practical purposes. The disappearance of Elliot Patterson with Mrs Curtis's $50,000 bond had left the Committee struggling to maintain a semblance of normality. But the murder of Carter Sprague, the obvious interest of the police, and the endless destructive publicity featuring one actionable heading, WHAT DO THESE THREE KNOW?, had exploded all such pretension.

The office of the president, phoning from Coburg, glibly rattled off specifics of the chaos obtaining in Brunswick admissions in three separate calls. 'So we've decided,' said the voice nervously, 'that our New York interviews will be handled by one of the deans. Of course, we're grateful . . .'

Marsden and Dunlop were apathetic. Only Ralph Armitage retorted that this looked like a lack of faith.

'No, no!' Coburg protested. 'But be reasonable, Ralph! Things are such a damned mess!'

There was no disputing this.

But even without a formal reason for being, the Committee found itself still united, this time by growing tension, by anxiety, even by fear.

'We've got to find Elliot!'

At one time or another, Neil Marsden, Jim Dunlop and Ralph Armitage each muttered this to himself.

And each in his own way and for his own reasons tried to do just that. If each man wanted to act independently, he wanted also to know what the others were doing. It was an alliance born of necessity.

Ralph Armitage, with stolid realism, appointed himself clearing-house for information, passing on developments and trying to impose order. He listened to Neil Marsden's plans to interview the remaining boys, for example. If his only answer to Marsden was a noncommittal shrug, he at least went on to block attempted interference by Whelby Kitchener.

'But, Ralph, this is upsetting the applicants,' Kitchener protested. 'Mrs Hughes called me to complain.'

'They're none of them applicants any more, Whelby,' Armitage reminded him. 'Leave Neil alone. If he comes up with anything, he's promised to let me know, first thing.'

With Jim Dunlop, Armitage had his troubles. But he had ultimately dragooned the young man to a Saturday trip to Portsmouth, New Hampshire, in order to check out the $50,000 bond that had emerged there.

'After all, Jim,' he had said, 'I'm the one who's been doing the running around until now. I'm the one who got on to Alec Baxter's place, I'm the one who prodded the banks on these bonds, I'm the one who – '

'Yes, Ralph. I admit you've done most of the work.'

'I can't get away myself, tomorrow. But I've got things set up so that someone in the collateral loan division will be available.'

'All right. All right,' Dunlop had said wearily, like a man worn down by persistent cajolery. He was ashamed to admit, even to himself, that he was going to Portsmouth because the alternative was a Saturday alone with his wife.

For himself, Armitage had reserved the problem of Sally Patterson. He had travelled the length of the subway system to an obscure shop in Brooklyn called 'Consett's Coins & Stamps' in order to interview her brother-in-law; he had been soundly snubbed by her broker; he had contacted every conceivable source of information about her movements and her intentions.

Therefore, two things happened at approximately the same time on Monday morning. Jim Dunlop, freshly returned from New Hampshire (Sunday alone with Lou had seemed no more attractive than Saturday), reported that the Portsmouth bond was the wrong bond.

And Gabriel Uhlein, primed by progress reports from Armitage, was not the least bit surprised to discover that his first visitor of the morning was going to be Sally Patterson. Carefully tuning down his ebullience in deference to the circumstances, he went forward to meet her, his expression grave, his voice lowered, his arm slightly outthrust to usher her to a chair.

'My dear, I'm so glad you've come to see us. Marian has told me how brave you've been.'

This mode of address was far more congenial to Sally than Uhlein's normal cavortings. 'Marian has been very kind.'

Perhaps it would have been better if she had not sounded quite so much like a kindergarten teacher awarding a gold star; still, it promised to be the first exchange between Gabe and Mrs Patterson where they were both operating on approximately the same wavelength.

Gabe settled behind the desk with the feeling that this might not be as bad as he had expected.

'You must tell us if there is anything we can do to help. I know it's hard, my dear, but you must begin to think in terms of long-range plans. For the sake of the children.'

Uhlein was proud of that last line. He had discovered, like many others before him, that it made palatable a practical turn to the conversation which would otherwise have been barbarously premature.

Sally nodded approvingly and said, 'I'm pleased that you agree with me. I felt that as long as Elliot's disappearance was unexplained, the right thing to do was to keep his home going. But now that's pointless.'

Uhlein frowned. In his view the disappearance was still unexplained. Did Sally know something? He doubted it. He had listened to the Armitage theory of a Patterson conspiracy and had branded it nonsense. It was more likely that Sally, now that her husband's disappearance was avowedly premeditated and with malice aforethought, required no further explanation.

But Uhlein was surprised at her behaviour. He would have expected her to treat Elliot's defection in much the same light that knowing mothers treat running-away-from-home in adventurous small boys. Elliot would show up, ashamed, tired, and possibly in need of a Band-Aid – but more appreciative than ever of the security and comforts of a good home. Well, maybe Sally was more realistic than he had anticipated. But Uhlein didn't like the way the house in Rye had become *his* home.

'Naturally, I can't make any plans until I know what my resources are,' Sally continued. 'I have been going through Elliot's desk at home. In a general way, I was already familiar with its contents.'

'How wise of you!' Now that the conversation was openly monetary, Gabe allowed himself a small measure of rubicund joviality. 'There's nothing like having a good, firm groundwork for your plans.'

Sally accepted the tribute unmoved. 'And I have come across this item about Elliot's pension plan.'

'I'm glad you brought that up, Sally,' Gabe said heartily. It was his stock phrase when he saw troubled waters ahead. If Gabe had been afloat in a small craft and the weather forecaster predicted a typhoon, the words would have come automatically to his lips. 'Now, with some of our Target wives, I might have to explain about our pension plan, but you have always taken such an intelligent interest in Elliot's affairs that I'm sure you know the plan is under the control of the pension trustees.'

Sally might not be the Einstein *manqué* that she thought, but she was far from being a fool. Her lips tightened.

'The money in that plan was put in by Elliot,' she ground out.

'Not entirely, my dear.'

'Elliot's right to it has vested.'

Uhlein expelled a soft sigh. That one word told him more

than Sally realized. He now knew that she had consulted a lawyer, a lawyer who had told her exactly what Target's lawyer had told him. Sally had no right to Elliot's share in the plan. Characteristically, she had jettisoned the lawyer and was preparing to bulldoze ahead on her own.

'Exactly.' Gabe beamed at Sally. 'I can't tell you how much easier it is when I talk with someone who understands these intricacies. Let me just review the situation briefly.'

By now Sally looked definitely mulish. 'Go ahead,' she said.

'Elliot joined our plan when he first came to Target and made a contribution monthly towards his retirement. That contribution was matched by Target Associates. But for the first ten years Elliot had no right to Target's share of the deposits. That is to say, if Elliot had left for other employment, he could have taken only his own share with him. Now, at the end of ten years, his right vested, as you yourself said.'

'That's right. And now it all belongs to Elliot.'

'Oh, yes. Elliot could do as he liked with it – leave it as a pension for his old age, or withdraw it. Or, of course, it would be payable to his widow upon death.'

Sally was finding Uhlein more intelligent than her lawyer. Her voice was more encouraging: 'That's exactly what I said. But I don't want to leave it in as an old-age fund. I want to take it out now. You just said that could be done after the first ten years.'

'I said that, under the terms of the plan, *Elliot* could take the money out. And he is the only one who can.'

'But that's absurd. I'm Elliot's wife!'

'I'm afraid you would have to be his widow to have any rights.'

Sally didn't believe it for a minute. 'Elliot isn't here. And you know perfectly well that he intended me to have everything. That's clear from the way he signed everything over to me. I'm sorry to say it, but I do feel you're being unreasonable. Surely you must understand that an unusual situation like this calls for flexibility.'

'I really am sorry, my dear, but it's not in my power to make any decisions or exercise any flexibility,' Uhlein replied. 'The pension document is perfectly clear. The only ones who have the power to pay out that money are the trustees of the fund, and they are bound by the terms of the plan.'

'It's outrageous! I knew you might try to make difficulties about the Target contribution, but to try to keep all the money for yourself is unbelievable!'

'The trustees will be keeping all the money for Elliot.' To his credit, Gabe Uhlein had not moderated his cordiality by one jot.

Sally settled down to go to work on him. Her self-assurance was immense. In her experience, her tactics always worked when she really wanted something. It did not occur to her that she had never asked the PTA or the Garden Club for a substantial sum of money.

At the end of fifteen minutes she was beginning to realize that she had met her match in this cheery little man. Indeed, the outcome of the duel went a long way towards explaining the success of Target Associates.

'No, the only thing I can advise is that you approach the trustees, Sally. Although I think I know what they'll say. Wait seven years and then, if Elliot hasn't appeared, you can have him declared legally dead. After all, it's not a question of your immediate needs.'

'Waiting seven years is out of the question!' snapped Sally, who seemed more annoyed by this suggestion than by the outright refusals which had preceded it. 'How do I know what will happen in seven years? I have no intention of letting this situation drag on and on.'

Uhlein let his inquiry show.

'I am certainly not going to be drawn into something not of my making. It wouldn't be fair to the children, and it wouldn't be fair to me. Whatever Elliot has done, he has done for reasons of his own. He left me out, and I intend to stay out!'

'What do you think Elliot is up to?'

'I don't know and I don't care! But *he* is going to pay the price for it, not me!'

'But things may clear up,' Uhlein reminded her.

'You sound just like my brother-in-law!' Sally's tone did not imply a compliment. 'I suppose you both mean well; you just don't understand the situation. Bill tells me not to make any hasty decisions. As if staying in Rye weren't the result of a decision, like anything else. I could be trapped simply because I let things go for twenty-four hours too long.'

'Trapped?' Uhlein was genuinely at sea.

'I am going to sell the house and move myself and the children to someplace where no one has heard of Elliot Patterson, as fast as I can.'

'Well, I can see how that might be something you want to do eventually, although I think you'll find that the furore over Elliot will die down. What I don't understand is all this rush. It's scarcely three weeks since Elliot disappeared. What if he turns up?'

She took a deep breath:

'That's what I'm afraid of.'

'Afraid of? I thought you wanted Elliot back.'

'I wanted my life back. The life I've worked for all these years. And what chance of that do I have? If Elliot walked in tomorrow, he'd be arrested in a riot of publicity. Is that what I've worked for all these years? Is that what I've raised my children for?'

Gabriel Uhlein ducked the question. 'I'm sure there's some explanation for Mrs Curtis's bond. I can't believe that Elliot – '

'Bond!' Sally choked over the word. 'Elliot will be arrested for murder!'

'Oh, now, it may not come to that.'

'You have to face facts,' Sally said defiantly. 'I can't afford to deceive myself by wilful blindness. And the fact is that Elliot will be arrested for murder.'

Sally was writing off Elliot with a vengeance.

Natural perversity led Gabe to support him. 'But what if he didn't do it?'

'What makes you think that?'

'Elliot wouldn't,' said Gabe weakly.

'How do I know what Elliot would or wouldn't do? He's

destroyed everything we've built together. It's not my fault it's gone, but it would be silly to pretend that it's still there.'

Uhlein could scarcely say that, in that case, he would have preferred a slightly sillier woman. But he could say something else.

'Then you don't want to be around when Elliot is caught?' The words were hard and blunt.

'So that people can expect me to stand behind him? So that I can pretend to be a loyal wife to a man who has nothing to do with the husband I was married to?' Sally's voice quickened so that whole phrases blurred together. 'I won't, I won't! I must get away!'

Suddenly Uhlein realized that Sally was afraid of herself. She knew that without the protection of distance and anonymity she could not resist the pressures to play Rye's casting.

From the point of view of Target Associates, that was all to the good. Sally would not put up an extended battle over the pension plan. But, as Uhlein escorted a temporarily silenced Sally to the hallway, he was graver than usual. He stood for a moment watching Sally march to the elevator, but he was not thinking of her. He was reviewing the events of the past few days – not the open events but the little reactions he had noted, the silences and sudden smiles which his shrewd antennae had dutifully recorded. Then he came to a decision.

When he turned, he did not go back to his own office. Instead, he marched with new firmness to Marian Knightley's.

Entering, he assured himself that they were alone, closed the door, seated himself directly in front of the desk and said, 'Marian, I think it's time we had a talk.'

Marian Knightley believed in facing facts just as strongly as Sally Patterson. She laid down her pen, took in the situation with one swift look, and nodded silent agreement.

'Yes, Gabe. But prepare yourself for a shock.'

Marian Knightley began to speak slowly. She kept her tone studiously neutral, her eyes firmly fixed on the desk top, as if she wanted Gabe to receive her information free from any taint of bias or suggestion. Perhaps she hoped to keep all emotion out of the situation.

If so, she failed.

As she spoke, Gabriel Uhlein first became very red, then almost white. A few incoherent syllables emerged, but when she halted questioningly to invite comment, he waved her on. With the next piece of data, he began to sputter cholerically.

'But, then you mean . . .? And he was doing this while he was at Target?'

Marian Knightley left no room for doubt. 'I'm afraid so, Gabe.' At last she looked at him squarely.

'And you expect me to go along?'

Marian did not resort to any evasions about doing what he thought was best. Her answer was totally uncompromising.

'Yes. Yes, Gabe, I do.'

For a moment their eyes locked.

Then Gabe Uhlein went off into peal after peal of wild laughter.

23. Please Read Instructions Carefully

John Putnam Thatcher was not laughing aloud. But he was quietly enjoying a richly deserved day at the Sloan Guaranty Trust, terrorizing everybody unwise enough to cross his path. With unwonted brutality, he interjected into the debates of the Investment Committee a scathing reminder to Walter Bowman of the red ink produced by recent Research Department recommendations. When Bowman's ancient enemies from International Division looked pious, Thatcher pounced on them:

'Let me put it this way,' he said astringently. 'There may be money to be made, but I do not propose to let this bank risk millions of dollars solely because you see – for reasons that still elude me – a high degree of political stability in Chile, Greece and Ghana!'

After bringing the Investment Committee to its knees, Thatcher proceeded to rout George C. Lancer over lunch. 'George, I've come around to your point of view!'

Alerted by Thatcher's relish, Lancer looked up inquiringly.

Thatcher continued. 'These attempts to shore up Brunswick College are inadequate. What we need at this juncture of affairs is a grand gesture. Why don't you give them a new dormitory?'

George choked slightly over his onion soup. Nevertheless he might have taken this seriously if Thatcher had not felt inspired to add, 'A show of confidence, George! Something on the order of Morgan buying!'

He referred to a dramatic incident in 1929. With pardonable indignation Lancer pointed out that he, like Thatcher, had lived through the succeeding débâcle on Wall Street. Then firmly he discussed the Sloan's new bank letter.

Such a morning could not fail to refresh. John Thatcher had been on the receiving end of too much discomfort lately. It is always more blessed to give than to receive. True, Brunswick College was the author of most of his recent trials. So, in a way, Walter Bowman and International Division were innocent victims. But both Walter Bowman and International Division were sure to rise up and smite him before the year was out. There was no harm in being beforehand in these things.

Miss Corsa, on the other hand, had not been designed to be an innocent victim. She greeted her employer's return to his own desk and responsibilities with approval suggesting that his recent derelictions had been a selfish search for worldly pleasure. Then she produced a large pile of documents requiring Thatcher's attention, declared herself ready to take dictation whenever needed, promised to intercept phone calls, and withdrew. Thatcher was left in no doubt: dealings with Lucy Lancer had enabled Miss Corsa to add to the already long list of his shortcomings.

He was at his own desk ready for his own work. For precisely twelve minutes he continued this performance. Then, without being quite aware of the transition, he found himself swivelled around, staring out the grimy window at a lowering sky.

Thinking about Elliot Patterson.

This did not surprise him. As far as he was concerned, Brunswick College could minister to its own. These small select colleges were always prating about the value of a liberal education through the thick and thin of life. Well, here was an acid test.

Thatcher shook his head. Carter Sprague? In the last analysis, Carter Sprague could be left to the police. Sooner or later they would find a witness, a fingerprint, a button – and a murderer. They were paid to think about bloodstained young bodies. He was not.

And his initial sympathy with the put-upon George? Thatcher, a realist to his core, decided that his supply of sympathy was not unlimited. George had been drawing pretty heavily these days.

But he could not rid himself of a persistent buzz of curiosity about Elliot Patterson. Where had the man gone, and why? This was a nuisance – like the tantalizing tune that dances out of recollection or the name of the ninth Supreme Court Justice. Whether the information is of any use or not, the tickle remains.

Thatcher straightened, suddenly struck with a thought. The quintessence of these intellectual gnats is that they represent misplaced familiar facts, not the great unknowns. No one, after all, is tormented for days wondering what the moon is made of: no, it is always the name of that chap we saw at lunch, the one we met in 1954.

Was Elliot Patterson that – rather than a great X? Were the bits and pieces of information aimlessly afloat concealing a complete explanation that would appear once they fell, or were put, into place?

Methodically, Thatcher began an inventory of what was known about Elliot Patterson. He was, or had been, unremarkable, similar in many respects to thousands of the men who churn between suburb and Manhattan. A competent, valued, middle-rank executive at Target Associates.

'But was he?' Thatcher asked himself, recalling Gabe Uhlein and Mrs Knightley. Exactly what had been the currents and cross-currents at Target Associates? At this stage it was not easy to tell.

Well, then, Elliot Patterson had been a devoted father and husband.

Immediately an unbidden Sally Patterson marched into Thatcher's mental line of sight. Sally Patterson in both phases: complete faith in Elliot followed by a rapid sale of assets.

No, even the most uncritical advocate of life in Rye could not claim that Elliot Patterson's domestic happiness was axiomatic.

Thatcher gave a low interior growl. All of this bore out the conclusions of a lifetime. Human beings and the tangles they create are endlessly fascinating, but they do not lend themselves to systematic classification. Thatcher prided himself on never running hard against the possible; facts might be less multifaceted, but they could be manipulated.

Well, then. One afternoon, Elliot Patterson had finished meeting with the Brunswick Admission Committee – Neil Marsden, Ralph Armitage and Jim Dunlop. He had helped interview four young men – Sprague, J. Hughes, D. Younger and Maestro Fursano's offspring. Then, Elliot Patterson had disappeared with Mrs Curtis's – and Brunswick's – $50,000.

There was a hard fact, or rather, a series of hard facts. Nothing slippery or elusive about them. Or was there?

'Hmm,' said Thatcher, running rapidly down a vocal history he had mentally compiled. Voices saying that Mr Patterson was in a hurry. Voices saying that Elliot was so pleased to have Mrs Curtis's bond. Young voices, older voices; sober voices, drunken voices.

'But . . .'

A discreet cough told him that he was not alone. He twirled around. Miss Corsa was present and waiting.

Too old a hand to be embarrassed at being caught in self-colloquy, Thatcher continued.

'You know, Miss Corsa,' he reflected aloud, 'I've just been visited with a strange notion. About Elliot Patterson. The more I think of it, the more I'm convinced that it bears investigation.'

Miss Corsa had already done her bit in the great hunt for Elliot Patterson and his like. She let her eyes rest on the untouched pile of documents reposing on Thatcher's desk. Left to her own devices she could speed them on their various ways, but tribal custom demanded that Mr Thatcher examine them. Miss Corsa was torn between her loyalty to the system and her instinct for efficiency. Thus are the saints tempted. Miss Corsa said nothing.

'What I need,' said Thatcher suggestively, 'is someone to help me for just twenty minutes. Down at the Ivy League Club.'

Outwardly unmoved, Miss Corsa braced herself.

'We could be back quite soon,' Thatcher said.

Miss Corsa had had enough. It was bad enough for Mr Thatcher to be haring off in all directions. Let him entice her away from the Sloan Guaranty Trust, and who knew what might befall the Trust Department?

'What you should do, Mr Thatcher,' she said kindly but firmly, 'is to call Mrs Lancer.'

In reply, he stared at her for quite a long time. Then:

'Lucy! Of course. That's what I was thinking of. By God, Miss Corsa, you are absolutely right!'

Miss Corsa, who had never doubted it, began dialling.

Women, or 'the ladies' as club rules describe them, are not allowed in the Ivy League Club until after five o'clock. Accordingly, when Lucy Lancer swept into the lobby at three o'clock that afternoon, it was with all flags flying.

'Herman! How nice to see you. Mr Thatcher here and I are running upstairs for just a moment. And Franz! I do hope your wife is feeling better? Oh good . . .'

Thatcher, bringing up a poor second, saw that when it came to routing opposition he had much to learn. The issue was never in question. When the Ivy League Club staff was asked to weigh Mrs George C. Lancer against the bylaws, they abandoned the field.

She watched them leave with a discreet smile, then turned to Thatcher.

'Well, here we are, John. Knowing you as I do, I realized that you were not suggesting an elopement – '

'I'm not sure that I take that as a compliment.'

'But now, will you please tell me exactly what you have in mind?' she finished.

'We-ell,' Thatcher temporized. 'I have three separate conversations in mind,' he went on infuriatingly, looking around the big lobby. 'They gave me the beginnings of an idea ... Lucy, I think fate is taking a hand in all this.'

'I do not regard that as an answer,' she told him sternly, but Thatcher had already moved from her side.

For as he spoke, his eye had fallen upon the occupant of the chair near the stairwell. There, in a posture of polite expectancy, was a familiar figure. Two swift steps brought Thatcher to him.

'You're ... now let me see ...?'

'Fursano, sir,' said the young man, jumping to his feet with promptness. He then bestowed a blinding smile on Lucy that caused her, she later admitted, to regret her age and station.

Without hesitation, Thatcher performed introductions and demanded to know the reason for Fursano's presence.

'I'm not quite sure,' the boy replied honestly. 'Mr Marsden and Mr Dunlop want to talk to me.'

'I wonder why?' Thatcher asked. Then, briskly dismissing this further evidence of the incalculability of human beings, he continued: 'Well, you come along with us, will you, Fursano? We can use you.'

Pete was amenable. Thatcher led the way upstairs.

'Now that I have an ally,' said Lucy cheerfully, trotting along obediently, 'I insist on knowing what we're doing. You do too, don't you, Pete?'

Pete did.

'Oh, didn't I mention that?' Thatcher asked. 'We're going up to settle once and for all what has happened to Elliot Patterson.'

There was a brief, respectful silence. Then, with only a slight tremor in her voice, Lucy said, 'We have perfect faith in you, John.'

'Yes, sir!' said Pete Fursano bouncily.

Thatcher grinned and privately hoped that he could prove worthy of his troops.

They arrived at the door of the offices of the New York Brunswick Club, site of the recent deliberations of the

Brunswick Admission Committee. Down a side turning, the quarters of the Pleydell College Club were brightly lit. Upstairs, members of the Tiverton Alumni Association hurried in and out, concerned with the Christmas descent of the Tiverton College Choir. By contrast, the Brunswick Club stood empty and deserted. It was not a matter of neglect, they saw as they entered and Pete Fursano switched on the overhead light. No dust had settled on the waiting-room furniture. There were even fresh flowers in the vases. Nor had the office beyond really been left derelict. Affairs at Brunswick had become so convoluted that, Thatcher knew, platoons of secretaries were coping with correspondence during frenzied mornings, while deans dashed around to placate irate schoolmasters, test-officials and parents. Even as they stood there, the telephone in the inner office erupted, chattered angrily, then flounced back into silence.

'We'll just ignore the telephone,' said Thatcher. That would show Miss Corsa.

'I adore masterful men,' Lucy Lancer said, gracefully settling on the sofa and regarding her companions with benevolence.

No, reality did not shadow the Brunswick Club. Ghosts did. The ghost of a policeman standing guard at the door. The ghost of Elliot Patterson shovelling papers into a briefcase, then walking out into a void.

The ghost of Carter Sprague.

Thatcher looked around for a moment, intercepted a bright expectant glance from Lucy and set about his exorcism.

'Now, Fursano,' he said, turning to the youth looming above him, 'I want you to act as all four of the boys who were here during that last meeting.'

'Right!' said Fursano. 'We're going to reenact the whole thing?'

'Right!' said Thatcher absorbing a certain youthful directness. 'And you, Lucy, you're Elliot Patterson.'

'Right!' she said, immediately adopting an expression of deep seriousness.

'Say, that's good,' said Pete Fursano admiringly.

Thatcher saw that this cast was going to require firm direction.

'And who are you, Mr Thatcher?' asked Pete Fursano with lively and intelligent interest.

'All the rest of them,' said Thatcher vaguely. This was not true. But he was not ready to make any identifications. 'Now then, Patterson and the committee were in the conference room when you boys arrived, weren't they?'

The exceedingly amateur dramatic performance commenced, with young Fursano checking on authenticity as they proceeded.

'Yes! The door was closed!' he yodelled.

Lucy and Thatcher stationed themselves in the conference room.

'I'm Elliot Patterson,' she said, getting into the spirit of things with a busy little frown. 'The committee isn't ready for the boys yet. You're Jim Dunlop, just putting the files back in the office.'

Thatcher was not misled. Lucy's eyes were intelligent too.

In quick, short sentences, Thatcher reproduced their script, culled from remembered accounts by Jim Dunlop, by Neil Marsden, by Ralph Armitage. Together they mimed a series of actions. Then, in response to a muffled yelp of time from outside, Thatcher opened the door.

'Now, Elliot, you and the rest of the committee start talking with the boys. Right, Pete?'

It was right. Lucy settled down once again. Pete Fursano, opposite her, looked eager and alert. In an undertone, he described the disposition of his fellow applicants, together with the rest of the committee.

'And we talked, oh, say, thirty-five minutes,' he said.

'Fine,' said Thatcher. 'I think we can telescope that a little. Now, Pete, you and I leave. This is the point where Carter Sprague stops you, Lucy.'

They had moved to the doorway.

'May I speak to you for a minute, sir?' asked Pete Fursano, so like Carter Sprague that he shocked Thatcher.

The model of the busy man of affairs. Lucy shot a cuff and peered at a heavy wristwatch. 'Well, I'm in a hurry.'

'It won't take a long time, Mr Patterson,' Sprague-Fursano

wheedled. 'You see, I've been wondering if Brunswick is really the right place for me . . .'

'I guess we'd better talk, fella!' Lucy said idiotically.

Fursano emitted an irrepressible guffaw.

'That's too athletic,' said Thatcher critically. 'Patterson was a more . . . er . . . intellectual type.'

Not one whit abashed, Lucy rewrote the speech. 'I see. Yes, for a matter as important as that, Sprague, I think I can spare you some time. Nothing is more important . . .'

With Thatcher standing in the corner, Carter Sprague and Elliot Patterson reentered the waiting-room and resettled themselves, carrying on a lunatic discussion of higher education that could have taught Lyman Todd a lot.

'Then you drop the papers, Elliot,' said Thatcher.

With a grin, Fursano dived to simulate Carter Sprague's ingratiating deference. Lucy was shovelling invisible folders back into an invisible briefcase with altogether unnecessary vigour when the door to the corridor was flung open.

'What the . . . !'

Neil Marsden froze in the doorway, dumbfounded by the tableau.

'Just come inside and stand over there,' said Thatcher impatiently. 'Come in.' The last was to Dunlop, who appeared on Marsden's heel. 'All right, Carter. Now you and Patterson get up and leave the office together' – Lucy and Pete got up, Lucy ostentatiously placing one folder on the table, then hoisting a briefcase which apparently weighed several hundred pounds – 'you go downstairs together, you go out as far as Fifth Avenue, then separate. No, no, that's enough!'

His hero and heroine showed a willingness to push this thing to extremes.

'What's going on?' Neil Marsden demanded furiously. 'What are you doing? We have to talk to Fursano . . .'

Abruptly Lucy ceased being Elliot Patterson and became Mrs George C. Lancer. At her most dauntingly gracious, she said, 'Why, Neil, aren't you feeling well? You don't sound like yourself. Does he, Mr Dunlop?'

Dunlop simply muttered something indistinguishable and took a step backward.

Marsden turned a bright, almost fevered gaze from Lucy to Pete Fursano to John Thatcher.

'What's the matter? I'll tell you what's the matter!' he declared bluntly. 'This is too serious for playing games!'

Thatcher cut in. 'We're not playing games, Marsden. On the contrary.'

Marsden bared his teeth. 'Well, what are you doing?'

Thatcher looked at him almost pityingly. 'We're establishing something that I have suspected for some time. Elliot Patterson did not steal the Curtis file when he left. He did not take the $50,000 bond.'

Dunlop gave an unguarded exclamation that drew Marsden's hot glance.

Lucy Lancer looked at the two newcomers, then at Thatcher. 'Of course,' she said slowly. 'Of course!'

Pete Fursano knit his brows.

But Neil Marsden did not relax. 'To hell with $50,000! For that matter, to hell with Brunswick College! They're not important now – and you know it. Carter Sprague was murdered, Thatcher. Stabbed in the back with a knife. There's a murderer loose. Who cares about the lousy money? We've got to track Elliot Patterson down. That's the only thing that's important now!'

'Take it easy, Neil,' said Jim Dunlop nervously.

Thatcher smiled at them both. 'No, I'm afraid that we can't dismiss the bond. That was the beginning – and the end – of this murder.'

'Theories!' Marsden burst out. 'That's all you've got, theories! We have to find Elliot Patterson! That's what counts!'

Thatcher's voice hardened. 'I agree that we need to verify this theory. And I agree that Elliot Patterson can do it. But don't worry about finding Elliot Patterson. We know where he is.'

He had silenced Neil Marsden and Jim Dunlop. They stared at him.

'We know where Elliot Patterson is?' asked Lucy faintly.

With affection he smiled at her. 'Yes, my dear, we do.'

There was a rumble of noise in the doorway as a latecomer arrived in time to catch these words.

'You mean to say you've finally tracked Elliot down?' Ralph Armitage was struggling for words in his excitement. 'How'd you ... no, that doesn't matter! Listen, what are we waiting for? Tell me where he is – I'll go down and get him. We can talk to him before the cops get their hands on him. And the newspapers. No, I'll go get him and I'll help him keep out of sight for a day or two. We may be able to save something yet ...'

John Putnam Thatcher was no longer smiling.

'I think not, Mr Armitage,' he said with cold emphasis. 'You've done enough already. Be content with it. Stealing $50,000 – and killing Carter Sprague. That's enough for any one man. Leave Elliot Patterson alone.'

24. Final Results Will Be Posted

The State of New Hampshire had reached the same conclusion as John Putnam Thatcher. Ralph Armitage had indeed murdered Carter Sprague. Thereafter a warrant for arrest followed, a phalanx of trial lawyers emplaned for northern New England, trial was set for January, and the remaining participants in the Brunswick drama were free to pick up the fragments of their shattered lives. This activity preoccupied them until late December, when a rain of subpoenas pattered down from the White Mountains and formed the principal topic of conversation during the intermission of the annual Town Hall Christmas concert by the Brunswick Glee Club (in cooperation with the Mount Holyoke Choir).

The Lancers and John Thatcher had joined forces with Neil Marsden and the Dunlops in a corner of the lobby. Swedish and German carols were behind them; English madrigals were yet to come.

'Ralph Armitage, of all people!' Lou Dunlop marvelled. She

was holding her husband's arm affectionately. 'I still don't see why he did it. After all, it all started with Elliot Patterson taking that bond, didn't it?'

'Elliot Patterson didn't take the bond,' Thatcher corrected gently. 'That was the key to the whole situation. Remember, nobody at the Monday meeting of the Admission Committee actually saw it. Elliot Patterson simply announced that he had succeeded in obtaining the bond from Mrs Curtis. Then the Curtis file was returned to the office, along with other folders, by your husband. The next thing we know is that the folder was missing on Thursday afternoon when Whelby Kitchener got access to the file cabinet under police supervision.'

'And that,' Lucy Lancer exclaimed in excitement, 'is where our famous reconstruction comes in.'

In the tension of murder, suspicion and arrest, Neil Marsden had achieved a more relaxed view of the Lancers.

'You scared me to death when I walked in on you,' he confessed. 'I was afraid that everybody was going to concentrate on the bond and forget about Carter Sprague's murder. And it was the murder that I wanted to clear up.'

Thatcher surveyed the curator mildly. 'I suspect that you understood the basis of the mystery all along.'

'I did think that Armitage had stolen the bond,' Neil conceded, 'but it seemed irrelevant to the murder. I was sure *that* hinged on Elliot Patterson's disappearance.'

'You thought Armitage had stolen the bond and you didn't say anything?' George Lancer demanded with a disapproval that would have wilted Marsden two months earlier. 'How did you know?'

Neil Marsden refused to be apologetic. 'Because it wasn't the sort of thing that Elliot would do. But I could see Ralph doing it very easily.'

Lancer dismissed this as frivolity. 'Extraordinary! You didn't have any evidence at all.'

'What does evidence have to do with what I knew about those two? But I was wrong just the same. I didn't connect Ralph with murder.'

'In a way you were right,' Thatcher reflected. 'Armitage was not born to be a criminal. He was an accidental criminal if ever there was one.'

'The bond,' Lancer reminded them. 'This reconstruction that Lucy's so proud of. What did it prove?'

'It proved that Elliot didn't steal the bond,' said Lucy impatiently.

'Well, not quite,' Thatcher modified. 'It proved that he didn't take the Curtis folder. After Mr Dunlop here returned it to the office, Patterson was continually in the presence of the entire Committee until they left. Then we have Carter Sprague's word for it that Patterson did not leave the waiting-room for the office.'

Lancer could be just as impatient as his wife. 'So? You yourself admitted that no one saw the bond. We don't even know whether Patterson brought it to the meeting.'

'Then who removed the Curtis file folder?'

'Is that so important?'

'It's why Carter Sprague was killed. Think for a minute. We know that Elliot Patterson was tidying up his affairs in preparation for a voluntary departure. He was being scrupulously honest in his professional and personal life, right down to reducing his Target Associates accounts to apple-pie order. What then would you expect him to do about the Curtis bond? When he doesn't have time to take it to Kitchener, the man who should have it?'

'Oh!' It was Lucy who leaped in. 'He would give it to some Committee member and ask him to deliver it to Kitchener!'

Thatcher and Lancer spoke almost simultaneously.

'Exactly!' said Thatcher.

'But if the meeting ended with the bond in somebody else's pocket,' Lancer asked, 'then why was the file folder stolen?'

'The explanation for that lies in what we have been told about Patterson. We've heard about his desk at home with everything neatly docketed, we've heard about his attention to detail, we've heard Kitchener praising his meticulous business methods. And what do you think that Elliot Patterson got in exchange for that bond?'

A great light broke on George Lancer. 'Good heavens! How obvious! He got a receipt from Armitage.'

Thatcher grinned. 'Right, George.'

Jim Dunlop slapped his knee. 'My God! Elliot and Ralph were alone before Neil and I showed up at the Committee Meeting.'

'As Carter Sprague told us, when he complained about being forced to wait. They were alone for some time before the two of you' – Thatcher nodded at Neil Marsden and Dunlop – 'arrived. In that ten minutes, Patterson said that he was going out of town and asked Armitage to deliver the bond to Whelby Kitchener. Armitage agreed, and a receipt was given as a matter of course. Then, when you were all shuffling folders around, Patterson announced his coup and casually slipped the receipt into the file.'

'He never said that Ralph had the bond,' Jim Dunlop interjected.

'Why should he? He was announcing a great stroke, accepting congratulations. Nobody was interested in the physical location of the bond.'

'And Ralph decided to steal it then and there? Neil Marsden was incredulous. 'But it wouldn't be safe.'

Thatcher shook his head decidedly. 'By no means. That's what I meant by calling Armitage an accidental criminal. When the meeting ended, Elliot Patterson carried out his disappearance – deplorable, but certainly not illegal. And Ralph Armitage left with a $50,000 bond he had every intention of delivering to Whelby Kitchener. But look what happened. The next day, Armitage is told that Patterson has disappeared.'

'I told him,' Marsden offered. 'In fact, I called him from the reception for the Friends of the Gary during our gouache showing.'

'And how did he take the news?'

'At first, he pooh-poohed my anxiety,' Neil answered. 'Said Elliot was just out of town. Then, when I told him that Sally wasn't the only one who was worried, that Target Associates had the wind up too, *then* he began to take it seriously. In fact, he leaped to the conclusion that Elliot had been embezzling.'

Thatcher almost purred with satisfaction. 'There! You see?'

'I don't know about seeing,' Marsden said stiffly. 'It was exactly the sort of thing Ralph would think of. But, when he told me that Uhlein was calling in the auditors, I had to admit that he might be right.'

'There is the whole situation in a nutshell,' Thatcher announced.

His audience looked at him blankly.

'Armitage was being perfectly logical. Six weeks before disappearing, Elliot Patterson converted all his life insurance with his insurance broker – who was Ralph Armitage. On Monday he tells Armitage he's going out of town. By Tuesday night Armitage has learned from you that his departure is a complete shock to his family and to Target Associates. Armitage leaps to the conclusion that Patterson has stolen millions from Target – a conclusion which receives support when he learns that the auditors are on the job. At that point, he remembers that he has a bearer bond worth $50,000 in his pocket and nobody except Elliot Patterson knows he has it.'

'I can see the temptation.' Jim Dunlop was turning the situation over in his mind. 'It looked perfectly safe.'

'I'll bet it was more than safety,' Marsden said shrewdly. 'Ralph always was a little contemptuous of Elliot. Thought he was too soft, too goody-goody. He would have been furious to think of Elliot getting away with something like that, furious and envious and admiring, all at the same time.'

Thatcher was inclined to agree. 'I think you're right. But don't underestimate the safety factor. When Armitage removed the receipt – and the whole Curtis file – on Wednesday morning, he thought he was committing the perfect reversible crime.'

Lucy's forehead puckered into a frown. 'Reversible? I don't see that, John.'

'He thought the Patterson situation would clarify itself before he was committed. Either Patterson was an embezzler in full flight to Brazil, in which case he had stolen so much money that the bond would fade into insignificance, or he was innocently absent, in which case he would return almost immediately under his own steam. If that happened, Armitage would quietly slip the folder back and deliver the bond to Kitchener.'

Lucy nodded her comprehension. 'He would be safe either way. How very intelligent!'

'It would have been, if it had worked,' said Thatcher dryly. 'What actually happened was that accident in Putnam County. The last thing in the world Armitage wanted was to have the police baying after Patterson for some reason other than theft.' He turned to Lancer. 'You remember how things went, don't you, George? We came back from Rye and the word spread that Elliot Patterson was a hit-and-run driver. The next day you found Armitage white and shaken because the police had put a guard on the Brunswick Committee files. I'd be willing to bet that Armitage had raced around to the Club, intending to restore the Curtis folder. Bear in mind that an embezzling Elliot Patterson probably wouldn't have been caught. He would have been out of the country before the alarm went off. But an Elliot Patterson without money, in panic-stricken flight from a car accident, was bound to be picked up and bound to tell the truth about the bond. So Armitage decides to reverse and gets the shock of his life when he discovers that he can't. While he's still in shock, Whelby Kitchener publicly demands to know if anyone knows about the bond, and Armitage lets the opportunity go down the drain. Before he knows it, his crime is no longer reversible. At first he must have been in an agony of suspense. The Target Associates audit swept away his last hope that Patterson was an embezzler, and he expected the police to find Patterson any minute. But days passed and nothing happened. Armitage began to breathe easily. He hadn't committed exactly the crime he intended, but he had gotten away with it and that was all that mattered. His confidence must have been almost restored by the time of the reunion weekend. Then, when he was least prepared for it, Carter Sprague suddenly emerged as a fullblown threat.'

'But Carter could have proved that Patterson didn't take the folder all along,' Lancer pointed out. 'He'd already been questioned. Why was he suddenly a threat?'

Neil Marsden turned to Jim Dunlop in high satisfaction. 'That's what I thought all along. One of the boys had noticed something and didn't realize its importance.'

'More or less,' Thatcher agreed. 'We were there when the penny finally dropped for Carter Sprague. If we had recognized the significance of what he said that night in the Deke house, we could have prevented a murder.'

'The Deke house?' It was Lucy's turn to be surprised. 'But that poor boy didn't know what he was saying. He was just casting around for anything that would make him the centre of attention.'

Thatcher nodded. 'And he cast around to some purpose. You may not know this, Lucy, but the police tried to find out from Sprague exactly which folders Elliot Patterson had in the waiting-room. This was after they knew he had left the Alec Baxter file in mistake for the folder with the college-admissions scores. The admission folders were buff with green labels and the alumni folders were white with red labels. The police asked Sprague if he remembered anything about white folders versus buff folders, and he said he didn't. Unfortunately they asked him the wrong question.'

Lucy took the point immediately. 'Oh, they shouldn't have concentrated on the colour of the folders. That difference would be much less noticeable than the colour of the labels. Suddenly she broke off with a gasp. 'Red labels! That's what Carter Sprague was talking about! How stupid we were!'

George Lancer was a little slower. 'What are you talking about? Why were we stupid? I don't see ... red labels! Of course!'

Neil Marsden intervened firmly. 'I wasn't there at the Deke house, you know.' A sudden grin made him seem years younger. 'I was otherwise occupied. But the Fursano boy said that they all spent that afternoon discussing the business of the folders.'

'Yes,' Thatcher continued. 'Carter Sprague's attention had been drawn to the entire question of folders and labels. Then, in the Deke house, somebody on the way to the bar began to recite orders. In that list was one item consisting of two Red Labels.'

'What's a Red Label?' Lou Dunlop blushed prettily as everyone turned to look at her.

'A brand of Scotch,' Thatcher explained kindly.

Lou blushed even harder.

Thatcher hurried on. 'Carter, now thinking in terms of labels rather than folders, immediately said that was wrong. The man, thinking that Carter wanted to add his order, changed it to three Red Labels. Then Carter Sprague, right under Ralph Armitage's nose, said loudly and clearly that there was only one Red Label. Carter was very drunk at the time. But Ralph Armitage saw the threat immediately. Elliot Patterson had the Alec Baxter file, and that was the only red-label file that he had. By the next morning Carter, who was a very sharp boy, would have figured out that Elliot Patterson had not left the Ivy League Club with the Curtis folder. The minute the police ceased to be obsessed with the guilt of Elliot Patterson, suspicion would focus on the other members of the committee. Armitage had been to the office to remove the Curtis file. He had made an abortive attempt to restore it. He couldn't afford to have questions asked. He was very busy thinking when he left the Deke house hard on our heels. Then luck played right into his hands when you, Mr Marsden, collapsed at Franklin House.

Marsden's face darkened. 'Luck may have been playing for him, it certainly wasn't playing for me. The police were certain that I sneaked out of Franklin House, went over to the Inn and murdered Carter Sprague.'

'The police must have abandoned that idea very early,' said Thatcher with quiet conviction. 'We should all have recognized the importance of your collapse.'

Dunlop was still sensitive on the subject. 'You weren't the only one they suspected, Neil. They didn't much like the fact that I was the one who promoted the move from the Deke house back to the Inn. They thought I was setting up Sprague.' He smiled reassuringly at his wife and squeezed her hand when she made an involuntary sound of protest. 'Come on, Lou, you half thought so yourself, for a while.'

'I didn't know what to think,' she confessed. 'If you could forget you were married, you could do almost anything!' Then she smiled radiantly. 'But now I realize you didn't really forget. You were just reliving your college days.'

'That's it.'

They were both lying. But they were both happy again, because Lou had learned to live with the idea that she was married to a man who could get drunk at a reunion weekend, and Jim had reconciled himself to the fact that a wife must grow into knowing her husband.

Thatcher hastened to prevent further revelations. He turned to Marsden. 'The police decided you were innocent very soon.'

'Ralph certainly didn't help,' said Marsden bitterly. 'He made me sound as suspicious as possible. After that, I did my damnedest to find out what he was up to.'

'I think he was trying to divert suspicion from himself,' Thatcher mused. 'The police were looking at him closely long before they learned his motive.'

Marsden was doubtful.

Thatcher began to spell it out. 'Ideally, the murderer should have known two things – first, that your room at the Inn would be vacant, and second, that Carter Sprague was at the Inn. How could you have known where Carter Sprague would be? And if you simply seized the opportunity to murder the boy, then why did you leave Franklin House surreptitiously? And how could Mr Dunlop have known that your room would be vacant? But there was no question that Ralph Armitage knew both. I wouldn't be surprised to learn that he engineered the move from the Deke house to the Inn in the first place.'

Jim Dunlop tried to recall the hazy events of that memorable evening. 'He may have,' he finally admitted. 'I think he did say something about the Deke boys wanting the place to themselves when he came back to pick up his car. But I'm almost certain that I was the one who mentioned getting Carter Sprague out of there.'

'He could count on that. You had already sympathized with Lucy's concern over Sprague earlier in the evening. If somebody then said that the night was about to turn into an orgy unsuitable for older graduates, you could be relied on to think it would be even more unsuitable for a teenage boy.'

Jim Dunlop remained unconvinced. He did not appreciate the idea that Armitage had used him as a cat's-paw.

Lou, with a tact that was beginning to develop without conscious volition, turned the conversation. 'And then Mr Armitage didn't have anything to worry about, after he had murdered Carter Sprague?'

'Far from it,' Thatcher retorted grimly. 'The only thing standing between Armitage and the position of number one suspect was the mystery of Elliot Patterson. He set out to capitalize on that immediately. Before the night was out, rumours had started that Patterson was in Coburg.'

Lancer remembered their Sunday-morning breakfast at the president's house. 'Was it Armitage who phoned to say Patterson was in Franklin House?'

'I wouldn't be surprised. He was certainly up very early doing his bit to keep that particular ball rolling.'

Marsden nodded to himself as if some earlier suspicion were being confirmed. 'And he really didn't know where Elliot was?'

'No. That was precisely his problem,' Thatcher said energetically. 'Patterson was now a greater danger than ever to Armitage. He could provide the motive for the murder. Armitage was determined that he should find Elliot Patterson before anybody else did. I doubt if he was very clear in his own mind what he was going to do – whether he was going to try to bargain or resort to murder again. I do know that he was rapidly going to pieces under the hourly suspense, never knowing when he would hear that Patterson was safely locked up in a police cell, out of his reach. That's why he virtually abandoned his business to chase down Patterson.'

Jim Dunlop confirmed this information. 'He did, you know. At the time I was amazed how much running around he was doing. I even compared him unfavourably with you,' the young man said to Neil Marsden. 'He didn't really ask me to do anything except make that trip to Portsmouth when a bond turned up there.'

'And he knew it was the wrong bond,' Thatcher told them. 'For the excellent reason that the right one was in his safety-deposit box.'

Lucy pounced instantly. 'They've actually found the bond, then?'

'Oh, yes. I suppose once Armitage committed murder for it, he couldn't bring himself to destroy it.'

'Well, Mrs Curtis will be happy about that.' Marsden smiled. 'She's probably doing a war dance of triumph.'

A warning buzzer shrilled into the silence as reminder that Elizabethan music was just around the corner. Everybody began to stub out cigarettes and pick up programmes.

'She isn't the only one to come out of this well,' Dunlop reflected, pocketing his wife's cigarette case and lighter. 'I hear that Brunswick's fund raising is going to be handled by Target Associates in the future.'

Thatcher lifted his eyebrows in amused inquiry. He knew only that, with the latest rash of publicity, Lyman Todd had retreated into the hands of his medical advisers.

George Lancer avoided Thatcher's eye as he picked up Lucy's purse. 'Lyman has been ordered to take things easy,' he said carefully. 'Regular hours and no travelling. So he had a long talk with Gabriel Uhlein.'

Heroically Thatcher refrained from comment. Not so Neil Marsden.

'Apparently it pays to have absconding employees. At least people get to know about you. I'm surprised Uhlein isn't here tonight, looking over the prospects.'

John Thatcher was inspecting the slow seepage towards the main aisle. 'He is,' he said suddenly, indicating a group of three people coming into view. 'Target Associates is out in full force.'

Gabriel Uhlein, Marian Knightley and the tall grey-haired man by Mrs Knightley's side paused in their progress. Greetings were exchanged.

Enthusiastically Lucy seized on Marian Knightley. 'How nice to see you again. What are you doing here?'

Marian Knightley was unabashed. 'We thought it was the least we could do for Brunswick College.'

'And how is Alec Baxter?' Thatcher asked dryly. 'I suppose you hear from him?'

'Oh, yes.' Marian smiled. 'Alec is very happy. He feels he did the right thing.' And still smiling, she passed on.

She left a dissatisfied Louise Dunlop in her wake. 'But what about Alec Baxter?' she protested. 'Didn't he have anything to do with it? And whatever happened to Elliot Patterson?'

'That,' said Thatcher gently, 'is another story.'

25. The Sheltering Pines

After the raw biting winds and the soot-laden smog of New York in December, John Thatcher and George Lancer were almost mesmerized by the quiet cloister in Gethsemane, Alabama. It was not so much the warmth as the heavy languor of the air, laden with a hundred sweet scents from shrubs and flowers in bloom. The stillness was reinforced, rather than interrupted, by an occasional rustle of leaves or the single clear call of a bird. Already shadows were creating a glade of coolness by the west wall.

The three men had been silent for some time.

'Yes,' said Thatcher at last. 'I'm afraid that you will have to testify, Mr Patterson.'

Elliot Patterson continued to gaze sightlessly at a single white cloud low on the horizon. 'Of course, it was all over when they found out I wasn't Alec Baxter.'

'They were bound to find out some time,' said Lancer, but his voice held none of its usual impatience when stating the obvious.

'Not necessarily,' Patterson continued with the same dispassionate detachment. 'That's why I chose Baxter. It had to be a Protestant bachelor, somebody whose paper background I knew very well. I was hesitating among four names when Alec told me he was going off to Europe for a couple of years. It seemed almost providential.'

Under the circumstances Thatcher and Lancer could do

nothing but stare at each other wordlessly. Their silence seemed to communicate some message to Patterson.

'I suppose you don't understand,' he said. 'I'm not sure that I do myself. But when I tried to explain it to Sally, she started to talk about Sunday schools. I tried, for weeks I really did try. But everything became very confused. I suppose I didn't make myself very clear. She didn't seem to understand what I wanted at all. Then, when I began to want more, the whole situation became impossible. Of course, now, I realize that I was wrong, very wrong. I should have gone on trying.'

Lancer shuffled his feet. 'It must have been hard.'

Elliot Patterson looked at them earnestly. He had exchanged his hornrim glasses for round steel spectacles. Behind the glass, his faded blue eyes shone with sincerity.

'I deceived myself. I pretended that I was taking Baxter's name only for conversion. But all along I knew I intended to go into orders. I was planning it all, but I wouldn't admit it to myself. Not until I actually applied to the Brothers of Silence.' He expelled a soft breath. 'It seemed so safe. I was sure no one would ever know.'

Thatcher was relieved to introduce a pedestrian note.

'Marian Knightley knew.'

'Marian?'

'Yes. Alec Baxter told the Knightleys all about his plan to go to Europe and drop out of sight while he worked quietly. They even saw him off on the boat. And he's written to them since. As soon as she saw the letter of recommendation you wrote for yourself, she guessed what happened.'

It was very curious. Elliot Patterson seemed to recall his wife and children only with difficulty, as if stretching his mind back over a gulf of decades. But he spoke naturally, with perfect ease, about Marian Knightley.

'Marian wouldn't understand. I suppose she was the one who told you about me.'

Thatcher was quick with his denial. 'Oh, no. Not only did she keep your secret, she persuaded Gabriel Uhlein to do the same.'

Elliot Patterson evinced his first emotion. 'I wonder why she did that?'

'She doesn't believe in interfering. Or at least, that's what she told us.'

Thatcher inspected Patterson closely. Did Elliot have the slightest idea of the compassion that had motivated Mrs Knightley? No, certainly not. It was not surprising that he had been unable to communicate his feelings to his wife. Elliot Patterson was kind, considerate, conscientious. But he had not the least understanding of people. If his wife had failed to understand his needs and desires, he had been equally at fault in failing to detect hers.

Now Elliot dismissed the enigma of Marian Knightley's behaviour.

'But if she didn't tell you, how did you find out?'

'We would have found out one way or another. As it was, Father Martin described you all too accurately. A man in a business suit, he said, looking like a lawyer.'

Elliot frowned. 'But how did you know that was me?'

'We didn't have to. We knew it wasn't Alec Baxter,' Thatcher replied.

Patterson lost interest in the history of his undoing. 'The Brothers have been very kind. But of course, they are sad and disappointed.'

Thatcher felt every sympathy with the Brothers. As he watched Patterson struggle for some further expression of his thoughts, he was aware of an elusive resemblance to someone – or something. What was it that Elliot Patterson reminded him of so persistently?

A gentle sigh from the black-garbed figure broke the silence. 'The whole thing is very unfortunate.'

'Yes,' Thatcher agreed sadly, 'very unfortunate.'

Was now the time to break it to Elliot Patterson that the explanations and apologies he anticipated would not be necessary? Should he explain that Sally Patterson, undeterred by her husband's innocence in the eyes of the law, had departed for places unknown? That the house in Rye was now occupied by some people called Fenster (a charming couple with three small boys)?

No, he decided, joining Lancer in farewells, there were some burdens that Elliot Patterson would have to shoulder himself. Presumably he would have the support of the Brothers – those saddened and disappointed Brothers – in his forthcoming trials.

As they passed through the entranceway to the courtyard, a newly arrived priest carrying a heavy overcoat and a black briefcase was busily talking to the monk in the lodge.

'Yes, yes, Father Martin,' the lodgekeeper was saying. 'I'll let him know that you've arrived.'

And suddenly Thatcher knew what elusive recollection had been stirred to life by Elliot Patterson. He was the slow, careful driver entering a speedway at a thoughtful twenty-five miles an hour. Behind him brakes are jammed on and seventeen cars pile up in a chain collision. Or, as in this case, he leaves in his wake a murdered boy, a middle-aged man sitting in a jail cell, a wife and mother suddenly staring at her three daughters in wild incomprehension.

But the careful driver proceeds slowly forward, his ears forever sealed to the sounds of grinding metal and splintering glass directly behind him, to the cries of human distress and bewilderment.

'Did you hear who that was?' George Lancer demanded.

'Yes, yes I heard.' Thatcher shook himself and spoke more briskly. 'That was Elliot Patterson's latest victim.'

More about Penguins
and Pelicans

Penguinews, which appears every month, contains details of
all the new books issued by Penguins as they are published.
From time to time it is supplemented by *Penguins in Print*,
which is a complete list of all titles available. (There are
some five thousand of these.)

A specimen copy of *Penguinews* will be sent to you free on
request. For a year's issues (including the complete lists)
please send 50p if you live in the British Isles, or 75p
if you live elsewhere. Just write to Dept EP, Penguin
Books Ltd, Harmondsworth, Middlesex, enclosing a cheque
or postal order, and your name will be added to the
mailing list.

In the U.S.A.: For a complete list of books available from
Penguin in the United States write to Dept CS, Penguin
Books Inc., 7110 Ambassador Road, Baltimore, Maryland
21207.

In Canada: For a complete list of books available from
Penguin in Canada write to Penguin Books Canada Ltd,
41 Steelcase Road West, Markham, Ontario.

Green Grow The Tresses-O

Stanley Hyland

An Italian mill girl is found horribly murdered in a small town in Yorkshire. Who would murder her and why do such a strange assortment of suspects have connections with the girl? Is it the work of a fanatic lover or are there more sinister implications? Is her death connected with the unsolved murder of another girl two years previously? The plot intensifies as the key witness dies and evidence is found which seems to connect her with a nearby high-security American base.

Stanley Hyland unravels this mystery with combined force and subtlety. He portrays with humour and sympathy the tensions of the local police battling against time and against the threatened intervention of the Yard to solve a crime that is casting a cloud of suspicion over the town.

'Ingenious as our old friend the madman's fly trap and told with his infectious maniacal zest' – *Observer*

'A splendid book, at once convincing, controlled, extremely well contrived, and written with much gaiety' – *Evening Standard*

'Bravura piece of crime writing ... Mr Hyland even holds a genuine surprise for his last paragraph' – *Financial Times*

Not for sale in the U.S.A.

More Rivals of Sherlock Holmes

Collected by Hugh Greene

'She drew off her left glove, a delicated, crinkled suede affair, and offered her bare hand to the surgeon . . . from the polished pink nails of the tapering fingers to the firm, well-moulded wrist, it was distinctly the hand of a woman of ease – one that had never known labour, a pampered hand, Dr. Prescott told himself.

'"The forefinger," she explained calmly, "I should like to have it amputated at the first joint, please."' – from Jacques Futrelle's *The Superfluous Finger*, just one of the stories from this first-rate collection of Edwardian tales of cosmopolitan crime.

Not for sale in the U.S.A.

When in Greece

Emma Lathen

The Sloan Guaranty Trust, the world's third largest bank, invested in a hydroelectric project in the Greek mountains.

During the Colonels' coup the Sloan's representative, Ken Nicholls, gets arrested at Salonika railway station.

A second Sloan man, Everett Gabler, is sent to retrieve him – but hasn't a chance: he is arrested too, within hours of his arrival and in broad daylight.

Against all advice, John Putnam Thatcher, the bank's vice-president, sets out for Greece and, with the help of two female archaeologists, pulls off the biggest coup of all ...

Not for sale in the U.S.A. or Canada

The Longer the Thread

Emma Lathen

The setting is Puerto Rico. A series of accidents at Slax, the sportswear manufacturers, begins to look more like industrial sabotage. Sloan Guaranty Trust is worried about its $3,000,000 investment. So they send out Thatcher.

Then there is a murder. The Slax warehouse goes up in flames. Zimmerman, the company president, is kidnapped as a political hostage. The Governor declares a state of emergency, and a nation-wide manhunt begins.

All is confusion. But quietly, patiently, John Putnam Thatcher carries out his own investigation . . .

Not for sale in the U.S.A. or Canada